# Freein' Pancho

## PRAISE FOR *Freein' Pancho*

*Freein' Pancho* is brilliant. It is a modern Tom Sawyer...funny, sad and deeply moving. It is superb.

—**Jay O'Callahan**, *storyteller, performer, author, workshop leader*

Prentice has gotten the voice of the stressed teenager just right. You can trust this narrator, whether he is explaining details of making a lariat and working around a stable, or showing us a San Francisco Bay Area still undeveloped enough to allow teenagers to ride their horses to the local hamburger joint. This is the well-paced, absorbing story of Calvin Moore, unhappy at home, unsure of his friends, trying to figure out which choices to make. You'll be in Calvin's corner but you won't always be sure he's going to make it.

—**Katherine Dibble**, *Dir. of Public Services, Boston Public Library (retired)*

As a person who hung out at horse stables in my youth and then spent 20 years of my professional life as an equine veterinarian, this story hits close to home. The characters in this novel are people that I have known from a time that has mostly passed us by. *Freein' Pancho* is an evocative, gritty and surprisingly sensitive story involving a subject dear to my heart.

**Jenny Maas**, *veterinarian*

This book grabs you on the first page and pulls you into the gritty, hard life of 14-year-old Calvin, who is wracked with self loathing for his part in the death of his horse; a horse who was his passion and his main reason for rising in the morning.

Prentice lets us see the golden foothills above San Francisco Bay slowly nibbled away before encroaching development. The poetry of Prentice's words mesmerizes us as Calvin explores his landscape; finding life bone weary, cold and harsh; receiving little sustenance from his home with an alcoholic stepfather and a loving, yet weak, mother.

Still, there are a surprising number of people in Calvin's life who believe in him and who offer him choices, choices that he often turns his back upon, going his headlong way alone.

This excellent story swept me along. I especially liked China, the woman who owns the local riding stable and who gathers lost young people to herself, holding them with her love, her palms held open, letting them leave as they would.

There are many prisons, some built by others and some built by ourselves. It takes maturity to find the key and turn the lock to become free.

I highly recommend this book to anyone who wishes to understand another human being with all the terror and sweetness that entails.

—**Carolyn Ryder DeHart**, *teacher, writer, storyteller*

# Freein' Pancho

Lloyd R. Prentice

WRITERS GLEN
PUBLICATIONS

Marshfield, MA

Copyright © 2011 Lloyd R. Prentice

Published 2011

Printed in the United States of America

ISBN: 978-0-9825892-0-5

Library of Congress Control Number: 2009943183

cover photo: Mark Vincent Müeller - www.markvincentmueller.ch

cover design: Pinkham Advertising & Design - www.pinkhamadvertising.com

## Publisher's Cataloging in Publication

Prentice, Lloyd R.
    Freein' Pancho / Lloyd R. Prentice.
p. ; cm.
Summary: Set in the mid 1950s, this story tells how childhood ends for Calvin Moore when he finds his beloved show horse strangled in her broken halter. His alcoholic stepfather and loyalty-torn mother are of little help. His friends reach out, but grapple with their own life challenges. As the hills above San Francisco Bay turn from green to golden, Calvin confronts perilous temptations and heart-rending choices as he struggles to understand who he is and what matters.
    ISBN: 978-0-9825892-0-5

1. Life change events–Fiction. 2. Horses–Fiction. 3. Adolescence–Juvenile fiction. 4. Life change events–Juvenile fiction. 5. Horses–Juvenile fiction. 6. Adolescence–Fiction. I. Title. II. Title: Freeing Pancho

PZ7.P746 Fr 2011
[Fic]                                                              2009943183

# Freein' Pancho

To Laurie for love and support.

And to Jack and Pat for their kindness, generousity, and refuge.

*...the creation of freedom for oneself for new creation—that is within the power of the lion. The creation of freedom for oneself and a sacred "No" even to duty—for that, my brothers, the lion is needed.*

Frederich Wilhelm Nietzsche

# A Matter of Devotion

I WANT to ride on forever. The hills are green with new grass pushing up through brittle stalks. The grass is greener, deeper, over every hill. China is in the lead, heavy, bulging over her saddle, but as graceful as water weeds in a slow moving stream. She's riding a giant sorrel.

We see deer on the slopes. Pause for a jackrabbit poised on the trail. Two hawks hang high over the hills.

Shorty Hollister rides with us for awhile, silent.

Now we're riding on asphalt, clatter of hooves. We're riding down into the zoological gardens, down under eucalyptus towering dark against white sky. We come to a deep culvert under the road. The creek is dry.

Now, afoot, I'm pushing through a rusted and jagged grate into the culvert. Violent marks etched and painted on the crumbling concrete warn me not to enter but I must. It's black and fetid under the road. I'm sinking in mud, ready to turn, when something dark, monstrous, rises under my feet, lifts me from sleep, heart pounding.

The shame spreads over me before I'm fully awake. I'm pressed hard against the wall, knotted wood just inches from my eyes. The rumpled sheets are wet and clammy as I lift the quilt. The acrid smell burns my nose. The floor is cold, sending a piercing ache into my feet. I hear Curly's tail thump against the floor in the living room. He knows I'm awake. I hear the clank of his dog tags and the clack of his paws on the linoleum as he pads into my bedroom. He licks my hand. I stand naked on the cold floor and scratch his ears. I open my bureau drawer, but it's empty. I step into the underpants I wore yesterday—pull them over my hips. Curly curls up on the floor and watches me. I sit on the bed, step into the left leg of my Levi's, then into the right. I sit, thinking,

1

remembering. Then I stand, pull up my Levi's, slip a clean tee shirt over my head, run a comb through my hair, and look for socks.

The house is dark and quiet with long shadows of morning. A thin leaden bar of light falls through the closed drapes. Mom's door is closed. Teddy, my stepfather, leaves at five. Mom sleeps in. I turn the stiff brass key at the base of the gas heater. It turns hard. Cold metal bites into my thumb and first knuckle. Makes me nervous. Sometimes the heater backfires and flames shoot out the vent and singe my hand. This morning it lights with a dull wop. I stand over the heater and warm myself and listen to the tick tick tick as the metal heats up. I watch the clay corncobs glow red through the mica windows in the enameled door. Curly pads into the kitchen. I follow.

The sky is gray with early morning fog. The water in the Mason jar in the kitchen window is the color of horse piss. In the night a pale yellow sprout has forced a crack in the golden skin of the avocado seed. The roots are delicate and white in the jar. They look like blind worms. I find a cereal bowl in the dish drainer. I open a new box of Nabisco Shredded Wheat, can't find sugar so I use powdered sugar. The wilderness tips inside the cereal box show how to build a dead fall, how to carve a whistle out of a willow branch, and how to recognize game tracks. The whistle card is new. I throw it on top of the yellow AC-DC radio at the back of the drain board before leaving the house. Might be interesting stuff to try sometime.

I pause at the back door. For weeks I couldn't leave the house through the back door. That was after my horse, Dutchess, died. Now, opening the back door, I catch myself looking toward the barn, look away. I look toward the empty corral, see shadows, scattered straw, dried horse droppings. I concentrate on jumping from splintered boards to islands of grass. The yard is muddy from the rains. My school shoes slide into the mud. I look at the fog covering the hills, see Dutchess, in that ravine, above the muddy creek, wedged in rain-soaked greasewood and poison oak. Across the yard, next door, Harris' horses are pushing against the fence. They nicker and push the fence when they see me. I push them away to climb the fence but they continue to nuzzle me. I shout and clap to shy them away. The rusty barbed wire screeches in the staples as I vault the fence. I'm thinking about telling Harris that I can't feed his horses anymore. I'd like to buy parts to build a ham radio set but I can get the money other ways. I scatter sheaves of hay, vault the back fence, and follow the narrow path through the back pasture that slopes down to the pond.

New green grass has sprouted under the dried mustard weeds down near the pond. Water trickles down from the hills clear and shimmering through the grass and runs into the pond. Last week millions of black polliwogs churned the water around the weeds at the edge of the pond. Now, as I walk, hundreds of tiny brown frogs hop in every direction to escape my feet. Ducks used to follow me around the edge of the pond, but three Oakland cops came down from the pistol range one morning and shot them. After the cops drove off in their dusty black and white car, laughing, trading insults, I waded in amid the floating feathers and pulled out the ducks. They were lead in my arms, waterlogged, bleeding. Mrs. Levinson drove us down to the police station, the ducks piled up in a soggy cardboard box on my lap, blood-tinted water spreading stains down the legs of my Levi's and across her front seat. The police laughed, made Donald Duck sounds. I climb the hill toward Huey's house. Huey lives with his grandparents at the pistol range. I don't know why I walk to school with Huey. Boxes of brass shell casings and lead ingots are stacked outside his door.

"Huey here?"

"Huey— Calvin's here. Don't forget your lunch money, honey."

Huey's grandmother releases the screen door, lets it slam in my face. Huey's skinny Labrador tries to jump me but his paws are black with mud so I push him away, hold him down, and scratch his tawny head. A fat silvery tick is sucking blood under his left ear, ready to burst. Normally I'd pull it out but I don't feel like it. I'd need matches, iodine, to do it right. The screen door slams again. Huey's eating a Hostess cupcake, his fat freckled cheeks smeared with frosting. His dog pulls out of my grip and lunges at the cupcake.

"You shit!"

Huey's foot lands with a thud and the dog yelps and runs under the porch.

"I'm goin' to shoot that fuckin' dog!"

"Why don't you feed your dog, Huey? He's skin and bones."

"Look at what he did to my shirt!"

The screen door slams as Huey retreats inside to change his shirt. I

decide to walk to school alone. I take the road through the zoo instead
of cutting over the hill like we usually do. I don't want Huey to catch
up with me, but he does. I hear his flat feet slapping the asphalt and his
heavy wheezing behind me before I reach the eucalyptus grove.

"Christ, man. You could've waited. It wouldn't have killed you."

He's out of breath. I know he wants to rest, but I keep walking.

"Slow down, man. I want to show you something."

I keep walking.

"Hey, look at this." He hits my shoulder with his middle knuckle.

"Wise off, will you!" I turn.

He waves a Heathkit catalog in my face. "What do you think? My
grandmother said she'd buy it for me."

"So—"

"So, what say? Think this is the best one— the one I should get?"

I slow down, take the catalog.

> *Drives any 4-16 ohm high-efficiency speaker with power to spare.  Excellent
> frequency response and low distortion. Inputs for ceramic phono cartridges, AM
> or FM tuners.*

I take in the picture in the catalog, a smiling blonde in turquoise pedal
pushers, red lips, standing in front of the gold amplifier, hand caressing
the case—proud guy looking on. I look at the gleaming knobs, cocked
hips, the books in the bookshelf, the blazing orange fire in the stone
fireplace. It's the same catalog I showed Huey weeks ago when I'd told
him my dream of building a hi fi.

"Think it's the best one?"

"You'd still need a turntable and speaker—"

"I'll help Vinnie melt lead at the range."

I hand the catalog back to Huey, walk on in silence. The fog swirls
around the tops of the eucalyptus trees.

"So you think it's the best one, Calvin?"

I don't feel like talking about it.

"Will you put it together for me, Calvin?"

"Put it together yourself—they tell you how."

"I'd fuck it up."

"They tell you how, dumb fuck. Step by step."

"But I'd mess it up. Like everything. You're the only one who could put it together for me, Calvin. I'll give you ten bucks if you'll put it together for me."

"I'm too busy—"

"Please, Calvin—"

"You can do it yourself—you can read can't you?"

We walk through the picnic area. People park here at night. I look around the ground for rubbers, don't see any. The ground is littered with dry eucalyptus leaves, air filled with eucalyptus scent.

"I can't, Calvin. Will you do it for me?"

I think. "Maybe—" I say.

Huey shuts his mouth for awhile. We come to the the place where I saw the hawk. I tell Huey about the hawk. I was walking along this part of the road, staring at the ground, when I saw this huge hawk dragging its wings on the ground not ten feet in front of me. The hawk stared at me and I froze. The hawk's beak was wide open, bone yellow, fleshy red inside, hissing at me— more like a snake than a bird. Suddenly it turned and started hopping down the road. It bounced on the road once or twice and then spread its giant wings. It was beautiful— graceful as it rose into the air, but in a second it was gone. All was silent in the park and my heart pounded for a very long time.

"Ever shoot a hawk, Calvin?" Huey asks.

"No."

"I shoot 'em all the time with my .22 when they fly over the range. If they're low enough you can hear the slugs whomp into 'em. But they keep flying anyway. Once I shot this big old sucker with Vinnie's .30-06. Man it come down like a brick shittin' feathers!"

"That was a dumb fuck thing to do."

"It was a blast!"

"You fucker. That's what was wrong with that hawk. Wounded, probably, by some dork like you."

"Just a dumb shit hawk."

I feel like smashing Huey's dumb shit face. My eyes burn in the morning air. We pass the mountain lion cage. I stop at the cage and Pancho paces out of the darkness of his house. Pancho is blind in one eye. He puts his neck up against the cyclone wire like a kitten. I scratch his neck.

"I wouldn't put my hand in that cage."

"Pancho's OK," I say. "He knows me."

"He could tear your arm off. Vinnie told me about a mountain lion that killed a dog he had. Broke its back and ripped its guts right out through the throat."

"Fuck off." I push Huey away.

I look at the sun, silver flare through fog swirling above the trees. I walk faster. Huey breathes hard to keep up.

"Calvin, meet me after school and I'll buy you a Coke."

"I've got stuff to do," I say.

"Calvin— You know June Ann Rogers?"

I used to ride with June Ann Rogers, but I don't anymore. I almost asked her to a Friday night dance. But I didn't.

"Yeah, what about her?"

"I'd like to fuck her in the ass."

"What do you mean in the ass? That's not where you put it."

"It is so."

"It is not."

"That's where I put it when I did it with that chick in Fresno."

"You never did it with no chick in Fresno."

"I did so."

"Like shit."

"That's where Vinnie told me you put it."

"Vinnie puts it in knot holes."

Huey's eyes are red. "Vinnie knows more than you—"

"Vinnie puts it in raw liver and bitch dogs."

"What do you know?" Huey says.

Huey stops, stands at the corner as I walk away. I glance over my shoulder. His back is to me, his shoulders hunched, quivering.

At lunch I head over to Reds for a donut and a Coke. The morning fog has burned off and it's hot as blazes. I have a quarter for lunch. I was saving the money Harris gave me for feeding his horses, but Teddy took what I had to help pay his business debts. Now I'm saving half of my lunch money without telling anyone. So far I have $18. The kids are noisy in Reds. I push my way to the counter. It's too hot to stand in the crowd. I love the donuts at Reds. They're big and golden brown— so puffy they feel like air in my mouth. They're covered with thick sugary glaze that makes my teeth ache when I bite into them. Sometimes when I'm really hungry I buy two, but today I buy one.

"Hey, Calvin!"

I turn. Huey is sitting at the counter at the back of the store. He's eating a cheeseburger, pretzels, two donuts, and a Coke. "Hey, Calvin!" He jerks his head for me to join him. I shake my head no. I push my way toward the door. "Hey, Calvin! There's something I forgot to tell you this morning." I push on out the door hoping he won't follow. I wait for traffic to pass, then cross Bancroft.

"Calvin!"

Huey runs up behind me, his mouth stuffed with donut, an open box of pretzels in his hand.

"Hot, eh?"

"What do you want, Huey?"

"There's something I forgot to tell you this morning."

We walk through the cyclone gate. Eighth graders are playing touch football in the yard. We walk past the shops. I hear old Carter the metal shop teacher chewing out some seventh grader. Carter's drunk as usual. The hall monitor tries to stop us, but I show him my library pass. It's cool in the long empty corridor. Our footsteps echo as we walk toward my locker. Huey's mouth is stuffed with pretzels. He offers me the box, but I shake my head.

"Calvin— I was goin' to tell you that Joe Pacheco and me were up in the hills last week. You know, up by your horse?"

"What were you doing up there?"

"I told him about your horse and he wanted to see it."

"Why'd you take him there?"

"He wanted to see it."

Old Bouknight sticks his head out of his classroom and glares at us. We hurry down the corridor.

"You didn't have to take him there."

"How'd I know you'd care? It's only an old dead horse. No need to spaz up. You should see it now. Looks like a mummy all ballooned up— flies thick as smoke. Flies, or something, have eaten a hole in its side." Huey starts laughing. He offers me the pretzels again. I start to walk away.

"Hey, Calvin, you know what Pacheco did?" Huey's laughing so hard I think maybe he won't be able to tell me and I'm not sure I want to hear.

"You know what Pacheco did? He got this big stick see—"

"You fucker, Huey, shut your mouth," I whisper.

"Pacheco got this big— this big stick see—"

I push Huey against the lockers. "I don't want to hear it, see—" Huey is still laughing in my hands.

"Pacheco got this big stick see and he shoved it— he shoved it up its— he shoved it up its ass!"

I hit Huey hard and his head bounces against the locker. He doesn't seem to feel it. He keeps laughing. I hit him again.

"He got this big— big stick and he shoved it up its— he shoved it up its ass and when he pulled it out it was covered— it was covered with maggots and pus—"

Tears blind my eyes and I keep hitting him and he keeps laughing although I know I'm making him bleed. I keep hitting him until hands grab me and jerk me down the hall through the gathering crowd. Huey is crying. His scream echoes down the hall.

"Hot shit!" he screams.

"Vinnie's going to shoot your ass!"

The hall is filled with teachers and kids but I'm too blind to see.

# Teddy

TEDDY is home early today. I see him through the kitchen window popping a beer. Usually he's home late. He falls asleep on the couch when he's late. I squeeze between his Ford truck and the old Studebaker parked side-by-side in the narrow dirt driveway. I hate the smell of Teddy's truck—death smell of greasy sawdust and rancid meat.

"School called—" Mom says when I enter the house. I go straight to my room.

"She's talking to you, bub—" Teddy says, following me into my room.

I stand, stare at the riding trophies on my desk.

"I'm talking to you, bub—"

I hate the trophies— meant to throw them out— can't stand to hear Mom brag about them.

"Don't listen then," Teddy says. "Way you're goin' you won't amount to shit."

He leaves the room and slams the door. I feel like lying down— sleeping maybe.

"Dinner's ready—" Mom says outside my door. The hill behind the pond, silhouetted in my window, is dark. The sky is blazing red behind it. On clear nights I watch the stars, wondering.

Sis sticks her head through the door. "Dinner's ready, Calvin—"

"I'm not hungry," I say.

"In here— NOW!" Teddy yells from the kitchen. When I was a little kid Teddy forced me to eat everything on my plate. Even slabs of fat.

"NOW!"

"Shove it!" I yell. I grab my Levi jacket.

Teddy stomps into my room. He smells like his truck— rancid fat, sour sweat, mold and blood. His khaki work shirt is bulging over his pants.

"Just who do you think you're talking to, bub?" His skin is gray, darkly stubbled. I look away, avoid his eyes, flat green irises in yellow pig fat.

"I'm not hungry," I say.

"Look at me, buster—" He says. "Think you're so high and mighty. Think you're so tough."

I hear Mom slam the door into the bathroom. Sis is standing behind Teddy, staring.

"Look at me tough guy— Screwing up in school. Making them call— Upset your mother."

"Out of my room!" I yell.

"Whose room?" he says.

Teddy once held out a twenty dollar bill— "Take it and leave the house forever," he yelled.

I never told Mom.

"Get out!" I scream.

Teddy stands, breathing through his nose. The veins on the side of his neck throb. Teddy used to hit me when I was a little kid. Sometimes used his belt. But then he stopped. I don't know why. Usually I try to stay out of his way. It's not hard. He leaves early. Usually he stops at the 296 Club after work, comes home late, chugs a beer, and falls asleep on the couch. I hate the smell of his feet on the couch. When he comes home early it's hard to stay out of his way. I just don't hang around the house. On weekends I hang around China's. I find things to do.

"You got a choice to make here, bub— Join the family or move your ass out."

"It's a free country," I say.

Mom opens the bathroom door. I hear her shuffling down the hall in her sheepskin slippers.

"Leave him alone!" she says.

"That's right. Stick up for mama's boy."

"Want some dinner, hon?" she asks.

"I'm not hungry," I say.

"Give it to the dogs then," Teddy says.

"Shut up! Now! Both of you—" Mom says.

Sis is crying. Mom's bathrobe is stained. I grab my Levi jacket and go.

I don't know where to go. I used to sit in the barn—in the box stall—listening to Dutchess chew hay in her manger, lean my head on her side—feel her warmth, listen to her organs. I used to think I could just saddle up and hit the road. I know horses. I could lie about my age. I could find a stable— get a job. That would make Teddy happy. Mom would be sad, but she's sad now. Sis always was Teddy's pet.

But now Dutchess— I mean, well— Now I don't know where to go.

I walk for awhile— sit by the pond. The grass is wet, but it doesn't bother me. The frogs are loud and soon it's too cold.

I remember, when I was a very little kid, playing in the two-wheeled trailer parked next to the house. It must have been Sunday because cars were parked up and down Stella Street. I could see, across the field, people coming and going, laughing, dressed in riding clothes. Then, coming down the road, I saw my dad's car— or so I thought. I saw my dad get out of the car. I dropped down into the trailer and scrunched into a ball in the corner of the trailer waiting for my dad to come and lift me out. But he never came. I waited, shivering with joy in the corner of the trailer, expecting his big hands to reach in. But he never came. I know now— it wasn't my dad. But then I only knew that I wanted my dad, but he never came. I don't know why this comes to me now.

I walk down through the park. Huey's house is blazing with light. I walk around it and down the road through the eucalyptus grove. It's dark under the trees but I know the way. I feel rather than see Pancho's cage beside the road. I sit on the picnic bench. Pancho is pacing behind the cyclone wire. I feel rather than see him—smell his hot breath, his musty cat urine. I kneel beside the cage. The galvanized wire cuts into my cheek. The cold zinc is metallic—sour against my tongue. "You've got a choice to make," I say. Now I'm crying—really crying. It's the first time since—that time. I can't stop. Pancho brushes against me, pads to the back of his cage.

Suddenly, between sobs, I hear a shuffle and a cough behind me. Someone is sitting at the picnic bench. I see the glow of a cigarette.

"*Señor Gato*," a voice says softly, "He should be free, don't you think?"

# Julieta's Funeral

I CAN'T talk.

"*Señor Gato*—" the voice says, "He's an easy one to talk to. Some of these furry people— they're not so easy. But it is understandable— They have many things on their minds."

I try to stand.

"I'm Emilio. I see you around here all the time. You like coffee?"

"I—" My legs are cramped. Needles jab my feet. I slump against the cage. Pancho presses his head into the wire, pressing against my shoulder.

"Coffee is good at a time like this. Come. I make you coffee. That fat one— this morning— what's his name?"

"Huey—" I get out.

"That one—" I sense the figure shaking his head. "A *gringo*— *Gringo* for sure. I watch you with *Señor Gato* this morning— then tonight.

"You're no *gringo*— in your heart. Come!"

I can't say why, but I start walking down the road with this strange dark figure, walking deeper into the park. The road is a wraith of faint black against the denser black of brush and trees.

"Who are you?" I ask.

"Emilio—"

"Where did you come from?"

"When?"

"Just now."

"Back there— by the tree."

I feel shame flooding my face. "The whole time? Why didn't you say something?"

"Anyone could see that you were deep in your thoughts. Sometimes

13

it is best not to interfere when a man is thinking such deep thoughts."

"But—"

"Such things happen. Put it out of your mind. It is good that you choose *Señor Gato*. He's not one to pass judgment."

"But why were you by the tree?"

"Same as you— things to discuss with *Señor Gato*. We have things to decide."

We pass the wolf cage. Moonlight illuminates the thick wire cage.

"Now, *Señor Lobo*, there— He is not an easy one to talk with. He is *loco*, you know. He misses his people. But he has forgotten everything.

"He knows only the pain in his heart. See how he walks back and forth— back and forth— even now in the night— But he's watching us— oh yes, a shadow in the moonlight watching us— trying to remember the old feeling in his heart."

"He's not a real wolf, is he? We thought he was just a big dog they kept in a cage."

"He is a real wolf for sure. But, then, he is not truly a wolf anymore. Wolves need their people. They need wild places where they can hunt— play. For wolves hunting and playing are like food for you and me. But this wolf has been— how you say it, *en la reclusión solitaria*— in solitary confinement. His whole life. I try to tell *Señor Winter* that it is not right. But *Señor Winter* won't listen to poor Emilio. I talk to *Señor Lobo* sometimes. But if you listen to *Señor Lobo* too long, you get mixed up, you go *loco* for sure."

"Does Pancho need his people too? Is that why he should be free?"

"No—*El Gato* walks the world alone. *El Gato* never forgets. He is the god of the old and the weak. He is the bearer of the final mercy."

"How can you say mercy? I've seen cats play with their prey—"

"Who is to say the prey is not playing with the cat?"

"But the prey is only trying to escape—"

"*Sì*. The final race. The last chance for *Señor Ratòn* to prove himself."

"But old Pancho isn't a god. He's my friend. I give him my roast beef sandwiches."

"*Sì*. We are all many things."

"So how do you know so much about the animals?"

"I am their god."

"What do you mean—"

"Forgive me, *mi estamados Dios*. I mean I feed them— clean their cages. In their real homes God looks after them. Here, it is my duty. I bring them food— clean up after them. So here I am their god. We talk of many things."

"You mean you work for the zoo?"

"For me it is not work. I worked once when I was like you—more than a boy, less than a man. It didn't suit me."

"Are you the one I see hosing out the cages?"

"At your service, *Señor*."

"I see you all the time too— But I didn't think of you like— like a real person."

"It suits me. Sometimes invisibility is best. *Los Niños* come to see the furry people, not poor Emilio hosing out the cages."

"Do you live here, then, in the zoo?"

"There is no difference between *Señor Gato*, *Señor Lobo* and me. But I am invisible. That is my advantage. People don't see me so they don't bang on my cage and throw cigarettes at me and say— 'Hey, *Señor*, eat my chewing gum!'"

Emilio is silent for a moment. Then he says, "In the zoo I am free— but not free— I am like the peacocks eating crumbs under the picnic table."

Emilio leads me past the refreshment stand and past the outdoor monkey cages. We pass under the cold light of one bare bulb on the side of the zoo train station and into darkness again. In the darkness, behind the train station, I make out a small house trailer that I'd never noticed before.

I'm surprised when I finally see Emilio in the light. His jaw, on the right, is caved in, giving his face a cadaverous look. Prickly gray and black stubble covers his chin. His green workman's shirt is buttoned to the neck. He's frail, like a child. His khaki work clothes hang on him. I think of a child playing dress-up in his father's clothing. He has a fat jangle of keys on his belt. His feet, in steel-toed shoes, seem to belong to a man twice his size. But his eyes— I've never seen such— happy— eyes in a person older than me.

"My coffee— Best in the west!" Emilio grabs a handful of ground coffee out of a Folgers can and throws it into a battered sauce pan on the narrow gas stove. He fills the pan with water, then opens the rusty

Frigidaire behind him, removes an egg, cracks it, dribbles the yoke into a bowl, drops shell and whites into the water. "But my coffee is better in the mountains," he says, lighting the gas burner with a large kitchen match.

"Why is that?" I ask.

"In the mountains you look into your cup and what do you see?"

"What?"

"*Señor Moon!*"

Emilio's eyes dance with delight.

"Sit."

The only place to sit is a narrow couch, gray and stained. Spread open on the couch, cover up, is a textbook—*Elements of Algebra*. The book is old, more faded than the couch.

"You're reading this?" I ask in surprise.

"*Caramba*! Makes my head spin!"

"But why are you reading it?"

"Found it under a picnic table. This algebra— you know it?"

"I'm learning it. You do all the problems and stuff?"

"Some I know the answers in my head. But some—"

"It must be hard— without a teacher."

"But I have teachers— All over the place!"

"What do you mean?"

"This very room— it looks small to you, *Sì? Un cuarto para los enanos*, a room for midgets. But this very room is filled with algebra teachers." He holds up a tin measuring cup in one hand, the Folgers coffee can in the other, and drops his voice— "If 4a equals— c—" he says, shaking the coffee can, "Then how many eggs do you want in your omelet, *Señor*?"

Gritty coffee, spicy omelets, toast toasted on forks over the gas burner— Emilio makes it easy to talk. I tell him about Huey. I tell him about Dutchess. Soon my face is streaming with tears again, but Emilio doesn't seem to notice.

"This horse seems like one smart *caballo*, all right. A genius. She must have loved you for sure."

"But I killed her."

"Maybe she chose it— how you say *suicidio*, suicide—"

"But I knew the halter was broken."

"But maybe she threw herself over the bank. It happens."

"No. I was stupid."

"So you know the future, *Señor God*— Tell me, please—"

"You're making fun—"

"*Sì*. It is not right of me— I think maybe you are too young to have such a crack in your heart. But I see that you have met the dark one all right— *El Gato*, he knows the dark one. He knows that you can't hide. The dark one is behind every door— in this very room!"

Emilio looks over my shoulder, his eyes wide.

"But it was my fault."

"Maybe she want to teach you a lesson. Horses are like that. Very dramatic. Not like a burro. Burros have four feet on the ground."

"I did it— Don't you see? The ground was muddy. I slipped in the mud myself. The rope was too long. The halter was broken. Teddy is right. I didn't deserve her— I killed her."

"This *Señor Teddy*— who is this please?"

"My stepfather."

Emilio looks very serious. He draws out his words. "Your stepfather! You have a stepfather? Is he *los jinete*— a horseman?"

"Used to be. I think."

"He must know everything about horses then, *sì*?"

I don't know how to answer.

"And *Señor Teddy*, your stepfather— He tells you before you take your horse down that big hill to that place where the grass grows high— 'Today the ground here is too muddy, *mi hijo*. The rope— is too long. The halter— is broken.'"

"He wasn't there."

"And he told you— 'Take this horse out in the rain. She needs her breakfast.'"

"It was the only way I could feed her— To stake her out. We were out of hay."

"But you must go to school. How can you watch your horse— protect her when you go off to your school?"

"I'd bring her in when I came home from school."

"And this *Señor Teddy*— He doesn't help you buy hay and oats for your horse?"

"No. He said if I wanted to keep her I had to take care of her myself."

"And you did— for sure. You told me you and your horse won

many trophies."

"Only in small shows— Her conformation wasn't much. But I had her really well trained. I used to work her in the show ring before I went to school."

Emilio gets up, stretches. The acrid smell of burnt coffee grounds fills the trailer.

"Before— Before this terrible thing— You wake up every morning with the birds, *sì*?"

"Yes," I say.

"And you train your horse, teach her, in the show ring, this place where all horses are judged. All this before school? *¿Sí?*"

"Yes."

"And you talk to your horse when you train her?"

"Yes," I say.

"She talk back to you too?"

"In a way—" I say.

"And you ride her up to that place where the grass grows high so she can have a good breakfast because you don't have hay in your barn, *sì*? All before you go to school?"

"Yes," I say.

"This *Señor Teddy*. With all respect. I think he don't understand about horses."


One minute it's utterly silent, but I'm not aware of it until, suddenly, outside, a thousand birds start singing. I hear the peacock screech and the gathering chatter of monkeys.

"Ah— My friends. They are hungry. 'You are late this morning, *Señor Emilio*— Where are you, *Señor Emilio*?' They will have harsh things to say to me, for sure."

"But you haven't slept— When will you sleep?"

"Sleep? I have no time for sleep."

"But you must sleep sometime."

Emilio looks away, distant.

"In truth I sleep my whole life away— hosing out cages."

Emilio looks back at me, his face alive again.

"But I sleep with one eye open— Come!"

Emilio leads me through the monkey house, monkeys jumping up and down in the dark and howling. Emilio turns on dim lights. He talks softly in Spanish, makes faces. We squeeze down a narrow passage behind the cages. He turns on harsh fluorescent lights and opens a walk-in cooler. With practiced motion he pulls a rolling cart in behind him, reaches into a green plastic bin.

"You like chicken heads? Lettuce? Oranges? Don't mind the green stuff on the skin, *Señor*, we wipe that off on our pants like this, *sì*?"

Sides of meat hang in the back of the cooler. I think of Teddy's failed butcher shop, smell the ammonia he made me use to clean his meat cases. Emilio weighs and sorts and stacks quickly, silently. Rolling the cart out of the cooler and back down behind the cages he starts talking again, in Spanish, softly. The monkeys calm down and listen.

I'm surprised when we leave the monkey house. It's light outside. Red dawn light paints the trees and cages. Emilio's carrying three small oranges, juggling them and grinning as we walk.

"What time does your school start today, *Señor Calvin*?"

"I'm not going to school today—"

"But it is a school day, no?"

"But I'm not going to school—"

"But you must go to school."

"Well, I'm not going— they wanted to suspend me. But they didn't. But I'm not going anyway."

Emilio stops and looks at me, deeply, his eyes sad. He puts the oranges in his pocket and looks away. When he looks back he's grinning again— "Then, today, *Señor*, you must learn the zoo business. Today you are my personal assistant!"

We walk to the elephant compound. A fat man, dressed like a big game hunter, is inside the compound. I know him and hesitate. Emilio leans against the railing. "Ah— *Señor Winter*!"

The fat man nods.

"This is *mi amigo*— *Señor Calvin*."

Mr. Winter turns slowly. The baby elephant beside him rests her trunk on his shoulder.

"I know Calvin— Pay your membership this year?"

You're not allowed in the zoo unless you're a paid-up member of the Zoological Society. Or unless you pay at the gate. Mr. Winter asks for my membership card whenever he catches me, then he lectures me about trespassing on private property. Once he made me sit in the zoo office until after dark. Mom was worried, yelled at me. Mom says that $20 is too much, that I should take the long way to school. But it's too far to walk the long way around.

"It is all right," Emilio says. "Today Calvin is my personal assistant."

Mr. Winter grunts. The elephant pushes him. He staggers to stay upright— "You're late today, Emilio," he says.

We walk around behind the elephant compound. Emilio pulls the keys off his belt and opens the elephant house. Emilio hands me a fat green hose with a brass nozzle. He shows me how to fill the watering trough, then drags a bale of hay into the compound. Elsi, the elephant, is stretching toward the hay. But Mr. Winter is tapping her knees with a short stick. "Hold—" he says.

"That elephant is *Señor Winter's* obsession." Emilio says. "Since she come he has no time for the furry people. They are very jealous."

"Mr. Winter brought her to my school," I say.

"You like Elsi's car?"

Mr. Winter drives Elsi around in a pink Cadillac. The back has been cut away and the seats taken out to give Elsi room to stand. Elsi's name is printed on the side of the Cadillac in bright violet letters.

"I liked his joke about the drunk seeing the elephant in the pink Cadillac," I say.

"Now I want you to meet my lover," Emilio says. Emilio's walking ahead of me. It's not a cool morning, but I'm shivering—from lack of sleep I think. I have to walk fast to keep up.

"—I serenade her. I would marry her, but her brothers would kill me, I think. She is from a royal family and I am beneath her. I melt in her eyes."

Emilio leads me past Devil's Slide. "*Resbaladeros los Diablos,*" Emilio says. Devil's Slide runs like a red gash up the steep bluff that overlooks the zoo. Scrub oak and poison ivy cling to the precipice on either side but the earth and rocks are eroded hard and bare up the center where kids climb the ladder of protruding roots to reach the top. It's steepest under the dark oaks toward the top. That's where most kids give up, under the hanging oaks, too afraid to climb further and unable to find safe footing for the climb back down. Firemen have to rescue them with a rope. But it's not too hard to climb Devil's Slide if you know what you're doing and once over the top you can walk through the pale olive trees and then down through the scotch broom and the grease wood thickets and into the eucalyptus stand and then out behind Pancho's cage to the road. But it's easy to get lost up there unless you know the trails.

Emilio stops, finally, in front of the wallaby pen. Three emus, which share the pen with the wallabies, are standing at the wire fence. A low drumming sound rises from their breasts. They cock their heads left, right, to look at us. Emilio presses his hip against the fence. One emu arches its neck and plucks an orange out of his pocket with its horny beak. I laugh as the orange moves like a wave down the big bird's slender throat.

"—*amante*! My flower!" Emilio puts his cheek up to the wire and the emu caresses him. The other two birds peck at the first and crowd in.

"These two are jealous—" he says. Emilio pulls the other two oranges out of his pocket and hands them out.

"—such beautiful eyes," he says.

He's right. They're soft brown with long lashes. Emilio talks to the birds for a long time in soft Spanish.


The snake house is bright with morning sun. Streaks of red, green, and blue filter through the leaded stained glass in the door, coloring the glass cages. Emilio opens a locked white door that leads to the feeding ramp behind the cages. He opens a wire cage and grabs two white mice, first one, and then the other. He holds them up to his face and talks to them softly, calming them. "Close the cage please, *Señor*—" he says, breaking into English. He is reverent, serious. He paces up and down as though unclear about his intentions, then stops in front of the rattlers. When he turns back to me his hands are empty.

Emilio catches my eye and nods his head toward the far end of the feeding ramp. His face is oddly intent. At first I'm confused, thinking he's ready to leave, but then I notice a tin brooder filled with yellow chicks. Bands of warm light spill out, illuminating the floor. At the same moment I become aware of the soft insistent sound of the baby chicks and realize that Emilio wants me to catch one. Emilio nods again more emphatically. I take a tentative step, then another. The chicks rush to the door of the brooder, peck my hand as I reach in to grab. It feels so odd. The chick struggles in my hand. I don't want to hurt it. The soft, warm, pulsating sensation throbs in my hand long after I've dropped the struggling chick into the boa constrictor's cage.

"*Señor Calvin*—" Emilio says. I turn. He's inside the alligator pool, kneeling on the bamboo island, hand on the snout of a four-footer. "Julieta—" he says. His face is ravaged.

"*Ella es muerta*—" he says. "Julieta is dead!"

I look more closely— notice a dull film on the bulging eyes. The other gators are piled up at the far end of the pool, sides heaving slowly.

"I tell *Señor Winter*— Julieta is not well. He don't listen."

Emilio looks at me, lost.

"Julieta is my daughter. She eats from my hand— Calvin," he says, "You know how to drive *un carro*— a pick-up truck?" I nod. I don't have my license yet, but Jimmy Root taught me how to drive the Chevy flatbed around the riding stable. "We must give Julieta a grand funeral."

Emilio gives me a key and tells me where to find the zoo's old Ford pickup. I drive it around from behind the train station, stalling it twice, and back up to the snake house. Emilio's waiting for me. Reverently he lifts the dead alligator in both arms and slides it into the bed of the pickup. The front of his shirt is wet. He bows his head and mumbles something in Spanish. I start to get out, but Emilio walks around and motions for me to slide over into the passenger seat. He slides in, shuts the door, and drives, hunched like a child over the steering wheel.

We bounce around the lion cages and up a dirt road. I know where the road goes— the zoo dump. I look at Emilio, but he's silent, intent. He wheels the truck around tightly, then stops and backs up, holding the wheel with one hand and looking over his shoulder. We stop.

I stand behind the truck, staring at the broken tail light, shivering from lack of sleep, as Emilio slides the gator out of the pickup bed. A smell of rotting vegetables rises up out of the dump. He cradles the gator again in his arms, rocking it like a baby, then, violently, pitches it over the bank where it raises a cloud of flies as it tumbles down the face of the zoo's festering garbage dump.

Emilio stands there, clearly wracked with pain.

"Emilio!" I say.

"*Sì, Señor Calvin*—" Emilio says, "We must light candles. Julieta was very poor."

# Jerry's

A HORSE is staring through my window. And another. The heads are haloed in harsh glare.

"Calvin!"

I feel like I'm at the bottom of the sea, crushed by tons of water. I rub my eyes.

"Calvin!"

I slide out of bed. It's Dixie, Alaska, and June, outside, on their horses, standing in their stirrups to stare into my window. "Come on out, Calvin—"

It's nearly noon.

"Are you goin' to sleep all day?"

I check the sheets. Maybe I'm OK again. It used to be a big problem when I was a little kid. Then, recently, I started having trouble again. Mom knows, I'm sure, but she hasn't said anything. I dress and go out back in my bare feet.

"We're riding down to Jerry's. Want to come along?"

"No," I say.

"You can ride behind June," Dixie says. Dixie is 16. Usually she doesn't have much time for me. June is two days older than me and never lets me forget it.

"Calvin—" they all say together, making eyes. Dixie, Alaska, and June go everywhere together. Dixie is on her buckskin. Alaska is on her sorrel mare. June is on her Arab. The horses snort and stamp around and twitch at flies.

"My treat—" June says.

"I have things to do," I say.

"Screw 'em," Dixie says.

"Need my boots—"

"Screw your boots," Dixie says. "Bare feet are sexy."

Alaska's mare nickers and nips my hand. Behind me, in the house, Teddy calls my name.

"Your choice—" Dixie says.

"Okay—" I say. June nudges her Arab close to the back porch and I jump on. Her Arab dances a bit and I have to hang on.

We squeeze single file between the barn and Harris' fence. June's Arab is skittish, but I hold on tight. June smells like apples. Her back is warm against my chest. Her stomach is hard, but I feel resilient flesh over her hip bones. Jimmy Root once talked about love handles. I wonder. Dixie leads us through Harris' back pasture and around the pond. The pond has flooded the lower end of the road that leads up the hill and the horses splash mud and water. June slows up. The two horses ahead of us look like they're dancing through diamonds.

"You weren't in school yesterday," June says.

"No—" I say.

"I heard about the fight. Are you in trouble? Did they suspend you or something?"

"No— They wanted to but Mr. James talked them out of it. They just sent me home."

"Then why weren't you in school yesterday?"

"Didn't feel like it."

"Mr. James read your poem."

"No! He had no right—"

"It was an assignment. He reads everybody's work."

"Not that poem. He had no right!"

"I thought it was beautiful. You should have seen it. You know how everybody is always talking and giggling and everything, even when Mr. James wants them to be quiet? Well after he read your poem you could have dropped a pin. Nobody said a thing for a long time after he read it."

"He had no right to read it."

"But it was an assignment. You gave it to him."

"I wish I hadn't."

"I'm glad you did, but it made me cry, last night, when I thought about it."

I feel like sliding off and walking home, but somehow June knows. She reaches back and pats my leg.

"Calvin," she says. "I wish I could share how you feel."

I want her to shut up— I don't want to think about it anymore. I have other things to think about. I stare out over the pond. Black-birds swirl up out of the marshy grass and settle down again. I slide back on the Arab's haunches as we start up the hill, holding tight to the Cheyenne roll rising from the seat of June's saddle.

Dixie and Alaska are waiting at the top of the hill. Beyond, the Bay Area, from San Francisco to San Jose, is stretched out like a rich kid's toy city. The air is shimmery, but clear as mountain water. We see houses, streets, tiny cars, trees, the bay. The towers of San Francisco, just above the Bay Bridge, gleam to the north. To the south the San Mateo Bridge, a dark shallow vee, cuts gracefully through the silvery glare of the bay. On the farthest horizon dark hills stretch from bridge to bridge like a purple bruise.

"Someday this will be my kingdom!" Dixie says, dropping the reins and spreading her arms wide. Alaska's just taking it in, quiet as usual.

"I like it at night—" June says.

"And who's been bringing you up here at night, Junie my love?" Dixie asks.

"I mean when we ride up here at night—" June says.

"I'll bet—" Dixie says. "You'd better keep your eye on her, Calvin. She's a wild little filly."

"I'm not her keeper," I say. "She can do what she wants—" I feel June stiffen in the saddle.

"Calvin—" Alaska says. I look at her. She has a way of looking, like she's looking through you. "Nothing—" she says. Dixie nudges her buckskin and we plunge down the hill.

June leans back in her stirrups as her Arab plunges down the hill. June's hair tickles my face and I can feel her ribs through her thin West-ern shirt and the bottom of her breasts bounce against my hands. The sun is harsh against the side of the hill. Hot air rises up the hill and into our faces. Rising air ripples through pale tufts of new green grass— makes me think of waves on a pond. The Arab picks his footing care-fully to keep from sliding. I shift my hands and push hard against the Cheyenne roll to keep from sliding forward.

"That was mean," June says. "Don't you really care what I do?"

"We're friends, June," I say.

"Didn't you care when you kissed me that night?"

"It didn't mean anything. I was drunk. The other kids were doing it too."

"But didn't you care?"

"Yes, but—"

"Calvin, when I heard about your horse, I— I know how much you loved that horse—"

"She was a good horse—"

"Daddy says you have potential. If you had the right horse you could go all the way—"

"All the way where?"

"You know— the Cow Palace, the Nationals. Maybe now you can get a better horse—"

"Dutchess was a good horse—"

"I know, but you know what I mean. A real show horse."

"I'm done with horses. Horses are for kids and retards."

"Calvin!"

We plunge down through a stand of emerald green anise. The feathery stalks slap against my bare feet. I pluck a sprig and another and pass one up to June to chew on. The taste of licorice explodes in my mouth.

At the bottom of the hill we pick our way through the construction sites. I smell new cut lumber and freshly poured cement. They're building a new house right across our trail. Sometimes the carpenters yell at us when we ride through but it's Saturday. The sites are deserted.

"I hate all these new houses," June says.

"Me too—" I say.

"They have no right to block our trail. Pretty soon we'll have to ride the long way around. It's not good for the horses to walk on pavement."

"Pretty soon they won't allow horses at all," I say.

"They have to!"

"Mr. Pritchett's been asking everybody on the hill to sign a petition."

"But who'd sign something like that?"

"More new people moving in all the time. They'll sign it."

"But the horses were here first."

"No," I say. "The Indians were here first."

"Yes, but—" June says.

"Then the Spaniards drove the Indians out—"

"But that was a long time ago."

"—and then the white people drove the Spaniards out."

"So—" June says.

"All these new houses are going to drive the horses out."

"I hate them—"

"That's probably what the Spaniards said," I say.

"Were the Spaniards like the pachucos?" June asks. June is afraid of the pachucos, Mexicans with slicked-back hair who hang around in gangs after school.

"No, they were different, I think. But maybe not."

"No wonder the pachucos think they own the streets."

"They're okay," I say. "They usually keep to themselves."

"They call us names when we wait for the bus. I never did anything to them—"

"Sometimes they get mad for no reason."

"Stuie Kramer says that the coloreds are going to take over every-thing anyway."

"Stuie Kramer doesn't know his ass from a hole in the ground."

"Stuie Kramer's driving Dixie out of her mind—" June says.

"Stuie Kramer's a jerk."

"Dixie thinks so too—"

The sound of the horse's hooves clattering on the pavement echoes against houses as we ride down Barrett Street. The houses are small, with flat roofs and narrow yards. A small terrier, rusty and white, darts out from behind a hedge and yips at Dixie's buckskin. The buckskin shys and kicks. Dixie holds her saddle well and gentles her horse with soft hands and voice. The terrier darts back toward us. "Here we go," June says as her Arab wheels sideways and slips on the slick pavement. June is thrown forward and it's all I can do to hang on. Thinking quick, Alaska moves her mare between the dog and us but the Arab scrambles for footing and bolts over a hedge and into someone's front yard then back down the street. June is half hanging out of the saddle, but I man-age to reach around and grab the reins. The spooked Arab fights my hand, twisting his head, eyes flaring, spraying us with froth, but I man-age to rein him in. He stands, trembling, snorting through both nostrils as we both slide off, giggling.

"You could have killed someone, you know!" a fat lady with pink curlers yells from her front porch.

"We know—" June says, still giggling. "Most likely us!"

"Want to ride in back for awhile?" I ask. The asphalt's hot under my feet. It makes me dance.

"Okay," June says, calming her horse. "I never know when this beast is going to lose his marbles." Back on the Arab she clings to me, resting her head against my shoulder.

We come to Lonnie Poole's house. Dixie dubbed him Pooh when he first showed up at the riding stable so now that's what everybody calls him. Pooh is in the street with Cliff Johnson, working on Cliff's '49 Merck.

"Hey, girls— Calvin— How's it hanging?"

"We're riding down to Jerry's. Want to come along?"

"Bitchin'!" Pooh says.

Pooh is short, with fiery red hair. He starts to climb on Dixie's buckskin, but Dixie says, "Not with those hands you don't! Go inside and wash!"

Cliff slams the hood of his Merck. "Hey, Calvin—" he says. "Heard about your horse. What a bitch, man!"

"Yeah—" I say.

"Yeah— Well, I better wash too."

We ride three abreast under the soft green eucalyptus trees down the shoulder of Foothill Boulevard, Pooh behind Dixie, and Cliff behind Alaska on Alaska's sorrel mare. Pooh brings his hands up from Dixie's waist and starts feeling her breasts. Dixie jerks her buckskin to a stop.

"If you start that now, Pooh, you can walk!"

"Ooo!" Cliff says.

Pooh grins.

"I mean it!" Dixie says.

Cliff starts humming. It's a familiar tune. He breaks into words. "I wish I was in Dixie, away, away— I wish I was in Dixie Land—" Alaska twists around and lands her elbow hard on Cliff's jaw. Pooh leans toward Alaska, crooning—

"Alaska— I think I'll aska for a piece of—" Alaska pulls her foot out of the stirrup and kicks Pooh in the shin.

"You guys!" June says.

They turn toward us and start singing together— "June is busting out all over!"

Dixie laughs, and kicks her buckskin into a fast trot.

"What a bunch of dorks!"

"Hey, Calvin—" Pooh yells as they trot out ahead. "We're sleeping out in the hay barn tonight. You up for it?"

"No—" I say.

"Come on, Calvin— We're goin' to wail tonight. Boots and Singer are sleeping out too."

"I can't—" I say.

"Bullll shit—" Pooh yells. "Bring Junie. It's goin' to be cold tonight." He starts singing at the top of his lungs, "Baby it's cold outside—"

"No way," June says.

I nudge June's Arab into a smooth jog to keep up.

Jerry's hamburgers cost 19 cents. Everywhere else hamburgers cost 30 cents. At Lot-A-Burger hamburgers cost 35 cents, but at Lot-A-Burger they're really great, big and juicy and piled up with cheese and lettuce and tomatoes and pickles. But Jerry's hamburgers are pretty good. French fries cost a dime at Jerry's. Milkshakes cost a quarter. Everybody comes to Jerry's now— kids with cool cars hang out in his big parking lot. You can't get near the place after school.

As usual Pooh has no money. He mooches enough from Dixie for a hamburger, fries, and a chocolate shake. Dixie always has money. She goes to Catholic school. She says she hates it, hates the long gray skirt they make her wear and the white blouse and the pink scarf and the gray jacket. I always think of Dixie in skin tight Levi's and tight western shirts. I'm always surprised when I see her in her school uniform, especially her brown and white saddle shoes.

We sit in the shade under Jerry's overhanging roof. I'm sitting between Dixie and June. Dixie's leaning against me, teasing my hair and blowing into my ear, trying to give Pooh a hard time I guess. The horses are standing together, just out of the sun, heads hanging down. Cliff finishes his hamburger before everybody else and goes back for another. Stuie Kramer pulls up in the black '54 GMC pickup that his mother had bought for his sixteenth birthday. Stuie's German shepherd, Stormtrooper, is sitting in the passenger seat.

"Oh, God!" Dixie says.

"Want to go?" Alaska asks.

Stuie slides out of his Jimmie and walks toward us, a stalk of hay moving from one side of his mouth to the other. He wears black alligator cowboy boots, faded Levi's, a black western shirt with pearl snaps and, as always, a black cowboy hat pulled low over his brow. Jimmy Root says he sleeps in the hat. When Stuie first showed up at the riding stable he wore tennis shoes and black chinos and white tee shirts and greasy hair with long sideburns combed back in a DA. But he started following Jimmy Root around and before long was walking and talking like Jimmy. Jimmy was a real cowboy, a champion bull rider until a Brahman fell on him and shattered his hip. Now Stuie walks like Jimmy, knees bowed with a slight limp, talks slow, and squints like Jimmy. He keeps talking about hitting the rodeo circuit, but everyone knows he's chicken shit.

"If he could ride a bull as well as he can sling it," Jimmy says, "he'd be up for Cowboy of the Year."

"Hi, Stuie—" Dixie says.

Stuie glares at Pooh and Pooh glares back, thrusting out his freckled chin. Then Stuie glares at me.

"What're ya'll doing with this horse killer?" Stuie says, turning to Dixie.

"Stuie!" Dixie says.

I start to rise, but June holds me back.

"I wouldn't hang out with no horse killer."

"Shut your mouth, Kramer—" Pooh says.

"Yeah?" Stuie says.

Just then Cliff comes back from the take-out window, takes in what's going on and walks up to Kramer, standing in his face. "Hey, Kramer— How's it hanging?"

Stuie steps aside. "I'm comin' over tonight," he says to Dixie, "You better be there—"

"Eat shit, Kramer—" Pooh says. "She's not your girl anymore."

"Alone—" Stuie says. Stuie glares at me again.

Stuie Kramer doesn't scare me, but my heart is pounding anyway. Stuie walks back to his Jimmie and peels out of the parking lot.

"Forget him, Calvin—" Dixie says. "He's just talking."

I don't feel like talking.

"It's cool, Calvin," Cliff says, "Kramer's got shit for brains."

"You could take him if you had to—" Pooh says.

I want to walk home. I stand, walk to the horses. My legs feel weak.

"Calvin—" June says.

Just then Jerry steps out from behind his building and hunkers down in front of Dixie and Pooh. Jerry's a good guy. Cliff says he's 29 and a millionaire already.

"Hey, guys—" he says. Sometimes Jerry gives us free burgers.

"Listen, I've got to ask you guys a big favor—"

"What's that, Jerry?" Pooh asks.

"I feel real bad askin'—"

"What?" Dixie asks.

"Listen, I've been getting complaints. I've got to ask you guys not to bring your horses around anymore."

"Jerry!" Dixie says.

"It's the insurance," Jerry says. "It makes me feel real bad."

# Crazy Pooh

THE smell of dog food fills the kitchen as I crank the can opener around the lid of the can. Curly makes a scratchy tattoo on the linoleum floor as he dances, jumps on me, and spins in circles waiting for me to spoon the food into his bowl. I kneel and spoon the wet food into his bowl and throw my arm over his tawny back as he wolfs down the food. He stops to lick me, then dives back to his bowl.

I dig my fingers in Curly's tawny neck hair— comb out cockle burrs with my fingers.

I open the refrigerator, see three six-packs and two cans of Budweiser in a torn six-pack wrapper, but not much to eat— pale green peas in a Tupperware bowl and a gray end of meat trapped in a white pool of congealed fat. I slug down a long swallow of milk from the brown milk bottle and, leaving the refrigerator door open, check the bread drawer. I find two stale slices of bread and a crust. I tear the bread into a soup bowl and cover it with milk. I rinse a dirty spoon under the tap and eat the bread and milk standing up— staring out the kitchen window.

From the kitchen window I see the riding stable across the road. Jimmy Root is forking hay into the box stalls from the back of the green Chevy flatbed. Shorty Hollister noses his light blue Caddie out of the driveway and onto the road, pulling his matching blue horse trailer. Jimmy waves and I see Shorty wave back, his pale hand bobbing up behind the roof of the Caddie. The stable house is silent, but when I hold my breath and listen hard I can just make out the jukebox in the clubhouse— *Your Cheatin' Heart*. The house is hot. The hills rise up behind the stable, glowing gold in the afternoon sun.

I finish the bread and milk and walk into my room. I sit on my bed and stand up again. I feel strange in my room, like I'm intruding on a stranger. I walk around the room touching my bow and raccoon quiver, my rock collection, my box of radio parts. I'll have to throw out a lot of this junk, I think. Maybe I can give it to a younger kid. I reach under my bed and pull out my sleeping bag. Outside, through my open door, I hear a truck door slam and the front door open. "Shit," I say softly, under my breath.

"Where do you think you're goin', bub?" Teddy says, standing in my doorway.

"Out—" I say.

Teddy's been drinking all day down at the 296 Club. Mom drove down the hill an hour ago in the Studebaker. She must still be there, or maybe she's following him home.

"Like hell—" Teddy says, "You're grounded."

"For what?" I ask.

"For one, not coming home the other night, worrying your mother sick. For another— for another—" Teddy has trouble getting it out. "For another— making trouble at school—"

"I can do what I want—" I say. "It's a free country."

"Not as long as your feet are under my table—"

"I don't see any feet under your table—"

"Don't smart ass me, smart ass— I'll whip your ass."

I put the sleeping bag under my arm and try to edge around him. He blocks the door and shoves me back. "You're not goin' anywhere, bub—" He steps into my room. I step around him, but he blocks me. I push him hard and walk fast out of the house.

"Don't come back to this house!" he yells as I slam the door behind me. He opens the door. "Don't come back, you hear me?"

"Maybe I won't!" I say. "Just maybe—"

I cross the road and cut up behind the box stalls to the hay barn. Water glistens in deep tire tracks slashed in the mud outside the door of the barn. Inside, on either side of a wide aisle, hay bales are stacked up into the darkness under the roof of the barn. The hay smells sweet in the cool darkness of the barn. I climb up a terrace of bales and back to our place under the eaves of the barn. Late afternoon light streaks through cracks in the wall. Hay dust gleams golden in the light. I see four rolled sleeping bags pushed up against the wall, but nobody's around. I leave my bag and climb back down.

I find everybody in the clubhouse. Pooh is dancing with Dixie, close, hardly moving, his face buried in her hair. Cliff, Boots, and Singer are flipping playing cards into Singer's greasy yellow baseball cap. They play for a nickel a card. Boots is pretty good. He can drop a card into a hat from 10 feet away.

"Hey, Calvin—" Cliff says.

"Hear you're gonna whip Kramer's ass—" Pooh says.

"Calvin's just about Kramer's size," Cliff says.

"Kramer's one bad son of a bitch—" Singer says. "Thinks he is, anyway."

"Calvin can take care of himself," Boots says. "Can't you, Calvin—"

Last year Boots and Singer were expelled from high school for setting fire to the auto shop. They were drunk when they did it, stayed drunk, knocked around the riding stable for a day or two until China kicked them out. Then they drove down to Tijuana, bought forged birth certificates, and enlisted in the Marines. The Marines found out that they were underage and kicked them out. Singer said that the DIs, the ones who missed Korea, rousted them out of their bunks at two every morning, marched them outside, and made them pray on their knees for another war. Now they both work for Boots' dad, doing construction. Singer's older brother is the leader of a motorcycle gang, in prison more than out.

Dixie and Pooh start arguing.

"The answer is— no!" Dixie says.

"Come on, baby—" Pooh says.

"I can't—" Dixie says.

"Do it, Dixie— Singer says. "You can't keep your precious cherry forever."

"Shut your trashy mouth, Singer—" Dixie says. "Calvin, ride me home—" Dixie lives in Chabot Estates. She has a swimming pool and a red horse barn and white fences all around her place. It's a long ride.

"I looove it when you talk nasty, Dixie babe—" Singer says.

"Up yours, Singer—" Dixie says. "Ride me home, Calvin."

"They won't know," Pooh says. "And I ain't tellin'—"

"They'll know—" Dixie says.

"Call 'em up, baby. Tell 'em you're staying at Alaska's tonight."

"The answer is— NO, Pooh!"

"Come on!" Pooh says. "Tell 'em you're sleeping over at Alaska's."

"No, Pooh! I won't lie to my parents!"

"Miss Goody Ass—" Pooh says. "Daddy's girl—"

Dixie turns to me. "Ask China—" she says. "She'll let you use one of the rent string horses."

I look at Pooh.

Pooh looks at me— back at Dixie. "Ride the bitch home, Moore—" he says, his face red with rage.

"You prick, Pooh!" Dixie says.

Pooh stands, his freckled face defiant. Then he softens. "You're right, baby," he says.

"I know I'm right—" Dixie says.

"You're right. I didn't mean it," Pooh says. "Go ahead, kid— Ride her home. I'd do it, but no way China'd give me a horse."

I ride bareback with just a half-hitch around the gelding's nose. We ride out behind the stable and up the hill. Dixie's silent most of the way, but at the top she pulls up to give her horse a breather.

"Poor Pooh—" Dixie says. "He's such a baby—"

"He wasn't very nice," I say.

"He's sweet. He was just showing off for Boots and Singer."

"You really like him?" I ask.

"You don't know much about girls, do you Calvin—" Dixie says. Dixie looks at me, softly. "You're a cutie," Dixie says. "You really are. Too bad I like Junie so much—"

"Junie's just a friend—" I say.

Dixie laughs. "There's no such thing as just friends between a girl and a boy, don't you know that Calvin?"

"What do you mean?" I ask.

"When you were kissing June in the barn that night— Didn't you feel something more than just friends?"

"I don't remember much—"

"Come on— You remember."

"I was surprised, mostly— I didn't think Junie liked me that much."

"You scare her, you know— June."

"What do you mean?"

"The way you been acting—"

"What do you mean?" I ask.

"Nothing," Dixie says, nudging her buckskin. "Just promise me one thing, will you Calvin?"

"What's that?" I ask.

"Don't hang around with Boots and Singer—"

"I don't— much—" I say.

"Pooh's OK. Poor crazy Pooh. Everything he does gets him into trouble. But he doesn't mean anything. He just can't help it. But that Boots and Singer— They're trouble— Promise?"

"But Boots helped me— That night—"

"Forget it—" Dixie says.

"Boots isn't so bad, really—" I say.

"Forget it—" Dixie says. "It's your choice, but he's real trouble." Dixie nudges her horse. "He'll get you in real bad trouble and you won't get out again."

We ride single file down the canyon trail. It's cool in the canyon, and dark with night shadows. Riding behind, I watch Dixie's swaying form, graceful, over my gelding's floppy ears. I see stars in the deepening purple sky through gaps in the towering laurels.

Stuie Kramer's Jimmie is parked in front of the clubhouse when I ride back into the stable. Light from the clubhouse glistens on the deeply waxed paint. I brush down the gelding, turn him loose in the rent string corral. Stuie Kramer's standing behind me when I turn. He's with Boots, Singer, Cliff, and Pooh.

"Hey, Moore, come on up to the show ring. I want to show you something—" It's dark and late. I can't see his face very well.

"Show me what?" I ask.

"Nothing much. Just want to show you something."

"What do you want to show me?"

"Come on up to the show ring— I'll show you."

We walk up to the show ring, passing through the yellow light of the stable yard. "What?" I ask. We climb the fence, our shadows long and jagged in the show ring.

"Over here," Stuie Kramer says. He leads me near the judging stand. It's very dark in the shadow of the judging stand.

"What?" I ask. Boots, Singer, Cliff, and Pooh close up around us.

"You been fuckin' around with my girl— I seen you tonight."

"What do you mean?" I ask.

"I hear you're fuckin' around my girl— And I seen you.  Nobody fucks with my girl—"

"What do you mean?" I ask.

"You cunt, Moore— I'm goin' to kick your ass, you cunt—" Stuie's so close I can smell the beer on his breath. "Fuckin' horse killer—"

"You goin' to let him talk that way, Calvin?" Boots asks.

My knees are shaking.  "I don't want to fight you, Stuie," I say.  "I didn't do nothing."

"Well I'm goin' to kick your ass from here to Monday, Moore— Nobody fucks around with my girl.  Horse killer cunt."

"You pussies gonna talk, fight, or fall in love?" Singer says.

"Looks to me like they're gonna fall in love—" Pooh says.

"Pussies—" Singer says.

Suddenly Stuie hits me, hard, beside my left eye.  At first it doesn't hurt, but then it does.  I fall, confused.  Tears fill my eyes but I fight them back.

I start to rise, but Kramer kicks me down.

"Son of a bitch, Kramer!" Pooh says.  "Pickin' on a kid— Kicking him when he's down.  How about someone your own size!"

I can't see well.  I feel sick to my stomach.

Next thing Cliff is pulling my arm.

"You okay, kid?" Cliff asks.

Pooh's standing over Stuie Kramer.  Stuie's down on one knee, head down.  It's dark but I can tell that Pooh's face is bleeding.  The blood is black in the darkness.

"Piece of shit," Pooh says, staring down at Stuie Kramer.  "Want some more?"

"You're a crazy son of a bitch, Pooh—" Boots says.  "Let's get out of here— This horse pucky is makin' me sick."

Pooh's eyes flash in the darkness.

"That Pooh's a real crazy son of a bitch, ain't he?" Singer says.

"Well I'm a thirsty son of a bitch," Cliff says.  "Let's go score us somethin' cold and wet."

"Later," Singer says.  "Wait until it's real late."

Boots puts his arm around my shoulders.  "He slugged you good, kid—" he says.  "You missed the good part."

I stare at Stuie Kramer, dark form, still kneeling in horse manure and shavings. Part of me wants to help him up.

Pooh pats my cheek. "You all right, cowboy?"

"Never let 'em get inside like that, kid—" Boots says. "Got to keep your distance—"

"He's still seein' stars—" Cliff says.

Boots pulls me in close, arm around my shoulders. "Kid didn't see it comin'—" he says to the other three. "Caught him by surprise."

I pull away.

"What's the matter, man?" Cliff asks.

"Why'd you do that?"

"Do what?" Cliff asks.

"Tell Kramer—"

"Tell Kramer what?"

"Tell Kramer that I was messin' around with Dixie. I was just ridin' her home because Pooh asked me to."

"Shit, man, we didn't tell Kramer nothin'—"

"You just wanted to start a fight—"

"Fightin's what we live for—" Singer says.

"Fightin's the second best thing in the whole world," Pooh says.

"Fuckin' A—" Singer says. "Next to fuckin'—"

"Fightin' and fuckin'— what else is there in life?" Pooh says.

"Beer!" Boots says.

"Fightin', fuckin', and beer!" Singer says. "Fuckin' A, man—"

"Forget it, Calvin—" Pooh says.

"We thought you could take him—" Cliff says.

"I'm not a fighter," I say. "I don't like to fight."

"He just caught you by surprise," Singer says.

"Stick with us, kid—" Boots says. "We'll make you a bad ass before you know it."

"Well let's bad ass to where we can get something wet and cold," Pooh says. "I think that fucker Kramer loosened my tooth—"

They climb the board fence— bounce over into the stable yard. I glance at Stuie Kramer, waiting for him to say something, but he's still— like a statue, staring at nothing. I climb the fence. The guys are waiting in the stable yard, shadows against shadows. They see me and start walking. I follow. The lights are out now in the stable yard but still on in the back of China's house.

"I wonder who China's fuckin' this week?" Boots whispers.

"Could be anybody—" Singer whispers back.

"China's too old. She don't do it no more—" Cliff says. "I don't think she does."

"I feel sorry for any poor fucker she does it with," Pooh giggles. "She roll over he'd be a goner for sure."

"She does it with that Rhona bitch—" Boots says.

"Think she's a lesbo?" Singer says.

"For sure—" Pooh says. "That China's a butch for sure."

I don't like what they're saying about China, but I follow anyway as they walk quietly to the hay barn, climb the tier of bales in darkness. Boots passes around a can of beer.

"Only got three cans—" he says. "Score more later—"

I hate beer, but drink anyway. Boots and Singer argue about motorcycles, waiting for it to get late enough, and I lie in the darkness thinking about how Boots helped me that night. I was sitting in the mud when he found me, trying to pull Dutchess up the muddy bank.

"Her neck's broke, kid—" he said. "You couldn't pull her up with a D9."

"I need a vet," I said. "Get me a vet—"

"I would if I could, kid—" he said and then he sat there in the rain with me while I pulled and cried and he talked to me.

He came to see me the next morning— told me what it was like when his mother died.

"It's time—" Singer says finally.

The floodlights are on at the golf driving range. We sneak down the fence line, keeping to shadows.

"I'll hot wire the Jeep," Boots says. "You guys get the beer."

"What jeep?" I ask.

"They got this jeep—" Cliff says. "Use it to shag balls from the range."

"Give me the key," Singer says. Cliff told me about the key. You take a key from any Master lock, the kind with the zigzag shape, and you file off all the teeth except certain ones, and you can open any Master lock. The beer cooler at the golf driving range has a Master lock, Cliff said. We climb the steps up to the driving platform.

"Hurry," Cliff says.

"Hold your wad, jerk off," Singer says. "Get two empty cases. We can only carry two cases up the hill."

I'm scared. I hear glass breaking back in the darkness, back near the office. "Look what I found in the office—" Singer says, holding up a full fifth of Jim Beam. "Now let's get the beer."

Boots drives the Jeep around to the base of the steps. The grass is green under the intense floodlights. White golf balls are scattered in the grass like mushrooms. Outside the ring of light it's dark all around.

"Hurry!" Boots says.

"Look what I've got!" Singer says, holding up the Jim Beam.

"That was stupid," Boots says. "That's breaking and entering."

"So?" Singer says.

"Get in," Boots says. He drives us up to the end of the fairway. "You guys carry the beer up the hill," he says, "And I'll return the Jeep."

We drink the Jim Beam and chase it down with beer— mostly Budweiser, a few cans of Miller High Life.

"That fucker!" Pooh says.

"Who?" Cliff says. "Kramer?"

"My old man—"

"What'd he do this time?"

"He slapped the shit out of my ma again—"

"What did you do?"

"Tried to stop him—"

"What'd you do?"

"Hit him with a chair—"

"Get a fuckin' .45—" Singer says. "He'll listen to that."

"Hey, look at Calvin—" Boots says.

"You ain't lookin' too good, Calvin—" Singer says.

"Fuck you," I say.

"Oooo, the kids got a load on—" Singer says.

"I'm gonna buy me a backhoe—" Boots says.

"What're you gonna do with a backhoe?" Cliff says.

"Shovel all the shit out of the world—"

"You'll be shovelin' from here 'til the next shit storm comes—" Singer says. "Which won't be long."

"But at least I'll be shovelin'—" Boots says.

"This kid ain't lookin' too good—" Cliff says.

"We've got to get this kid movin' around a bit— He ain't used to this horse piss—" Boots says.

"Can you walk, Calvin?" Cliff asks.

"Fuck you—" I say.

We're walking down the zoo road.

"So what's goin' on at old Castlemont High?" Boots asks Cliff.

"Same shit—" Cliff says, "Different year."

"Still playin' ball?"

"Season's done."

"Playin' next fall?"

"Yeah— Maybe."

"Then what?"

"College, I guess. If they'll take me."

"Way to go—" Boots says.

"College pussy—" Singer says.

"Shut your mouth, Singer—" Boots says. "Just because you're an ignorant son of a bitch."

We come to the mountain lion cage. I run to the cage. "Hey, Pancho!"

Pancho's at the wire. Shadows and moonlight dart around the cage. "Hey, Pancho—"

I push my hand through the wire as far as it'll go and scratch Pancho's ear.

"Stupid shit's gonna lose his hand," Singer says.

"We come to turn you loose—" I say. "Hey, Boots, give me the key."

"What key, kid?"

"You know. Give me the key. We're gonna turn him loose—"

"Bitchin'!" Pooh says.

"Come on, Calvin, we don't want to let that fuckin' mountain lion out of that cage— Fucker'll hurt somebody—"

"You fucker, Boots!" I shout. "Give me the fuckin' key!"

"You're funeral—" Boots says and gives me the key. "But I'm climbin' a fuckin' tree."

I run around the back of the cage. The key won't fit. "The fuckin' key won't fit!" I yell. "Get me a rock!"

Boots is pulling me away from the cage.

"We gotta turn him loose!" I say, pounding on the cage. "Shouldn't be locked up like that! Should be up in the hills! Should be free!"

"Poor fucker's really pissed!" Singer says.

"Get me a fuckin' hacksaw!" I scream.

"I know," Pooh says. "Let's roll garbage barrels down Devil's Slide!"

"Fuckin' A!" Singer says.

Next we're rolling heavy metal trash barrels up through the scotch broom, 55 gallon steel drums. Me, Cliff and Pooh are rolling one and Boots and Singer are rolling another. It's a hard climb.

"Fucker's heavy," Pooh says.

"We need a fuckin' front-end loader—" Boots says.

"We could carry 50 barrels!" Singer says.

"Fifty barrels down Devil's Slide!" Pooh giggles. "Fuckin' A!"

We reach the top of Devil's Slide.

"Who first?" Cliff asks.

"Calvin first—" Boots says.

"Fuckin' A!" Singer says.

Boots and Singer teeter the barrel at the edge and I push. The barrel clangs and clamors down the slide, breaking the black silence. The monkeys shriek, chatter, shriek again, piercing the echo of the clanging barrel. Lights come on down below.

"My turn!" Singer says— horses the other barrel over the edge.

I stand at the top of Devil's Slide and stare into the void.

"Fuck you! Fuck you!" I yell at the top of my lungs. "Fuck all of you!"

"Way to go!" Pooh says, stepping up beside me.

"And fuck Santa Claus too!" he yells, his voice echoing over the trees.

# China

DUTCHESS is loose in Pritchett's yard. I'm wading through the pond with a tie rope, trapped in mud. Pritchett is aiming a shotgun at the white blaze between Dutchess' deep brown eyes. She's eating roses, her mouth bleeding, thorns pierce her flesh, her blood spreads in a pool across the pond. I scream.

"Easy, kid—" Boots says. Boots is in his sleeping bag beside me. His face is shadowed and gray in the soft light, his left cheek inflamed and ridged where he was sleeping against the hay. His hair is matted, laced with hay. "You're just dreamin', kid—" he says. Morning light streams through the cracks in the barn wall.

I breathe through my mouth. Outside I hear the Chevy flatbed, Jimmy Root feeding the horses. I realize that I have a problem. Boots is sleeping again. The dream images fade.

I move crabwise in my sleeping bag, away from the others. I unzip my bag, the smell of urine sharp against the sweet smell of hay. I roll up my sleeping bag, hiding the incriminating stain. The right leg of my Levi's is soaked to my knee. I throw my rolled sleeping bag to the floor of the hay barn and climb down the stepped bales. Outside, in the stable yard, I turn on the faucet behind the watering trough. Pale green scum floats on the surface of the trough. The water burbling out of the black hose tastes like rubber at first, but then is cold and clean in my mouth.

"Mornin', sunshine—"

It's China.

"What'd you do to your eye?" she asks.

I touch the corner of my eye. It's swollen, tender.

"Banged it on something, I guess—"

"What'd you do to your pants?"

"I— squirted myself with the hose—"

"Oh—" she says.

China taught me how to ride. "The most important, thing," she said, "is the hands and the knees." She taught me to keep my knees over the balls of my feet so my legs could absorb the movement of the horse. "Guide your horse with your knees," she said. "Not the reins."

China taught me how to hold the reins in my right hand and how to hold my hand above my saddle horn— "Respect your horse's mouth," she said. "Use a gentle hand— Listen with your hand. Let your hand sense every fiber in your horse's being— every movement and thought— so sensitive that a mournin' dove lands on your hand you can sense when he wants to fly away— he wants to lift off, you give him nothin' to push from. Imagine you're trappin' mournin' doves on the back of your hand."

"Gotta pick up a horse in Turlock—" China says. "Could use some company—"

"What about Jimmy Root?" I ask.

"Jimmy's got to stay and manage the rent string and look after that wormy mare that Suzie Miller dropped off here last week. I was thinkin' about you, sunshine, hopin' you'd give me a hand, keep me company, like the old days—"

China could see my hesitation.

"Just goin' out the Valley and comin' back—" she says. "Back before supper."

"I guess so—" I say. "Okay."

"Had your breakfast?"

"No—" I say.

"Then you go in— tell Grandma to cook you up a couple eggs while I hook the trailer up to the pickup."

"I could help you with the trailer—" I say.

"Go in and tell Grandma to cook you up a couple eggs. And while you're there, see if she's got a pair of dry Levi's, your size, you could wear while she washes out the ones you're wearin'."

My Levi's are starting to dry so I decide not to tell Grandma about the Levi's but she gives me a bar of soap and a sack of pumpkin seeds while I'm eating her fried eggs at the kitchen table.

"Shower down good after you finish them eggs," she says. "And every night before you go to bed make yourself strong tea out of them pumpkin seeds and drink it down before you go to bed. I know all about your trouble, Calvin— You need any more pumpkin seeds, you come see me, you hear?"

Grandma sits beside me. She never leaves the big farm house kitchen except when there's dancin' in the clubhouse. Then she's in the middle of it and the last one to bed.

"My first husband was big and strappin' like you're gonna be, Calvin, but he had the same trouble you got. Peed the bed on our weddin' night— Happens to lots of folks."

Heat rises in my cheeks. "What'd you do?"

"What do you think I did? Kicked him out of bed. That's what I did. Mama never told me about that part. Made him sleep on the floor— It's the pumpkin seed tea cured him. More toast?"

"How— how'd you know?" I ask, looking down at the pumpkin seeds.

"Still got a nose, ain't I?" she answers.

The shower's hot, clears the throbbing in my head. The towel's hard and scratchy. I'm looking at my eye in the steamy mirror when Grandma barges into the bathroom without knocking. "Try these for size—" she says. "The way people leave perfectly good clothes around this stable you'd think it was a rummage sale—"

"Grandma!" I say.

"Don't you blush at me, Calvin—" she says. "I seen more'n you got plenty of times, but not many handsomer—"

"Ready, sunshine?" China yells from the back door.

"Give the boy a minute—" Grandma yells back. "He's still gotta zip up his britches."

Jimmy Root says that China's pickup is more lived in than some people's houses. It's high off the ground with heavy overload springs. The chipped paint on the side of the door says "China Seas Boarding Rental Trade" in a big circle around a horse's head. I once asked China about the China Seas part, what it meant. "My daddy always wanted to go to the China Seas and I always wanted a stable—" she said. "So when I got my stable I decided to call it 'China Seas.' Besides, I just like the sound of it— Sounds like a place I'd like to go someday—"

I open the passenger door and step up on the running board. I push stuff on the floor and shove more stuff behind the seat to sit in the passenger side— a hackamore, a hoof pick, two rain slickers, beer bottles, candy bar wrappers. A knitted baby bootie hangs down from the rear view mirror. The ledge over the dashboard is littered with feed receipts and parking tickets. China's keys hang down from the ignition. "I don't even know myself what all them keys are anymore— Never use 'em," she told me once. "Nothin' to steal I wouldn't give somebody they wanted it bad enough." Fine dust, stubble, oat kernels, sawdust cover every surface.

When China was taking me around to horse shows we slept in sleeping bags on feed sacks and saddle blankets in the bed of the pickup. When it rained we covered the bed with a tarp— never did much good. I never knew when China came in to sleep. I always gave up and crawled into my bag long before the laughing, talking, and partying that went on around the horse trailers ended. And China was always up before me too, feeding and watering the horses.

We pull out of the stable yard. China doesn't say much as we wind down the hill, roll past the houses on 106th Street, then head out Foothill Boulevard toward the freeway. I stare out the side window, thinking. China starts singing. She has a way of singing when she drives, softly, under her breath, so you can hardly hear. I turn to study her. She fills the driver's side. Her chest and stomach press up against the steering wheel, her legs are so tight in her Levi's that I think the seams are going to burst. Her face is delicate, beautiful in a way. Her hair is blond, platinum. The sun's shining through her window, making the frizzes of hair that halo her head look like white fire. She's wearing her turquoise barrette. I've never seen her without it.

"How you doin' with your stepdaddy—" China asks.

I don't answer. China drives without saying more.

"Kicked me out. Told me not to come back no more—" I say finally.

"Damned fool—" China says. "He drinkin' when he told you that?"

"Yeah—" I say. "Drinks all the time. Damned lush—"

"Then don't pay no attention to him. He's a damned fool when he gets to drinkin'— Just don't pay no attention when he gets like that."

"I hate him—" I say. "I really do—"

"Life's too short for hatin', sunshine—" China says. "Nobody ever told you that?"

"Well I do. He's stupid."

"That a crime?"

"What a crime?"

"Stupidity?"

"Well he's stupid—"

"Stupidity was a crime they'd lock up half the people in this county, me before anybody— lock us up and throw away the key for good."

"Well I'm never going back there—"

"Where you goin' then?"

"I don't know—"

"That hay barn gets wicked cold in the winter. Besides, your mama needs you."

"Well she's made her choice."

China's silent for a minute while she passes a slow tractor trailer rig, CenCal Lettuce, E. J. Gonzales and Sons.

"I remember your stepdaddy when he first started comin' up to the China Seas. He was a handsome buck then. Didn't have that potbelly he's got now. He was a drinker then too, but he could hold it. He had a lot of the women around the place interested, I'll tell you, but he was only interested in your mama. When you started to ride— took your first blue ribbon— he was proud as punch."

"Well he's not like that no more—"

"It ain't easy, sunshine— gettin' up every morning before the sun comes up— raisin' two kids, one not even your own flesh and blood. Money don't go very far these days, you know, even if you make a good dollar—"

"Money— He drinks every dollar he makes and pisses it away— Sometimes Mom don't even have enough to buy groceries. He only comes home to sleep— And to boss me around."

"That's a failin', I grant you— He's missin' out on something there for sure, not takin' time to know you good."

"Well I ain't goin' back there."

China looks me over. "Sunshine, your mama needs you. Without you, your mama be lost for sure."

I look at her, surprised.

"How long you think your mama could hold it together without you, Calvin? I think she married your stepdaddy so you'd have a daddy around. Without you around your mama'd be lost for sure—"

"I wish she'd up and walk out then— I don't need him for a daddy. I got my own."

"But what'd she do then, sunshine? Where'd she go? Your mama's strong in lots of ways, but in some ways she ain't. Sometimes you just gotta stay and fight it out."

"But—" I say.

China glances over at me. "You hear me, sunshine? Sometimes you gotta fight for what you love."

"Well I still hate him."

"Hatin' someone, sugar, just makes 'em bigger in your mind."

I don't want to talk about it anymore. The freeway ends. We circle down the ramp and head out through Castro Valley. The stores are closed. It's Sunday morning quiet. We pass Valley Used Cars, H & J Plumbing Supplies, Mia's Superette. We stop for traffic lights every other block. Soon we're passing small white houses, then houses with horses and fruit trees. We head up the long grade toward the pass. China shifts into a lower gear. The hills are steep, brown and bare with slashes of green in the folds. We see steers grazing on the side of the hills. We pass through Livermore Valley, emerald green with alfalfa fields, then climb again. At the summit the Central Valley heat hits us like a furnace.

"Been thinkin'—" China says. "Summer vacation's comin' on. What you doin' with your summer, sunshine?"

"Nothin', I guess—"

"Jimmy's hip's been actin' up on him. What's say I hire you for the summer to help him out?"

"I— I don't know—" I say.

"Can't pay you much— Will you think about it?"

"I don't know if I can—" I say.

"Well, it's a thought."

I let my hand plane in the hot slipstream outside the cab window. If I point my fingers just right my hand slips easily through the air. If I tilt it up or down it takes all my strength to keep my hand from blowing back against the side of the cab. The valley is flat and hazy. Battered trucks filled with sugar beets pass us, filling the pickup with hot, dusty diesel fumes.

"What's the trouble, sunshine?" China asks, sensing the black thing rising inside me.

"China?" I ask. "Why does it hurt so much?"

"Hurt?" she asks.

"You know—"

"Your mare?"

I nod.

"Of course it hurts when you lose something you love, sunshine—"

"But why?"

"I can remember the first horse I lost— It hurts, I can tell you that. Hurts like hell.But I can tell you something hurts a whole lot more—"

"What's that?" I ask.

"Losin' someone you love. Losin' family."

"But what if you don't love nobody— And nobody loves you— Then you can't be hurt, can you? And you don't have to fight—"

"Sunshine, it sounds like some crazy old country song, but it's far better to love somebody and feel the hurt of losin' 'em, then never to love at all."

"Have you ever felt it— that kind of hurtin'?" I ask.

China concentrates on driving. I think she's not going to answer.

"Yes—" she says finally. "When my daddy died. A couple of other times."

"Does it go away?" I ask.

"After awhile it doesn't hurt so much—" she says. "But it never really goes away. Not really— Leaves a hole."

"If it's better to love someone," I say, "how come you never got married?"

"Trouble with marryin' is you're saddled with someone thinks you're their exclusive property to boss around."

"But you just said that it's better to love somebody than not to love at all—"

"Love's different than marryin'."

"But didn't you ever want babies?"

"Now you gettin' personal on me, ain't you sunshine—"

"Didn't you?"

"Oh I've tried to have babies, believe me, I've tried that— Besides, I got plenty of babies now—"

"What do you mean?" I ask.

"You and all them other kids that hang around the China Seas—"

"We're not babies!"

"To me you are. Always will be. I get to watch you grow up— I see things even your mamas don't get to see—"

"But why don't you get married? Don't you like men?"

"Men? I can take 'em or leave 'em, I guess. But a good piece of horse flesh comes along— that's somethin' I can't resist. Keeps me poorer than a church mouse."

"Who'd you love?" I ask. "That hurt you, I mean—"

China takes a long time answering. "Someone—" she says. "Once—"

"Well I'm never going to love nobody— enough for them to hurt me anyway."

China reaches across the seat and pats my knee. "You will, sunshine," she says. "Someday you will, believe me."

China pulls into a truck stop just outside Turlock, Arnold's Fuel and Diesel—White Gas.

"Hungry?" she asks.

We sit at the bar. China orders a hamburger and a beer. I order a cheeseburger, fries, and a Coke. The Coke is warm, tastes like flat syrup. It's dark and cool in the bar. We're the only ones.

"What'd you do before you got the China Seas?" I ask.

"Tended bar for my daddy—" China says.

"So how'd you get the China Seas?"

"My daddy up and died and left me with the bar. I didn't like talkin' to drunks all night so I sold the bar and bought the China Seas. Ain't much— worthless piece of dirt and a bunch of sheds ready to fall down and kill somebody. But I like it well enough."

China stares into the mirror behind the bar. I can't see much in the mirror except the slow-moving fan on the ceiling behind me and fly-speckled beer posters on the pine-wood wall behind us. But China stares into the mirror in a way that makes me stop eating. I turn my head to look at her.

"You see all kinds wash up at the China Seas—" China says. "It's like my daddy's bar, I guess. You see rich people and poor people, good people and not such good people. But they're all lookin' for somethin' and somehow, don't ask me how, they all seem to find a little somethin' at the China Seas. Least they keep hangin' around— Sometimes I think the China Seas is like a little island, battered by storms. People wash up, find each other, huddle together against the storm."

"What storm?" I ask, but China continues talking like she's talking to somebody in the mirror.

"Don't ask me how, but somehow I know what's goin' to happen to every one of them. I see it clear as a picture show sometimes. Scares me— That Boots— Everybody's given up on that Boots. Thinks he's goin' to no good. He's been a hell raiser for sure, but he'll be okay. I've seen that, clear as day. But that Singer's gonna end up dead— dead or in the can like his brother. Now Pooh's gonna end up in the can, all right, but he's gonna be okay. In the long run. That Alaska's gonna end up with six kids and a husband she won't take no shit from no way."

"What about me?" I ask.

"You? I don't know about you, sunshine, but you're goin' places— you can bet on that."

"Where am I going?" I ask.

"You? I don't know for sure. Someplace I'll never get to see, I know that. But you're goin' places. Everybody 'round the China Seas is countin' on that. Now finish that cheeseburger," China says. "Let's go pick up my new stallion."

We drive past grain silos, a big yard that sells used tractors and combines, a tall water tower on steel legs painted green and orange. Well out of town, nearly to the Sierra foothills, we drive up a long gravel drive with white fences on either side. Rotating sprinklers cast long ropes of glistening water out over green alfalfa.

"Now you're gonna see a real horse farm," China says.

We pass a long low steel show barn with a bright white roof and a black brand mark painted big on the roof. "Rockin' Chair E and R—" China says. "Don't say much about how hard old Ellen and Rodney busted their butts to get this place and what they gotta do to keep it."

A blond girl with a white ribbon in her hair, younger than me, is exercising a big bay jumper. China pulls into the yard between the show barn and a newly raked paddock where stable hands are walking three horses in circles, parks in front of a strip of crimson and white roses. A heavy man in English habit and shiny boots walks out of the shadow of the show barn and greets us, smiling like his cheeks are going to burst.

"Top o' the mornin' to you, Miss Clark!"

"Well good mornin' to you, handsome," China says. "But my watch says it's pushin' on to one o'clock. Some of us have had our lunch already and done a good day's work to boot—"

"Well the early worm is bird chow— that's my motto," he says. "Come to pick up your Appaloosa?"

"Sure did!" China says.

"He's a handful. Glad to see you brought your top hand with you. Might wish you'd brought two or three more—"

"This here's Calvin. He's the best, all right. He's all I'm gonna need."

China turns to me. "Don't let this fancy pants pull the wool over your eyes. He could charm a cat out of a tree. He'll answer to most anything, but most folks call him Rodney. Why he lets 'em beats me. Name like that sounds like some fancy pants English lord or something. I knew him when the only thing to his name was a scuffed-up saddle with a broken tree and a pair of cast-off Levi's."

"And those were the days—" Rodney says.

Rodney opens the truck door for China. "Well come on in. Sit yourselves down— Cup of coffee or somethin'? Strain the road dust out of your teeth? Plenty of time before we load that firecracker into your trailer."

The kitchen is gleaming, shiny copper pots hanging on hooks over a big black stove with white enamel handles— fancy tile around the sink.

"Rather have a beer?"

"You know me, handsome—"

"What about you, Calvin— You a beer drinkin' man?"

"No thank you," I say.

"So you're finally goin' to get that outfit of yours on the right foot, are you, China?" Rodney says when he returns with a beer for China and a Coke for me. For himself he pours a big mug of coffee out of the porcelain coffee pot on the stove.

"If that Appaloosa you're sellin' me has half the fire in his balls you're claimin'."

"Wouldn't be sellin' him if Ellen, precious dear, wasn't always tellin' me that Appaloosas is for redskins, not for civilized Christians. Wouldn't even be sellin' him then, but she went and sold all my western tack right out from under my nose. Thinks that people who ride western is the next best thing to sheep herders and stoop labor. Personally, I think Appaloosas is the coming thing."

"Rodney, the way you talk that woman's got you on a short rope and hog tied. You jump the fence, we'll go into the Appaloosa business together."

"Believe me I'd jump at it. But I do love that woman even if she is the worst blue blood stuck up this side of St. Louis."

"Who's a blue blood stuck up?" Rodney's wife walks into the kitchen. She's tall, jet black hair, wearing a purple dress with Indian jewelry.

"Well, good morning, China—"

"Howdy, sugar. Rodney's just tellin' me how you sold all his western tack right out from under his nose."

"He tell you that?"

"Sure did—"

"Well don't you believe everything you hear from an overweight horse trader with a smile on his face. You oughta know that by now, China."

"Rodney?" China says, her eyebrows raised. "He stretch the truth, does he?"

"Stretch the truth? Want to know what this one told me before we said our marriage vows?"

"What's that?" China says.

"Now don't go tellin' tall tales," Rodney says.

"He told me—" Ellen starts to laugh, stretching her hands apart like a fisherman showing off a fish that got away. "Well, I'll tell you the truth of it when he ain't around to deny it."

"Now don't you spiteful ladies get started on me," Rodney says with a smile.

The Appaloosa is the most beautiful animal I've ever seen. He's small but fills his box stall with energy I can feel like nothing I've felt before. He's chestnut in front, feathering to black behind the withers. The large white spots on his rump stand out in the black like they were pasted on. The Appaloosa flattens his ears, charges the box stall door, and spins with a challenging nicker, ready to kick the life out of anything that enters his stall.

"Best be careful around this beauty and I'm serious about that—"

Rodney says. "He's got teeth sharper than butcher knives and jaw muscles that could snap a pitch fork like a tooth pick. And he's got a streak of pure evil, I swear. And he's smart— smarter than the bunch of us put together. Can't get but one of my hands to enter the box stall bare handed. And that only because the poor ol' boy is so rum dumb he can't remember his own name from day to day."

"So, this beauty trailer broke?" China asks.

"Sometimes he is and sometimes he ain't. Depends on the mood he's in and the price of wheat futures."

"Well let's load him up then," China says.

"You might want to lip cinch him," Rodney says.

"I don't think so," China says. She talks softly for awhile, enters the box stall carefully, dodges a few half-hearted kicks, and before long has the stallion sniffing her hair.

"I never seen no one handle an animal like that lady," Rodney says to me. "Wouldn't have sold that Appaloosa to anyone else for love nor money— See there? That animal loves her."

The Appaloosa loads easily. China writes out a check on the hood of the pickup.

"I'm goin' to need your help with an animal like this around the place," China says as we're pulling out of the yard.

"What do you mean?" I ask.

"Animal like this is a big responsibility—"

A stable hand, carrying a bulging feed sack, steps out of the shadow of the barn.

"Whatcha got?" China asks out the window.

"Damned cats—" the farmhand says. "Barn cat had another litter."

"Whatcha doin' with 'em?"

"Take 'em down the irrigation ditch—"

"No you ain't," China says, opening her door. "Give 'em to me. We can't have you goin' around drowning defenseless kittens."

Jimmy Root's waiting at the stable gate when we drive in— runs toward the pickup. It's past feeding time.

"China— China— "

China rolls down her window.

"Rent string rider got throwed. Hurt real bad. Called the ambulance. They came and took her down to the emergency—"

"Good Lord!" China says. "Anybody from here go down to the emergency with her?"

"Wasn't nobody much around, so I gave Boots the keys to my convertible and he followed the ambulance down."

"Boots?"

"Wasn't nobody much around and I couldn't just leave the place with all the kids around and stuff."

"You call Marty?"

"Yeah. He says he'll check tomorrow, but he's not sure you kept your insurance up to date. You did, didn't you, China? I pray to God you did. That little girl was hurt real bad."

# The Emergency

CHINA tells me to stay behind, help out at the stable. But no way she's going to kick me out of this truck. Just feels like she needs someone.

"Unhook me, Jimmy, and careful with the stallion— he's a fresh one," China says, pulling into the stable yard. Jimmy is running beside the pickup to keep up, limping bad.

"Put him in the last box stall— one down the end by Shorty Hollister's gelding. Want to keep him away from the mares. Calvin, you go home now; don't let your stepdaddy give you no more shit—"

But I stay in the truck, huddled up in the corner of the cab like I don't want to be seen.

China opens the door on her side and fishes the kittens out from under her seat. "Cutest damned things—" she says as she puts them back into the feed sack. Their eyes are still closed and she puts them into the sack gently, but I can tell she's in a real hurry.

"Jimmy—" she says, "After you take care of the Appaloosa, take these damned kittens into Grandma. They got took away from their mama too soon. She'll know what to do."

China flies down the hill to the emergency— tires squeal as she takes the turns. She drives with one hand, the other in her lap fingering the top of an empty Miller's bottle, turning it over and over in her pale fingers. She goes through a red light like she doesn't even see it. The streetlights turn on and I can see them all the way down Foothill Boulevard— a spear of lights. The sky is deepening. Clouds are tinged with orange.

China bounces into the parking lot. I hang on when she makes the turn. I see Jimmy Root's convertible parked up near the entrance— last spot before the sign that says Emergency Vehicles Only. China pulls in four spots down.

Boots is nowhere to be seen in the visitor's waiting room. China asks the nurse behind the desk. The nurse says check the third floor in the other wing. We go up an elevator smelling of medicine and down a long hall with a green stripe painted on the wall. Through open doors I see beds with feet sticking up under sheets and people sitting up— trays of food on rolling trays over their laps. China's walking so fast I can't see much else. I hurry to keep up— hold my breath as long as I can. I can't stand the smell.

Boots is in the waiting room on the third floor. He's reading a motorcycle magazine. A small woman with red hair and a green dress is walking up and down holding a Kleenex to her nose. A little girl with a teddy bear is curled up on a chair. Her legs are dirty and she has a dirty pink Band-Aid on one knee. When we walk into the waiting room the woman in the green dress looks at us like we're poison.

"Doctor says her spine is broke—" Boots says when we walk into the waiting room. "This here's her mother."

The woman in the green dress stomps up to China and glares up at her. She's tiny, not much taller than my sister. "You the owner of that stable?"

"I'm China Clark—" China says, holding out her hand.

"You the person broke my baby's back?"

"I'm sorry—" China says. "I wasn't there when it happened."

"That's the trouble. You wasn't there. You put those little kids up on a horse with no supervision."

"There was supervision. Boots was there. And Jimmy. Besides, renters ride at their own risk. They sign a form."

"I never signed no damned form. And I'm her mother. You put 10-year-old girls up on your horses and you claim it's at their own risk?"

"Calm down, sugar—" China says. "This ain't helpin' nothin'."

"Well who's goin' to help me take care of my baby with a broken back? Who's goin' to help her she can't get up out of her wheelchair to pee? And don't you sugar me!"

China's silent.

"Miss—" Boots says.

"And don't you 'Miss' me neither!" the lady snaps at Boots. "I'm a Mrs. and when I'm through I'll own your sorry butt!"

She turns back to China. "This your idea of 'supervision?' This—hoodlum."

Boots' face turns dark.

"Boots is a good boy—" China says. "He knows his way around a horse. Your husband here?"

"What husband? I don't have a husband! And just what business is that of yours?"

"Sugar—" China starts to say and then she goes silent. She walks over to the window and stares out into the parking lot.

"It was a birthday present—" the woman says softly. "She took her friend riding as a birthday present now she'll never walk again because she wanted to give her friend a nice birthday present." The woman starts to cry.

Boots puts his arm around the woman's shoulder. Helps her sit down. The woman doesn't seem to notice. Boots is wearing his leather vest with no shirt underneath. His face is black with stubble.

"I'm gonna find someone to talk to—" China says to me. "You wait here, Calvin, keep Boots occupied."

China comes back with a nurse. The nurse is carrying a tray with a pill and a glass of water.

"Here, Mrs. Anderson, this might help."

"How's my baby?" the woman asks, looking up.

"She's still in X-ray— It'll be a long time. You might want to go home. There's nothing you can do here now."

"I want to see her—"

"It's not a good idea right now."

The nurse turns to China. "It might be better if you all just go home. There's nothing you can do here now either."

"I'm stayin'" China says. "Boots— You take Calvin home in Jimmy's convertible."

"But there's nothing you can do—" the nurse says.

"I'm stayin', I say—" China says.

"You gonna be okay, China?" Boots asks.

"I'll be fine, handsome," China says. "You just take Calvin home. It's gettin' late."

"China—" I say. I want to hug her, protect her.

"What is it, sunshine?"

"China—" I say. "Thanks for taking me out to the Rocking Chair E and R today. I had a real good time."

China doesn't seem to hear. She walks back to the window.

Outside, I'm glad to breathe real air again. It's cold riding in the convertible with the top down. I wrap my arms around my chest to shield myself from the wind.

"It was Stuie Kramer's fault—" Boots says.

"What do you mean?" I ask.

"Kramer was sicin' that dog of his— Stormtrooper— on that Labrador from over at the pistol range. They was just startin' to mix it up when those kids rode through the gate. That little girl was on old Cricket. You know how gentle old Cricket is. Cricket wouldn't move more'n an inch if a bomb went off under his ass. But those dogs tumbled right under his feet. Poor Cricket didn't know what to do with two hundred pounds of fightin' dog under his feet so he kicked out a little and that little girl fell off backward right on that gatepost. Hadn't been for that gatepost she probably woulda just hit the ground and knocked the wind out of herself. Damned Stuie Kramer and that gatepost."

"Jimmy Root didn't say nothing about Stuie Kramer."

"Jimmy Root's covering up. Stuie Kramer lit out in his pickup right after it happened— before the ambulance even got there. Jimmy Root says it wasn't really anybody's fault. Kramer didn't really mean nothin'— Like shit."

"If I was Stuie Kramer—" I start to say.

"If you was Stuie Kramer what?" Boots says.

"If I was Stuie Kramer— After last night?"

"You know Kramer— Ain't got no shame. Told Jimmy Root he kicked Pooh's butt," Boots says. "Just like the little shit. Fuck me, it's gettin' cold!"

"What's going to happen, Boots?" I ask.

"What do you mean?" he asks.

"To China—"

"Nothing much—" Boots says. "Insurance take care of it. My daddy's gettin' sued all the time from guys gettin' hurt on the job. Insurance always takes care of it."

"But what if China don't have insurance?"

"I don't know—" Boots says. "You hungry?"

"But what if China don't have insurance?"

"Beats me, kid— Don't even think about it."

"But what if she don't?"

"China's up shit creek I guess. China Seas will be turned into ex– ec– u– tive housing I guess. Don't even think about it."

Boots pulls into Jerry's. It's Sunday night so there aren't many cars in the parking lot.

"How much bread you got?" he asks.

"Not much," I say. "A dime and maybe a nickel—"

"Ain't got much neither, but maybe I got enough we can share a burger."

I give Boots my money. He's got a dime and two pennies. He rustles through Jimmy Root's glove compartment and finds a nickel.

"Fat city!" he says. "We got just enough for a hamburger and fries."

We go up to the window. Jerry's working the window. "What's happenin' guys?" he asks.

"Hear about China?" Boots says. "Little girl broke her back up at the stable today— rent string rider."

"Broke her back?" Jerry says.

"Yeah—"

"Jesus," Jerry says. "Hope China's got a pot of insurance."

"China's down at the hospital now—"

"People sue their grandmothers these days. It's one of the things gives me the willies. But a broken back— I hope China's loaded up with insurance."

"Listen, Jerry," Boots says. "This is all the money we got and we want a hamburger and small fries. Can you spot us a couple of Cokes?"

We sit in the convertible sharing the hamburger and drinking Cokes.

"Calvin, I'm sorry about what happened last night—" Boots says.

"Nothin' much happened," I say.

"You don't want to get mixed up with that shit—" he says.

"What shit?" I say.

"Drinkin' all night— fightin' and stealin'."

"It was fun—" I say.

"It's okay for fuck ups— like Singer and me. But you got a choice."

"What choice," I say.

Boots looks at me, hard.

"That Stuie Kramer really cocked you one. I see you wearin' a badge on your eye."

"Why'd you tell Stuie Kramer I was messing around with Dixie?"

"Wasn't me. It was Singer. You know Singer. Shit for brains."

I'm silent.

"I was thinkin' about you and that mountain lion—" Boots says.

"Pancho?"

"Yeah. You was really gonna turn that sucker loose, wasn't you?"

"Don't remember much—" I say.

"You was really gonna turn that sucker loose. Get a few drinks in you, kid, and you're a wild man."

"Pancho don't belong in a cage," I say. "He should be up in the hills somewhere— livin' off of deer."

"We all in cages someway or another, kid. Don't you know that?"

"What do you mean?" I ask.

"I got people rattlin' my cage, I can tell you that— Goin' to school tomorrow?"

"I guess—" I say.

"Well we better get you home."

Before Boots can start the car three Harleys roar into the parking lot. Singer is riding behind his brother.

"Hey, man— Thought that was you. You drivin' Jimmy Root's short now?"

"Girl broke her back up at the stable today. Rent string rider. We was just down at the hospital."

"No shit!" Singer says.

Singer's brother swings his big boot over the Harley, almost kicking Singer in the face. He walks around the bike and leans on Boots' door. He has a tattoo on his shoulder, a skull riding on wings. The lights from Jerry's, red and white neon, dance on his dark glasses.

"Hey, Kirk, man—" Boots says. "When'd they let you out?"

"I got out—"

"Bitchin'!" Boots says.

"No shit—" Kirk says. "Need a gig. Talk to your old man."

"Don't know, Kirk man—" Boots says. "You know what he said last time."

"Talk to your old man."

"Sure, Kirk," Boots says.

"Don't forget—" Kirk says.

Kirk climbs back on the Harley and kick starts it. "Don't forget!" he says before gunning the Harley. "Talk to your old man."

Kirk does a donut in the parking lot and peels out into the street leaving a strip of gray smoke. Singer throws us the finger. The other bikes roar behind. My ears ring with the noise.

"That's one that belongs in a cage," Boots says. "Hate to see Singer ridin' with his brother again—" He starts the car. "Lets get you home."

Boots is quiet driving back up Malcolm Avenue. Jimmy's convertible coughs twice and runs out of gas half way up the hill.

"Shit!" Boots says. "I thought we could make it." He backs the convertible up to a wide spot on the road. We find a large rock to block the wheel. We start a small rock slide digging it out. We walk the rest of the way up the hill. Crickets are loud in the grass and frogs are even louder as we walk around the pond.

"See you, kid—" Boots says as he drops me off at my house.

He walks into the darkness to tell Jimmy Root about his car.

The house is dark. Curly's all over me. I sneak into my room. Sis tiptoes into my room behind me. "Where you been, Calvin?" she whispers.

I just give her a hug and tell her to go to bed.

# Roberts Surplus

JUNE asks if I want a ride home. Her mother is picking her up, but Lee Campo and I are headed down to Roberts Surplus.

"Moore—"

Mr. James brushes around the corner, carrying the PA amp from the auditorium, Cary George and Lisa Simon at his elbow. He pivots to walk backward a few steps, talk to me, before hurrying down the hall toward the principal's office.

"What're you doing this summer, Moore?"

"Nothing," I say.

"Well, keep that writing muscle exercised," he says.

"Writing muscle?" Cary George says.

"He wrote this really neat poem?" Lisa Simon says. "About a horse?"

"A horse?" Cary George says.

"It died—" Lisa says.

Cary George stares at me.

Mr. James turns with a half wave and hurries away down the hall. The others follow.

June touches me with her elbow.

"Well, see you then—" she says, cradling the stuff she'd cleaned out of her locker in her arms. She turns, starts to follow Mr. James down the hall, but then stops and turns back.

"Think we can ride together this summer? You can borrow my daddy's mare." Her blouse is bunched up over the top of her books and gym shoes.

"Don't know—" I say. "Maybe—"

"Well, bye then—" June says.

Someone bangs a locker door at the far end of the hall. It echoes in the empty hallway. The janitor's mopping the floor, pulling a battered bucket behind him. Light from the high windows glints off the wet swaths on the floor. The hall begins to smell less like steam tables and sweaty gym clothes and more like Lysol.

And that's about it, I think. End of junior high.

I meet Lee Campo on the narrow patch of burned crab grass in front of the school. He's staring up at the flag. The flag is hanging like a limp rag from a white pole over the front entrance.

"They ought to burn it—" he says.

"Why?" I ask.

"Supposed to burn a flag when it starts looking like that. Out of respect."

"They ought to burn the whole school." I say.

Campo laughs. "Out of respect."

"So what'd you get?" I ask.

"What do you think?" he grins.

"Even from Bouknight?"

"What could he do? I aced his tests."

"Smart mother—"

"You're smarter than me. You just don't copy from the right people."

"Copying's not my style."

"Ask me, you just kind of gave up this year."

"What do you mean?" I ask.

"Your algebra homework was hopeless. I had to copy from Lisa Simon."

"Had other stuff on my mind this year."

"They going to take you out of college prep put you in auto shop. You'll be in with all the pachucos— over at the high school there next semester. How're you going to get into college?"

"Maybe I'm not going to college."

"That's great! Got just the job for you then."

"What's that?"

"Cleaning spark plugs on diesel engines."

"Sounds better than hanging sky hooks."

"Or, got a better one— sex fiend like you—"

"What's that?"

"Counting teats on wild boars."

"My kind of job."

"Well let's shag it then, sex fiend," he says. "It's a long walk down to the airport."

The houses go from poor to shabby as we walk down 98th Avenue. Kids with big eyes and black hair stare at us. An old man is painting a '49 Ford with a paintbrush, sky blue. He's wearing a straw-woven snap brim hat and a sleeveless tee-shirt. *"Hola!"* he says as we walk by. We wave, walk past a vacant lot planted with corn.

"So what're you doing this summer?" Campo asks as we walk past the potato chip factory. The smell of fresh potato chips is faint at first, then overpowers the smell of the street—makes me hungry.

"Nothing much—" I say. "What're you doing?"

"That special program— up at Cal."

"Mr. James tried to sign me up for that."

"Should have signed up. We'd have a blast. Hang out on Telegraph Avenue– write poetry with those beat characters."

"Costs too much," I say.

"James didn't tell you about the scholarships?"

"Parents got to fill out the forms."

"So?"

"Didn't ask them."

"Why not?"

"Just didn't. Don't ask them for nothin'."

"Jesus—" Campo says. "Why not?"

I don't answer.

"I'm kind of lucky I guess. My dad's taking me up to Canada fishing in August."

"Careful you don't get eaten by a moose," I say.

"British Columbia— camping in a tent."

"Or a grizzly bear."

The airport is spread out across the mud flats at the edge of the bay. Walking down the frontage road we see shimmers of hot air over the runways— shiny reflections off the bay.

"Look, there's an old DC-3," I say. "You don't see them much anymore. Know how to tell the difference between a DC-3 and a DC-4?"

"How?" Campo asks.

"DC-3's got two engines, carries 14 passengers; and the DC-4's got four, carries 48."

"How do you know that?" Campo asks.

"My dad told me. My real dad. DC-6 has four engines also, but it carries 102 passengers. The Super Connie that TWA flies looks like it's got a hunch back. It's got four engines, but only carries 40 passengers. But jets are going to replace them all. Fly to New York in six hours."

"Your dad live in New York? Your real dad?"

"No. Philadelphia."

"You could go anywhere— where'd you most like to go?" Campo asks.

"Tahiti—" I say.

"I worked a guy in Tahiti once— on my ham rig," Campo says. "A missionary."

"You can talk to people that far away?"

"Right conditions in the ionosphere—"

"How long would it take me to get my ticket?"

"Need to learn the code first. Five words a minute for your novice ticket— thirteen for general class."

"What's the difference?"

"Novice is good for one year. And you can only work certain bands."

"What've you got?"

"General class. Advanced too. Test for advanced is tougher."

"How'd you get started?"

"My dad's a ham. We got our advanced tickets together."

I walk in silence.

"But I can help you learn the code."

"Code hard?" I ask.

"Work at it, take you a couple of weeks maybe. And the theory test is a joke. I'll give you a book. You can memorize the answers."

"Who'd you copy from when you took the test, your dad?" I ask.

"Wrote the answers on my fingernails," Campo laughs.

Roberts Surplus is in a low metal building next to the airport. Two bright yellow bomb cases stand on their fins on either side of the door. Open cartons bulging with GI canteens, telephone handsets, and olive colored metal boxes with weird knobs and dials block the doorway, make it hard to squeeze inside. We shimmy around the cartons.

"The neat stuff's inside," Campo says.

It's dark and cavernous inside after being out in the bright sun. Metal shelves sag under bulging boxes— dusty electronic instruments rise to the corrugated iron ceiling. The maze-like passages between the shelves are littered with airplane parts and more cartons filled with trench shovels, flare guns, broken typewriters, odd-shaped boxes snarled in wire tangles. One passage is lined with electronic consoles that look like stuff out of a science fiction movie.

"What are those?" I ask Campo, pointing to a carton overflowing with silvery metallic boxes.

"Filter capacitors," he says. "But lookee here—"

Campo's pointing at a pile of shoebox size black boxes with dials and tuning knobs on the front panels.

"I was hoping we'd find some of these suckers— ARC-5's. Change the coils, build a power supply, and you got yourself a dandy communications receiver."

"How do you know all this stuff?"

"My dad—" he says, "But I'll show you— I wonder what they're getting for them these days."

Campo finds a bald man with wireless rim glasses and a cigar. The man looks at Campo and me. He looks at the pile of ARC-5s like he's never seen them before. He looks up at the corrugated iron ceiling like he's reading a price list. Then he looks back at us. "Those going for $3.50," he says.

"Too much," Campo says. He starts shifting the ARC-5s around the pile, digging down to a deeper level. He finds one covered with gray dust. "Look at this— It's all dinged up."

The man looks at the unit like a jeweler looking at a watch. He takes a small screwdriver out of his shirt pocket and opens up a metal hatch on the top of the unit. Inside I see the silvery tops of vacuum tubes packed tightly in the box.

"That one you can have for a buck—" he says.

"Got a dollar?" Campo asks.

"No," I say.

"I'll loan you one. It's a good buy. You can pay me back next semester."

"How do we know it works?" I ask.

"Probably doesn't, but my dad can fix it," he says. "My dad can fix anything. It'll make a real good communications receiver."

"Okay," I say.

Outside, in the bright sun, the black thing that I'd felt in China's truck rises up in me again. I've been feeling it more and more lately. Campo doesn't notice, but then he does.

"What's the matter, Calvin?"

"Nothing—" I say.

"Come on, man. I'm your buddy, you know."

"All that stuff in there—" I say. "I feel like that sometimes—"

"What do you mean," he says.

"Nothing—" I say.

"Come on, man—"

"I feel like that—" I say.

"Like what?"

"Crap left over from a war."

Campo's mother asks me to stay for dinner. I thank her— say I can't.

"Why not, man?" Campo asks.

"Got to go," I say.

"It's just tuna casserole," Campo's mom says. "But it's real good—"

"Besides, I'm going to be up at Cal most of the summer and then up in Canada," Campo says. "I won't see you until next semester."

"I know," I say. "Have a real great summer."

"Why don't you stay," he says.

"I've just got to go," I say.

"Yeah, man— OK." Campo says. "Don't forget your receiver. When I get back from Canada me and my dad can help you fire it up."

"Yeah, sure—" I say. "Have a real great summer—"

"You too—" Campo says.

"Yeah—" I say.

Campo lives near the school. I walk down his block to Bancroft Avenue and then head up Bancroft toward home. The radio is heavy under my arm, the sharp edges cut into my ribs. I hear a roar and a motorcycle pulls up on the sidewalk behind me. It's Singer.

"Hey, man! Thought that was you. Want a ride, sucker?"

"New bike?"

"My brother's. Melinda bought it for him for gettin' out of the joint. We givin' him a comin' out party tonight—"

"He lets you ride his bike?"

"Yeah, well, let's just say it's a surprise party. Melinda's keeping him busy. Want a ride?"

"Sure—" I say.

"Got a few things to do before I can take you up the hill—"

"That's okay," I say.

"What's that thing?" he asks, pointing at the metal box under my arm.

"A communications receiver—"

"No shit," Singer says. "What's it do?"

"It's like a radio—" I say.

"No shit! Well I don't think you can carry it on the bike."

"Maybe I better walk then—"

"No, look man, hide it under that hedge there. I'll pick it up for you later—"

"Maybe I just better walk up the hill—"

"Your choice—" Singer says.

"Yeah, well, okay," I say.

I'm feeling needles in my arm from the weight of the receiver. It feels good to put it down, nestled in under the cool dark of the hedge. I straddle the jump seat behind Singer. It's the first time I've ever been on a Harley. Singer kick starts the bike and bounces over the curb into the street. The engine feels like it's alive between my legs. I feel like I'm going to vibrate off the seat. I tighten my hold on Singer's waist. His stomach is hard as steel. I feel a kind of sickness when Singer takes a corner. He hits a pothole and I clench my jaw to keep from biting my tongue.

"Where we going?" I yell.

"Get the beer," he says.

"You don't have an ID," I say.

"Don't need an ID. You'll see—"

We cross the line into San Leandro. Singer turns down a narrow gravel road. Dust and gravel spray out behind us. I try to bow out my knee. The tail pipe is burning my leg. But I need to hold the bike tightly between my knees to keep from bouncing off.

Singer pulls into a driveway. A grossly fat biker is working on a Harley next to a dirty white house trailer with rusty trim. His Harley has weird handlebars that rise up like the horns on a wild bull.

"Hey, skipper!" the biker says, wiping his hands on a rag.

"Hey, Cocky—" Singer says.

The biker has a red bandanna knotted around his neck, no shirt, and Levi's expose the crack in his butt. Folds of fat hang over the tops of his greasy Levi's.

"This here is Captain Cock—" Singer say.

Captain Cock's flabby shoulders and chest are dripping sweat. "U.S. Navy" is tattooed on his shoulder. A huge snake tattoo is wrapped around his fat arm, it's jaws open, fangs dripping, like it's going to devour his thumb. Captain Cock's front teeth are missing. He shoves his face into mine, exposing the black void under his lip. "My friends call me 'Sucker— Cap'n Cock Sucker.'"

"Leave him be—" Singer says.

"I looove fresh white meat—" he says, shoving his face even closer into mine.

"We're throwin' a party for my brother—" Singer says. "A comin' out party. Melinda wants you to get the beer."

"Party time—" Captain Cock says.

Singer pulls a hundred dollar bill out of his shirt pocket. I've never seen a hundred dollar bill before. Never even seen a fifty.

"Melinda says you know what we need—"

"Believe it," Captain Cock says. He nods at me. "Sweet Pea gonna be there?"

"Gotta go—" Singer says.

"You're ridin' the Kirk Man's bike—" Cock says.

"Melinda's keepin' him busy—"

"Better hope so—"

"She's keepin' him real busy 'til I come back."

"Well you want music forget Mouse," Captain Cock says.

"Why's that?"

"He's in five to ten for receivin'."

"Shit," Singer says. "Melinda was hot for Mouse."

"Why'n'cha ask the two Joes. They better anyway—"

"Yeah," Singer says. "They pretty good—"

Captain Cock winks at me. "See ya, Sweet Pea—"

We ride back into Oakland, almost to the Alameda line. Sinking sun glares in my eyes. I don't know how Singer can see without dark glasses. We pull in beside other bikes in front of a bar, The Hell Hound. Two bikers burst out of the bar, releasing a loud blast of country music.

"The two Joes in there?" Singer asks.

"Try the Transmission Shop—" one says. "What'cha doin' on the Kirk Man's bike?"

We ride back to east Oakland. The Transmission Shop is on MacArthur Boulevard. Singer rides through a cavernous door, through an empty auto shop, and stops in front of the office door, stomping down the kick stand. The Harley echos like thunder inside the garage.

"Hey, Singer—" the two Joes say with one voice.

They're identical twins, albinos.

"Sure, we'll do the music—" they say after Singer tells them about his brother's party. "The Kirk Man know you got his bike?"

"Ride me up the hill now, Singer—" I say as we ride out of the Transmission Shop.

"Sure—" Singer says. "But first got to get back to my brother's place— You ain't in no hurry, are you?"

MacArthur Boulevard is lit up with streetlights. Singer pulls out into the fast-moving cars. The red taillights are a blur.

We ride out through San Leandro, out to Hayward. Singer's brother lives in the hills. There're no streetlights on the winding road to his house. Bugs whop into my face and eyes.

"Hey, babe—" Singer's brother says as we walk into his bedroom. He's sitting up in bed with a woman sitting beside him. The woman's breasts are bare. Her left breast is decorated with a rose tattoo. It's hard not to look.

"That my new bike I hear you roll in on?"

"Just took it up the road—" Singer says.

"I oughta kick your ass, job my bike—" Kirk says.

"I told him he could ride your bike," the woman says.

"I oughta kick your ass too—"

"You'd like to try, wouldn't you—"

"Don't think I can?"

"I'd cut your BB balls off, honey buns—" she says. "Shove 'em up where they won't do you no good no more." She pats the bed. "Hey, baby brother, want to join us?"

"You'd do it too, wouldn't you—" Kirk says.

"What—"

"Cut off my balls to spite yourself—"

"Bet your sweet A— mess with me. What do you say, baby brother? Ask your friend too."

A roar of bikes assaults the house. The front door bangs open.

"Who's that—" Kirk says.

"Why'n'cha go see—" the woman says.

Kirk swings out of bed, naked. His neck is red and tanned— his back white, shoulder and back raked with scars. He walks into the living room.

"Party time!" someone yells and it sounds like a football game, vicious contact, people cheering.

"You, bitch, Melinda," Kirk says, leaning back through the bedroom door, a beer can in his hand. "You been plannin' this all along, ain't ya?"

"Plannin' what?" Melinda says. "I'm stayin' in here all night with these two sweet young things."

# The Kirk Man's Comin' Out Party

THE two Joes are setting up an amp and an awesome pair of speakers. Rowdy bikers, smiling couples, wary loners— pausing, sniffing— are crowding through the front door. Kirk's telling Singer how to move the furniture around but they're having trouble with so many milling boots on the orange and brown rug, so many people crowded into the red linoleum spaces between the furniture.

Kirk's wearing Levi's but no shoes nor shirt. He's carrying two beer cans, one in each hand, gesturing, telling Singer to move the sofa into the corner, the lamp into the bedroom, the TV on the floor.

They're rolling the rug when Captain Cock pushes through the front door with two kegs, one on each shoulder. The bikers, already loud, cheer and drum on the walls and tables and wave fists in the air. The Captain grins, his hideous tongue darts in and out of the gap in his mouth. "Kiss me, Buck Teeth," a tall biker, arm in a cast, yells over the din. "My tonsils itch." Captain Cock grins, makes like he's going to throw the kegs at the tall biker, handling the full kegs on his shoulders like basketballs. The tall biker ducks, knocking over a floor lamp with his cast. The Joes test the mike, making the speakers screech and squeal.

"Playin' our song!" someone yells.

"Sounds like Rudy's teeth scrapin' the curb when he hit that beer truck!" another answers.

More bikers come through the door, carrying cases of beer, bottles in brown paper bags— the men in leathers and faded black tees, or Levi jackets with the ripped out sleeves. The women wear revealing blouses, cut low, clinging skirts, tight black pants, heavy lipstick and mascara. The women all have long hair, sleek and shiny and newly brushed. Captain Cock, bulling his way out of the kitchen, sees me.

"Hey, Sweet Pea—" he yells. "We gettin' it on tonight?"

Melinda, standing behind me, presses my cheeks in the palms of her hands, pulls my head back between her breasts—

"Filthy hands off this boy, Dick Head," she says. "This one's mine tonight." Melinda's nails are long and crimson red.

"Tomorrow, then," Captain Cock grins, "His sweet ass is mine—" He pushes back out the front door, returns with two more kegs on his shoulders.

"Singer—" I say.

"Have a beer—" Singer says.

"Look, Singer, I've gotta go—" I say. "Can you ride me home?"

"Yeah," he says. "In awhile. Have a beer—"

One of the Joes sets up a drum set and the other snaps a contact mike on a Fender guitar.

"Baby— baby— baby—" the Joes sing and suddenly the sound of the drums and the guitar fills the room with pulsing rhythm. Someone shoves a beer into my hand and someone else shakes a beer can and sprays beer over my head, starting a beer fight with me as a shield. An old biker with a gray goatee unsnaps a saxophone case and joins in with the Joes. It's hot and close and leather and bodies are pushing me on all sides. I sip the beer. It's cool in my throat— cuts through the smoke that makes breathing hard.

I slump down, sit on the floor, back against the wall. Singer pushes through the dancers and sits beside me. "They're gettin' it on tonight!" he says. Singer's eyes are shiny. He takes quick sips out of the beer can that he holds in both hands.

A biker, leather vest over a body cast, pushes through the door. Angry black stitches crisscross his shaved skull like railroad tracks. He's leaning for support on two heavy blond women, gold chains hanging between their breasts.

"Hey, Rudy!" a voice yells.

"Rudy make it?" another answers.

"Yeah, Rudy—" a chorus of people pick up around the door.

"And this is dedicated to—" the Joes say, "Rudy!" and pick up an even fiercer rhythm.

"Piled into a beer truck," Singer says. "Slid right under that sucker. Totaled his bike. We thought he was a goner."

One of the blondes, cigarette dangling from her over-painted mouth, leering grin on her face, pulls her hand from behind Rudy's back, holds up a transfusion bag with a dangling rubber hose.

"Rudy's blood bag?" someone yells.

"Rudy's douche bag!" another returns.

"Rudy wants to thank you all for your donations—" the blonde says. "Says we're all blood brothers and sisters now."

"Hey, hey, hey!" the crowd yells.

"Fill it up with that Seagrams quick," someone yells. "Rudy's blood type."

Someone tilts a whiskey bottle by the neck over Rudy's mouth and Rudy chug-a-lugs it down, whiskey running down his chin.

"Singer, I've really got to go—" I say.

"In awhile," Singer says. "Gotta borrow a bike from a guy I know to get you home. Don't see him yet."

I push my way through the dancers to the kitchen. It's brighter in the kitchen but no less crowded. I'm pushed against a kid not much older than me. He's wearing full leathers. His face is pinched and pockmarked. "Watch it, fuck face!" he sneers. I raise my beer can, give him a salute, and slip further into the kitchen. A tall biker, bony, wearing a cowboy hat, is frying eggs on the top of the stove, sliding the skillet back and forth across the gas burner, making sparks. "Over easy comin' up," he yells over his shoulder. "Any takers?"

Empty beer cans and torn beer wrappers are piled up on the top of the stove behind the skillet. I push through to the sink. The sink is overflowing with empty beer cans and whiskey bottles. I look for a glass to get water but can't find one.

"Watcha lookin' for, kid?" someone shouts.

I turn. It's a biker with deep red skin, mahogany, almost as tall as the ceiling. His hair is long and black, pulled back tight from his face and tied in a ponytail.

"Water," I say.

"Beer's better—" he says, and shoves a full can of beer into my hand.

"Hey, Moon!" someone yells.

The biker with the ponytail, Moon, turns. "Born to Die" is embroidered on the back of his Levi's jacket. "Got uppers?"

Moon reaches into his jacket pocket, pulls out a prescription vial and tosses it over the crowd.

I push my way out of the kitchen.

"Jesus Christ!" someone yells. "Fire!"

People press hard behind me, push out of the kitchen. I turn and see orange flames through the jostling bodies, smoke rising to the ceiling, first white then black. The biker with the cowboy hat grabs a beer can, shakes it, pops the top, and uses it as a fire extinguisher.

"Shit!" he yells, slapping his bare forearm. "Fuckin' grease—"

Someone behind him shakes up another can.

Someone strong pushes me from behind, bulldozes me back into the kitchen. It's Kirk. "Fuck's happenin'?" he yells.

"Nothin', man," the biker with the cowboy hat yells back, blowing the grease burns on his arm. "Just a grease fire. Want some eggs?"

"Open the door," Kirk says, "Get some fuckin' air in here—" People push back into the kitchen.

I push through the dancers to the other side of the living room. The music is physical and loud. Hurts my head. I feel it in my teeth. A fourth biker's joined the group, playing an accordion in a way that I've never heard an accordion played before.

"Try this—" Singer shoves a paper cup into my hand. I sip. It burns like fire.

"What's that?" I croak.

"Tequila!" Singer giggles. "Taste the worm?"

Someone's pulled all the pillows off the sofa. I see them piled up in the corner, straight backed chairs making a fence. I look. Two infants, sucking their fists, are curled up in the pillows. Empty beer cans are piling up around them. The dancers are making the windows rattle. I wonder how the babies can sleep.

"Leave her the fuck alone!" someone yells and I'm almost pushed back over the chairs and into the babies as the dancers surge back against the wall. I recover— stand up on one of the chairs. Two bikers are standing in the cleared spot, one squeezing the other in a bear grip and the other shoving the first one's chin back with the heel of his hand. The hand is dark and grease-lined, fingers splayed out. The throat is bare and white as milk, tarnished black neck chain cutting into flesh, silver crucifix dangling. Kirk and Captain Cock step into the cleared spot and each grabs a fighter in a head lock, snaps his head down until he's bent double, and marches his captive, head under muscled arm, toward the front door. The dancers clear a path as Kirk and Captain Cock march the fighters toward the front door. "Fightin's outside—" Kirk says as he kicks his fighter out the door, moving aside to let Captain Cock do the same. Kirk's wearing motorcycle boots, but still no shirt.

I step into the bedroom. It's dark but I hear struggling, muffled cries, and moaning. I see dark forms kneeling over the bed, ten or more shadows, glint of bare buttocks. Someone grabs me and pushes me back toward the door.

"Outta here—" a voice says, low with believable menace.

I see Sergeant Joe Friday down on the floor through pounding legs— fuzzy gray image. If sound, it's drowned out by cacophony. *Dragnet.* I try to watch but mostly see flickering silver flashes behind dancing feet. The top of the TV is covered with beer cans and paper cups—a woman's bra dangles over the screen.

I see the dining room table pushed up against the wall. I squeeze through dancing bikers and crawl underneath. It's tight under the table but it's easier to breathe. I see spike heels, vermilion toenails, and mo- torcycle boots. I rest my chin on my knees, hug my legs. Another form pushes in behind me—a woman, short black hair, skin white as milk.

"Hi," she says. "I'm Andrea. What's your name?"

I'm startled.

"It's neat in here," she says. She sits, ankles crossed, on the other side of the dusty cross brace under the table. I see a bulge of white panties, dark underneath. Her thighs are white as milk. "Gonna tell me your name?"

"Calvin—" I say.

"Calvin," she says. "That's a beautiful name."

I can't tell how old she is. Her features are fine. Her skin is smooth. Her eyes are big and deep blue. She looks more like a doll than a woman. She looks like a little girl.

"Where you from, Calvin?" she asks.

"Singer brought me," I say.

"Singer—" she says. "You thirsty?"

"A little," I say. I start to crawl out from under the table.

"No," she says. "I'll get it."

She backs out from under the table. My heart's pounding. She's back with a jug of red wine. "I like this better than beer—" she says. "You like red wine?"

"A little—" I say, not meaning it. We drink the wine together, passing the jug back and forth. She asks me things. After awhile I tell her about Dutchess. When I'm done she's crying, or at least her eyes are filled with tears. She looks at me, into my eyes. She leans over and kisses me, gently, on the lips. I'm crying too.

"Poor baby—" she says. "Let's dance—"

The Joes are taking a break. The old biker with the goatee is playing his saxophone, softly, slowly. Andrea presses hard against me. "You're nice, Calvin," she says. She presses her face into my neck. I'm faint with the smell of her. I feel like she's holding me up. I've got a boner and want to pull away but she holds me tight. She's holding me like I've never been held before. The Joes come back and the rhythm gets hard. "Know how to bop?" Andrea asks.

"No," I say.

"Well just do what I do," she says and starts twisting her hips into me, drawing away, her eyes closed and her face dreamy. Dancers push us back together, crushing us. Andrea grinds her hips into me. She grinds her breasts into me. I've never felt a woman's breasts before, like this. When she pulls back her nipples show hard under her thin white blouse. The musicians take another break. The saxophone player pushes his way into the kitchen. A biker, with a black eye patch, climbs up on the coffee table, kicking beer cans and cigarette wrappers onto the floor. The biker's Levi's are splotched with white, cut with battery acid holes, gray flesh and black leg hair showing through. Andrea takes my hand as the biker's deep voice rumbles down.

> *"Dear Mother, dear Mother, the Church is cold,*
> *But the Alehouse is healthy and pleasant and warm;*
> *Besides I can tell where I am used well,*
> *Such usage in Heaven will never do well..."*

"Fuck's he sayin'?" someone behind me says.

"Fuckin' Bloom doin' poetry again—"

"The fuck Bloom know about poetry?"

"Used to be a professor."

"Bloom? That crazy fuck?"

"Shut the fuck up, Bloom—"
"Get him down from there before he breaks the fuckin' table—"
"Only does it when he's drunker'n a fuckin' skunk."
I pull away, but Andrea holds me, presses me closer to the table.

*"But if at the Church they would give some Ale,*
*And a pleasant fire our souls to regale,*
*We'd sing and we'd pray all the livelong day,*
*Not ever once—"*

"Shut the fuck up, Bloom!"

*"—wish from the Church to stray."*

"That's beautiful," Andrea says, childlike, looking up at the biker on the coffee table. "Did you write that?"
The biker looks down fiercely, seeking her out among the faces.
"Blake, my lady. Don't you know your Blake?" The biker then turns to me, fiercely with his one gray eye, shaggy black brow. He leans low, his gray eye boring into me. I draw back but bodies, jostling behind me, push me back into his face.

*"The night was dark, no father was there;*
*The child was wet with dew;*
*The mire was deep, and the child did weep,*
*And away the vapour flew."*

The voice yells behind me again.
"Bloom— Shut the fuck up I said!"
Beer splashes up into the craggy face and down onto me. Bloom's eyes snap cold as he spreads his arms, Christ like, while grappling fingers pull him down from the coffee table.
"No— no— Careful, his head— let him sing!" Andrea cries, clutching my hand and pressing close to me.
"Fuck's the band?" someone yells and the one-eyed biker falls into the pillowless couch, his words ringing in my ears.
Andrea grabs me, kisses me, fiercely, her tongue probing my mouth. I pull away. Andrea looks at me, probing, her eyes are all I see. But I

pull away, turn, and push my way to the bathroom. As I push my way into the bathroom someone pushes in behind me and closes the door. It's Moon. He pushes me up against the sink, traps me between his hard body and the sink, and leans over me and examines his teeth in the mirror.

"Hey, bro—" he says. "Let's you and me stay friends."

"What do you mean?" I say.

"Havin' a good time out there?"

"Yes," I say.

"Havin' a real good time?"

"Yes," I say, finding it hard to talk with his weight pressing me against the sink. He smells like beer and burnt motor oil and spices and something menacing that grips my chest, constricts my belly.

Moon picks at this teeth with his fingernails, examining his teeth in the mirror.

"Well that's my wife you dancin' with out there," he says. "Know what I mean? You dancin' with my wife."

"Your wife?" I say.

"The lady with the forever smile. So let's you and me stay friends."

Moon leaves the bathroom and I stare in the mirror, white face, black eyes and mouth. I sit on the toilet, trembling. A fist pounds on the door. "Hurry up in there before I pee on the floor—"

When I leave the bathroom Moon's dancing with Andrea and she's looking up at him, lovingly, like a child.

# Mom

WHEN I was a little kid I was always first out of bed. I couldn't wait for Teddy to come out of the bathroom. We'd sit in the kitchen, the kitchen light shining, the rest of the house dark, and darkness beyond the windows. We seldom talked. To break the stillness, as I remember it now, seemed forbidden somehow. Teddy would pour milk for me, stir in a spoonful of coffee, then he'd sit, sipping his black coffee, staring out the kitchen window, staring into the darkness beyond the glass. I'd color, or turn the pages of a picture book, or play quietly with a toy, afraid to break the silence, or maybe just sharing the ritual, the silence, the closeness.

Strange that I remember those mornings now. I remember so little from back then.

Later I'd stay in bed, wait until I heard the front door close and Teddy's truck drive off. Then I'd get up, dress warmly, go out to feed Dutchess, come back, wait for dawn to fill the house with leaden light before going out again to saddle Dutchess. I'd work her in the show ring for an hour each morning before going off to school.

Now I can't seem to get myself out of bed. It's three o'clock and I'm sweaty and my room is filled with hot blazing light. I have to pee in the worst way but I stay in my bed, watching a fly crawl around on the ceiling until I can't stand it anymore, and at last I get up, pull my top sheet over my shoulders, and pad into the bathroom to pee. The house is empty, still, just a buzzing of flies against the window panes.

In the bathroom I drop the sheet to the floor and stare at myself in the mirror, skinny kid, ribs showing, scraggly black hair over my cock, loopy black curls over white skin. Grandma calls me a long drink of water. I stare at my arms, stringy muscles, not rounded and powerful

85

like Boots or Cliff or hard with veins standing out like Kirk.  I have girl arms I think— one with a long bluish scar where I'd cut myself on barbed wire.  I stare at my face.  Brown eyes.  Messy brown hair.  A cowlick.  Ordinary.  I try a tough face.  And another.  It doesn't seem to work.  I have a plain face.  Nothing much even to shave.

I pad into my sister's room.  Her model horse collection covers the long bookshelf under her window, ceramic and plastic bays and sorrels and pintos and palominos.  Teddy told me that I would have to share Dutchess with Sis, let her ride Dutchess, or he would take Dutchess away from me, sell her.  I refused.  I'd trained Dutchess as a show horse.  Trained her to respond to secret signals, imperceptible commands.  Dutchess knew me.  Responded to me.  Trusted me.  I didn't want to confuse her, spoil her.  She was a good show horse, not much to look at, but always won top points for performance.  I fed her.  Groomed her.  Cleaned her stall.  She was mine.  I told Teddy that I would never ride again, that I would take his Winchester .30-30 and shoot Dutchess in the head first, and myself.  Sis cried and stared at me, hard, like she hated me, and then she came to me, in my room that night— "Don't kill yourself, Calvin," she said.  "I can save up money for my own horse."  I cried and told Sis that after the show season I would let her ride Dutchess, that I would give her lessons.  I told her about showing, what it was like.  I told her that I didn't know what else to say to make Teddy understand.  Teddy threatened to run an ad in the paper, sell Dutchess, but he never did.

Sis' room is messier than mine.  Her pajamas are on the floor and her play clothes and school dresses, her panties with pink teddy bears, and two bunched up white socks with dirty heels, her red school shoes.  Sis likes to paint.  Her watercolor set is sprawled across newspapers on the floor, black water in a glass, soaking brushes, rivulets of muddy brown and green paint.  She paints horses.  Her paintings are taped to her wall and one over the telephone table in the kitchen and two on the refrigerator.  I wish now that I'd let her ride Dutchess.

I pad into the living room, white sheet dragging behind me.  Teddy's slippers are on the floor in the living room and a beer can and newspapers.  Mom reupholstered the sofa but already it's stained and sagging, covered with golden hairs, Curly's favorite place to sleep.  Mom made the drapes and braided the rug on the floor.  When I was young Mom was always busy doing things, sewed her own clothing, made riding shirts for Teddy and me, but now she doesn't sew much anymore. The rug is unfinished. A tangle of woolen strips pulled through three metal cones pointed together at the end of the outermost braid is shoved under the sofa. There's a picture of Mom as a young girl with her mom, my grandmother, on the wall behind the floor lamp, a soft brown photograph in an old frame. Mom was beautiful then, faint smile, soft eyes. Harsh light streams through the drapes and falls in hard bars on the sofa and on Mom's unfinished rug. I turn. Teddy's run-down slippers smell up the living room, force me to leave.

I pad into the kitchen, open the cabinet door under the counter by the kitchen door. Mom keeps her leather working tools and scraps of leather and cans of leather dye and spools of leather stitching under the counter. Mom used to do beautiful carved leather work, wallets and belts and purses. I slide out the block of hardwood with all the holes filled with all the knurled metal stamping tools sticking up like flowers. I run my finger over the tools and enjoy the smell of the leather. Some of the tools are smooth and rounded and some are shaped like leaves and petals.

I pad into Mom's room. Her bed is unmade. Her pale blue nightgown is sprawled across the bunched up blankets and sheets. I lie down on the sheets and blankets and night gown, stare at the ceiling. There's a faint animal smell on Mom's bed. On the pillow next to me I catch a whiff of Teddy's rotten meat smell. On the floor, on Teddy's side, is a pair of Teddy's work pants, rumpled figure eight, left as he'd dropped them on the floor around his feet, gray pocket linings frayed and stained with ink, greasy belt stretched across the floor like a black and ugly snake.

I stand and look at Mom's things on her dressing table, a brush knotted with auburn hair, a padded round box, open, filled with crumbly flesh-colored powder, a tin ashtray with seven short and crushed and lipstick-stained cigarette butts, three pennies, seven hair pins, a paperback book, *Molly's Revenge*. I thumb through the book, looking for dirty parts.

I slide open Mom's closet— white blouses, pale green pants, three dresses, three sweaters, blue, white, pale rose, a fancy riding shirt, two empty wooden hangers and ten wire hangers. On the shelf above I find a suitcase with dented brass corners, empty, a pale blue cosmetics case, also empty except for one pink plastic eyeliner case with a broken mirror. Shoved in around the suitcase are five bright red boxes from Capwells filled with tissue paper, and four rolls of red and green Christmas wrapping paper.

On the floor below I find Mom's sheepskin slippers, scuffed up sandals, a rumpled nylon stocking, shiny black patent leather high heels, four wire hangers, her black riding boots, a ball of hair and dust, a dead fly. Mom never wears her riding boots anymore.

I open Mom's top dresser drawer, panties with bunched up elastic, four bras folded cup in cup, two pairs of nylon stockings, four pairs of white cotton socks, an unopened carton of Lucky Strikes, a penny, tarnished, 1948, Denver mint. I hold one of her sweaters up to my cheek, smell it.

Now I hear the front door. I scurry into my room, cover myself with the sheet, pretend sleep. My door opens, closes again, I hear mumbling outside my door. I hear footsteps, muffled voices, the refrigerator door slam, Sis squeal.

My door opens again.

"He sick?" Teddy asks.

I hear Mom's shuffling footsteps. I concentrate on relaxing my face, pretending sleep. I feel Mom's soft and cool hand on my forehead. I try hard not to blink. "His head's cool," she says.

"Shake him then," Teddy says. "Time he gets off his ass and does his share around here—"

"Let him sleep," Mom says.

"Five o'clock in the goddamned afternoon?" Teddy says.

"Must be exhausted," Mom says. "Let him sleep."

"Goddamned hooligan, runnin' around all night—"

"It's been hard for him," Mom says.

"Hard, my foot," Teddy says. "I'll show him hard."

"Shush up," Mom says. "Let him sleep." I hear the door close. I sleep. The room is dark with shadows when I open my eyes. Mom is sitting on the end of my bed.

"What's happening with you, Calvin?" Mom asks.

"What do you mean?" I ask.

"This isn't like you—"

"What isn't like me?" I ask.

"Running around all night. Sleeping all day."

I stare at the dark outside the window, surprised that I've lost a day.

"You feel all right? You feel sick?"

"No—" I say.

"Which?" she says. "You don't feel all right?"

"Yes. I'm not sick, I mean. I feel fine."

"Then tell me what's the matter— tell me what's bothering you."

"Just tired," I say.

Mom says. "All day. And you've been wetting your bed again."

"Just a little," I say.

"But you haven't done it for so long. I thought you were over that."

"I don't know," I say. "I think I am— sometimes I just can't help it."

"What's troubling you, Calvin? That horse?"

I'm silent.

"It was just a damned horse. Maybe we can find you another one."

I'm still silent.

"I found your report card," Mom says.

"I was going to give it to you," I say.

"I don't know what happened this year— last year you did so much better."

"This year was really hard—"

"I don't believe that," Mom says. "You're one of the smartest boys in your class. All the teachers say so."

"Really," I say. "It was really hard this year—"

"I talked with Lee Campo's mom. Lee did much better than you."

"Lee cheats. He copies from people."

"Calvin," Mom asks. "What are those seeds I found behind the cereal in the kitchen cabinet? Some kind of dope?"

"What seeds?" I ask.

"You know what seeds I'm talking about— In the paper bag."

"Oh, those," I say. "Those're pumpkin seeds. Grandma gave them to me. She said you make a tea out of 'em and they make you strong."

"Grandma?" Mom asks.

"Over at the China Seas—"

"I know Grandma," Mom says, "but why would she give you pumpkin seeds to make you strong?"

"I don't know," I say. "She just gave 'em to me."

"Mind if I ask her about that?"

"Go ahead," I say. "You don't trust me."

"Calvin, I don't know what to trust anymore—" Mom says. She's crying. "I just can't stand this anymore."

"I'm sorry, Mom," I say.

"What do you want to do?" Mom asks.

"What do you mean?" I ask.

"Do you want to live with your dad?"

"No," I say. "I want to live here—"

"Live with your dad in Philadelphia?"

"No," I say. "I want to live here."

"But you don't live here anymore. I never see you. I don't know where you live anymore—"

"I live here—" I say. "With you."

"Not really. You don't really live here anymore. I just can't stand it anymore."

I feel tears, but fight them back.

"I feel like I'm being torn apart between you and your stepdad. I feel like you're pulling my arms and legs right out of my body. Both of you. I just can't stand it anymore. I want to go off by myself, live somewhere alone."

"I hate him—" I say.

"How can you say that?"

"I do—"

"Not many men would take in a boy like you— Give you all he's given you."

"Gives me shit—" I mumble.

"What?" Mom asks.

"All he ever gives me is do this— do that—you'll never amount to anything," I say.

"Don't talk like that," Mom says.

"But it's true—"

"He's trying to help you learn responsibility. It's his way."

"What does he know about responsibility?"

"He's hard-working, your step dad. His job ain't easy, you know—"

"He's a lush—"

"After what he puts up with down at that shop all day he deserves a little relaxation— You don't know what he puts up with down at that shop just to keep a roof over your head."

"He can keep his roof— I'd rather live in the barn," I say.

"Calvin—" Mom says.

"I hate him," I say. "I don't know why you married him."

"You love your little sister?" Mom asks.

"What do you mean?" I say.

"You wouldn't have a little sister, you know— Wasn't for your step dad."

"I can't help it," I say.

"Calvin—" Mom says.

Mom looks at me, her face long and dark and hollow. She stands up, walks to the window.

"Calvin," Mom says. "Can't you try?"

She turns, eyes filled with tears.

"Can't you at least just try to get along with him?"

I cry. It's dark in my room. I cry, my pillow hot and slimy under my face. My door opens.

"You hungry," Mom asks.

"A little—" I say.

"Come on out and I'll make you a hamburger."

"No," I say.

"Your step dad's gone," she says. "Down to the 296 Club. Sis is asleep."

"Okay—" I say.

I get up, pulling my sheet around me.

Mom hugs me. I smell stale cigarettes in her hair.

The hamburger, fat between two slices of white bread, is red in the middle and juicy and tastes like I haven't eaten anything in a week.

Mom stares at me, eyes deep and brown, sunk in black hollows, silent, while I eat.

# Wild Horses

MOM shakes me hard.
"Wake up, honey. China needs your help."

"What—" I say, groggy from too much sleep. Mom's switched on the ceiling light. It hurts to open my eyes.

"Out of bed now, honey," Mom says. "China's at the door."

I squint at the window. It's light, but foggy outside. I slide out of bed. Thick morning fog presses against my window, silvery wet fog that hides the hill, hides the pond, hides the barn, even, and presses in on my window like glistening angel hair, reflecting back the yellowish light on my ceiling, reflecting back my naked frame. I pull up my Levi's, the faded denim cold and stiff.

China's framed in the front door against the white fog.

"Damned rent string horses busted out again," China says. "They're runnin' wild all over the hill."

China shoves a tie rope into my hand and starts to turn away, hurrying.

"I'll get my boots," I say.

"Shake a leg, sunshine," China yells over her shoulder. "They're in that damned Pritchett's yard again. And some are runnin' down through the pistol range." China's white Western shirt fades into the fog.

I find my boots, slip them on. I find a tee shirt in the dirty clothes hamper, slip it on. Outside, on the road, I feel lost in the fog. I hold out my hand, white against white. I look down at the ground, circle of dirt. My house is gone. The stables are gone. The hills are gone. I hear tires on the road. Yellow eyes come at me through the fog.

"I drove by Pritchett's, didn't see nothin'," China says, leaning out the window of her truck. "Go back and check the field behind Pritchett's house for me, will you sunshine?"

Red eyes fade into the fog.

I jog past Harris' field. Harris' horses know me, nicker at me, even though I don't feed them anymore. I hear them, but barely see them behind the fence in the swirling wet fog.

I jog past Sammy Burwin's place. His house is gone, his ivy lawn is gone, his brick steps are gone, obscured completely in fog. I take a turn into his driveway, see nothing but the hazy red side of his horse barn, the shadow of his horse trailer. Sammy's dog, locked in the house, barks as I walk back down the drive. Sometimes, but not today, the horses stray into Sammy Burwin's place.

I catch up with Jimmy Root on the road. He's a ghost-like shape at first, lurching through the fog ahead of me.

"Jimmy—" I yell.

He turns. He's wearing his deerskin roping gloves, carrying his lariat, iron-hard coils in his left hand, stiff loop drawn through the big-eyed honda in his right.

"Never seen 'em so frisky," Jimmy says.

"What do you mean?" I say.

"Catch your breath, son—" Jimmy says. Jimmy's face is scored with weather lines, shiny from the dripping fog. Shaving cream, hastily wiped, fluffs out under his smiling eye.

"Ain't worth bustin' a gut 'til this fog lifts," Jimmy says.

"I'm okay," I say, breathing hard. Fence posts beside the road look like soldiers in the fog.

"Tried to catch old Sally—" Jimmy says. "Back there in front of your house— But she took off down the road like a shot, tail flying high like a two-year-old filly. Lord knows where to in all this fog."

"Sally?" I say.

"Yeah, old Rattle Bones— Old gal's got to be sixteen if she's a day."

"So what's got into Sally, Jimmy?" I say. "Spooked by the fog?"

"A whiff of hot young horse dick, I'd say—"

"Horse dick?"

I realize what he's said after I say it. For some reason it embarrasses me. I step ahead.

"Slow down, cowboy," Jimmy says. "You're gallopin' too fast for these decrepit old bones."

"What're you talking about, Jimmy?"

"These old bones got more mileage on 'em than fleas on a dog," Jimmy says.

"No. You said horse dick—"

"That new stallion China brought in—" Jimmy grins. "You're old enough to know about the birds and bees ain't you?"

"The Appaloosa? He's locked up in a box stall, ain't he Jimmy?"

"And every she horse on the place knows which one," Jimmy says. "They keepin' me up nights, croonin'—"

"But the stallion's locked up in the box stall. How they even know he's around?"

"They can smell him. Or he can smell them. Don't matter. It's in the air. He's been singin' love songs and they been moonin' back ever since I backed him out of China's trailer. 'Come and get it, big boy—'" Jimmy laughs. "Especially that Tululla."

"Tululla?"

"Yeah, Tululla— That ol' whore's come into heat for the first time in five years by my recollection—"

We approach the Simpson's house. "So how'd they get out this time?" I ask.

"Give you three guesses," Jimmy says.

"That stretch of fence by the water trough," I say. "Busted it down again."

"I told China we gotta put a whole new fence around that rent string corral— Ain't nothin' but creosote and termite shit holdin' it together right now. But China wants to put in a breedin' pen first."

"Stuie Kramer said he fixed up the rent string corral real good the last time they busted out," I say. "Told China they'd never bust out through the fence again—"

"Don't matter who fixed it up last," Jimmy says. "Get a few fillies as horny as Tululla there, or that new paint filly, and they'd bust out of San Quintin to get themselves some of what that Appoloosa's got between his legs. Rest of 'em just went along to watch the show, I betcha."

"I'm going to run ahead, see if I can head 'em off at Pritchett's," I say.

"You do that, son," Jimmy says. "And give ol' Pritchett my regards."

I run. The horses are no longer in Pritchett's yard. But Pritchett is standing in the middle of the road, looking like a scarecrow in the fog.

"You're gonna pay for this!" Pritchett says, pointing toward his shattered fence, hooved up lawn. A yellow Caterpillar front-end loader is sitting in his driveway.

"I'm sorry, Mr. Pritchett," I say. "We'll fix up your lawn."

"Damned right you'll fix up my lawn. And you'll fix up my split rail fence too—"

"Yes, sir," I say.

"Next time I see those damned animals on my property, I'm gonna make dog meat out of 'em with my .30-06. You tell that woman."

"Yes, sir," I say.

Pritchett's standing in his bedroom slippers. His hair is white and curly. Stands out like wire.

"And you tell her another thing—"

"What's that, sir?" I say.

"You tell her I heard what happened to that little girl. And I've been in touch with that poor little girl's mother. I've got a petition up that I'm presenting to the city council—"

"The city council—" I say.

"Presenting it at the very next city council meeting. That stable's a public nuisance. Oughta be bulldozed into dirt. Them damned horses of yours are worse than sewer rats."

I'm silent, beginning to shake.

Pritchett turns, stomps up his driveway.

"Mr. Pritchett—" I say.

"What now?" he says.

I stare at him. He looks like Teddy, the way he's standing.

"Spit it out, sonny—" he says. "Ain't got all danged morning."

"Did you happen to notice which way the horses went?"

I run down past Mrs. Levinson's house. I see two ghostly shapes at the end of the road. It's Red and Long Tom. When I get near they clatter past me and back up the road. The clack of their shod hooves on the asphalt sounds hollow and muted in the fog. Mrs. Levinson's house is a low gray shape in the fog. I follow.

"Easy now, fella—" I say, walking up to Red. Red's looking at me, ears alert. He lets me get within touching distance then dances backward and skitters around me and clatters back down toward the pond.

I look around for Long Tom. I don't see him, but then he comes trotting out of Mrs. Levinson's driveway. "Hey, Tom—" I say. He clatters after Red, swerving around me, just beyond reach..

I jog back down toward the pond. Jimmy's leading Mavis and Corn Pone back toward the stable when I get down near the pond. Jimmy's leading Mavis with the lariat pulled short around her neck and Corn Pone by the long hair under her throat.

"Old Red and Long Tom come runnin' by me just now," he says. "You see 'em go by?"

"Yeah, I seen 'em," I say. "I'll get 'em."

"You see old Pritchett up that way?" Jimmy says.

"Yeah," I say.

"What's the old boy say for himself this morning?" Jimmy says, grinning again. "Invite you into tea?"

"Jimmy—" I say. "It's not so funny. He says he's got a petition and he's going to give it to the city council."

"The city council—" Jimmy says, shaking his head.

"That's what he said," I say.

"You ever wonder, Calvin," Jimmy says, "why there's more horses heinies around this town than there is horses?"

I stare at the dirt.

"Don't you worry about the city council none," Jimmy says.

"But he says he's talked to that girl's mother— the girl that broke her back."

"Don't you worry about that stuff none," Jimmy says, but I can see Jimmy looking me over. "China ain't no pushover. She's bulldogged worse before."

I turn away.

Jimmy stops me. "I think old Sally's down that way too—" he says, gesturing with his chin. "Now don't you worry about that Pritchett shit."

Red's standing in water up to his fetlocks when I get down near the pond. The pond, farther out, is smooth and gray, reflecting the gray fog. Closer in, Red's bony shape dances in oily ripples. Red's watching me— I swear, laughing at me. My boots sink into the mud when I wade in after him. He lets me get up to him again, almost close enough to loop the tie rope around his neck, then he turns explosively, splashing me with mud and water.

"You crow bait!" I yell.

I lunge after him, almost losing my boot in the mud. Red stops not ten feet away. This time he lets me clip the tie rope around his neck. I snub a half-hitch around his nose and swing on, Indian style, my boots dripping water and muddy pond weeds. My Levi's are soaked to the knees and I've got a line of mud up the front of my shirt.

"Now, Red," I say. "Where's Tom and Sally?"

Red's old and skinny, a rack of bones really, and his backbone feels like it's going to cut me in half lengthwise. Dutchess was well muscled. Her backbone was cleft into hard and sinuous muscle.

The fog's lifting some. I see Long Tom and Sally grazing on the high grass at the edge of the pond. They only stray to graze a couple of times as I herd them back up to the stable.

"Don't get off that horse," China says when I ride into the stable yard. She's putting her shoulder against a fence post by the water trough, nails in her teeth, a carpenter's apron hanging under her heavy belly. "Danny Boy and Elvis are still runnin' around down near the pistol range."

"I'll get 'em," I say.

Riding out through the gate I hear the crack of China's hammer driving staples into the shaky post to hold up the twisted barbed wire.

I nudge Red. He starts off at a jog and his bony spine about kills me. I nudge him into a full gallop.

Huey's granddad is staring at the horses in the middle of the pistol range. "Got a pistol meet this mornin'" he says, spitting tobacco.

"I'll get 'em out of there, " I say.

"Be obliged," he says.

I nudge Red down the steps, railroad ties sunk in dirt. Danny Boy and Elvis see us coming. They jog back and forth in front of the green shooting benches. Further down the range I see the targets, black torsos silhouetted on white. Danny Boy and Elvis dart back past us and up the steps and out onto the road in front of the range.

I chase Danny Boy and Elvis down into the zoo. When we hit the slick asphalt, clattering down the hill, I have to bring Red to a walk. The fog is high in the trees.

I see Emilio's truck near Pancho's cage. Emilio's holding Danny Boy.

He's using a twisted gunny sack for a tie rope. Pancho is chewing on a bloody carcass. Elvis is grazing across the road from Pancho's cage, ears alert as we approach.

"*Señor Calvin*—" Emilio says. "*Amigo!*"

"Hi, Emilio—" I say.

"I miss you, *amigo*. You don't visit me—"

Emilio's eyes are dark and deep. The bones in his face look like they're going to burst through his taut skin. He's skinnier than I remember.

"I've been busy," I say. "Just got out of school."

"Come see me," he says. "I have something for you."

"For me?" I say. "I'll come by——"

"I'm glad to see you back on your *caballo*," Emilio says. "But this one's a little skinny, *sí*?"

Emilio leads Danny Boy over to me. "This one says he's tired now and wants to go home again," Emilio says. "Let me get you a rope out of the truck."

"Emilio—" I say.

"*Sí*," Emilio says

"Thanks—" I say.

Emilio grins. "Come visit me," he says. "The furry ones ask about you all the time."

I lead Danny Boy and Elvis back to the stable. As I lead Danny Boy and Elvis through the gate and back into the rent string corral I hear the squeal of fighting horses, the hammering of hooves on hollow wood, the crack of shattering one-by-eights from over behind the box stalls. I jump off Red, unclip the tie rope, and slap his backside, hurrying him into the corral.

The back of the box stall is nearly kicked out. It's the Appaloosa's stall. The Appaloosa's shod hooves are still hammering on the wall, flashing silver shoe, white foreleg, through the splintering wood. Jimmy's waving his hat, jumping around, trying to shoo Tululla into the hay barn. Tululla's tail is in the air. She's prancing around the yard between the box stalls and the hay barn. Her eyes are wild. I'm still carrying the rope Emilio'd given me. I manage to dance in, flick the rope around Tululla's neck.

"Good move, son," Jimmy says. "We better get that Appaloosa settled down—"

We tie Tululla up to one of the fence posts. She's still backing off against the rope, snorting through her nostrils, eyes flaring, but she's calming down now.

We lean over the bottom door of the Appaloosa's box stall. "Look at that pastern," Jimmy says. "Must of cut it good kickin' out the back slats there. Wonder he didn't bring down the whole shebang."

"What can we do about that cut?" I ask. "Looks bad."

"Clean it out, wrap it good," Jimmy says. "China'll have a cow and a half that leg gets infected."

"What can I do?"

"Get the fixin's and I'll try to gentle him down some."

I run, get the big purple bottle of disinfectant and the red and white box of horse bandages out of the tack room.

"Stand out of the way," Jimmy says when I get back to the Appaloosa's box stall. "This ain't gonna be no walk in the park."

"Maybe we should halter him," I say.

"He's riled enough already," Jimmy says. "Let's just get it over with."

Jimmy enters the box stall.

"Easy, fella— Get me a clean sponge," Jimmy says.

I start, but suddenly the Appaloosa squeals and I hear a sickening thud, like a baseball bat on a watermelon, and shattering glass. When I turn Jimmy's rolled up in the corner of the box stall, purple disinfectant splattered on the wall, white bandage unrolled on the sawdust floor. The Appaloosa's head is stretched out like a snake, ears flattened back, flared nostrils snorting fire on Jimmy's rumpled form.

"Jimmy—" I say.

The Appaloosa turns, hindquarters cocked, ready to let fly again.

"Jimmy!" I say.

Jimmy yells. The Appaloosa jumps, skittish. Blood's still running black down his left hind pastern, leaving bright red crescents on the pale shavings.

"Jimmy, you all right?" I ask.

"Ribs stoved in is all," Jimmy says tightly, fighting for breath. "Get me outta here before that son takes another swipe at me."

I enter the box stall and the Appaloosa twitches his head, fires a look at me. I work my way between Jimmy and the Appaloosa. The

Appaloosa twists his head to bite me but I kick him hard in the ribs. He flips his ears forward, startled.

"Can you make it okay, Jimmy?" I say, keeping my eye on the Appaloosa.

"I can make it," Jimmy says. "But it's gonna cost me some."

Jimmy half slithers, half crawls on his hands and knees through the cedar shavings toward the door. "Lordy, Lordy," Jimmy moans.

"You okay, Jimmy?" I say.

"Dear Lordy," Jimmy says just above his breath. "How many more times—"

"How many more times what, Jimmy?" I say.

I hear harsh breathing behind me.

"Jimmy—" I say.

"—you gonna bust this poor cowboy's worthless bones?"

"Hurry, Jimmy," I say. "I got him distracted."

"I'll distract the son of a bitch— with a two-by-four—" Jimmy says, stronger, face twisted, reaching up for the latch on the box stall door. "I heal up from this."

I back out of the box stall behind Jimmy.

"How bad is it?" I ask.

"Three, four ribs is all," Jimmy winces. "Same ones I busted about ten times before." Jimmy's face is red with pain.

"What can I do?" I ask.

"Get China to look after that stallion's leg," Jimmy says through his teeth. "I'll drag these miserable bones into the bunk house some way or another."

"Let me help," I say.

"Just get China," Jimmy says. "I been stove up worse before."

China's pulling into the yard in her pickup, back from looking for the last horses.

"China!" I yell.

China comes running. Jimmy's leaning on the hitching post outside the clubhouse when she comes running around the corner. His face is twisted up, stringy black hair hanging over his forehead, clipped gray hair on his temples glistening with sweat.

"What happened, handsome?" China asks.

"Blamed stallion snuck one in on me," Jimmy says.

"Hurt you bad?"

"Just those same damned ribs I busted down Visalia that time."

"Well you was stove up pretty bad that time, handsome," China says. "Laid up six weeks— bitchin' like a baby the whole damned time—"

"Well I'm gettin' tougher in my old age—" Jimmy says. "But don't make me laugh none, like you done that last time."

"Well let me help you into the house you tough old buzzard."

"I can make it my own way," Jimmy says.

"Well just you lean up against me. Holler if it's hurtin' too much—"

China settles Jimmy in on her bed. Grandma peels Jimmy's shirt off. Jimmy's skin is white and loose like chicken skin, ribbed with old scars. His chest hair is gray. I'm surprised at how skinny he is. His ribs, on the left side, are angry red with pinpricks of blood oozing up along a white crescent.

"Looks like he connected real good—" China says. "We gotta get you down to the emergency."

"Better look after your stallion first," Jimmy says.

"You didn't bust 'im back?"

"He cut himself up gettin' all excited about the ladies. That's why I was in his box stall in the first place."

"My luck," China says. "How bad he cut himself?"

"Not bad," Jimmy says. "But you better tend to it."

"Well I'll tend to it after I get you down to the emergency."

"Don't worry about me—" Jimmy says.

"I ain't worried, handsome, but I'll feel better after they've looked at them ribs. And I still got a couple of horses to catch."

"Gotta patch up that box stall some too—" Jimmy says. "He tried to kick himself a new door."

"Think we could use that lumber we bought last week to build the breedin' pen?" China asks.

"Better use that to fix up the rent string corral," Jimmy says.

"Need a whole new barn, is what you need," Grandma says. "Surprised that horse of yours didn't bring the whole blamed thing down around his ears."

"We'll patch it up," China says. "Good as new—"

"Fat chance," Grandma says. "What'cha gonna do, China? You need help around this place. More'n just Jimmy even. You can't go on doin' everything by yourself on a wing and a prayer, and bein' mother to the whole world to boot."

"And just where do you think I got that bad habit from?" China smiles.

"Never you mind," Grandma says. "Just what're you gonna do now that Jimmy's hurt the way he is?"

"I can help out," I say.

"Shush up, Calvin. You're just a boy, you don't know what you're talkin' about," Grandma says. "This place needs man work and plenty of it."

"I'll find somebody—" China says.

"You tell me where, Missy," Grandma says. "Piss pot little you can pay."

"I can pay," China says.

"You spent every cent on that cursed spotted horse of yours— And don't you deny it."

"I can run an ad in the newspaper—" China says.

"And lucky to get some rummy or wetback or psycho running from the law for what you can pay— Good hands like Jimmy don't grow on trees, and you know it. Plus you got this lawsuit to think about."

"I can help out—" I say again.

"And I don't care what you say. At my age I ain't gonna go out there and shovel no horse manure to help you out of this kettle of fish," Grandma says. "I do enough of that around here already."

"Sometimes you just gotta fight for what matters—" China says. "Isn't that what you always told me, mom?"

"Maybe I can get Pooh and Cliff and Boots and Singer to help out too—" I say.

China looks at me.

"Well maybe I can't do back work," Jimmy says. "But I can do head work. And Calvin's stronger than he looks. Maybe two of us, workin' partners, can get a man's work done."

"We can," I say, looking at China.

China looks at us, softly.

"Jimmy," China says. "You want a beer? Ease the pain some before I take you down to the emergency?"

"Hell yes," Jimmy says. "Didn't think you'd ever ask. But ain't you got nothin' stronger?"

"Well maybe I can hose down the yard for you now and again," Grandma says. "But don't you ask me to do nothin' more strenuous, you hear?"

# The Water Fight

"DON'T you climb that ladder condition you're in, Jimmy Root!" Grandma yells.

Grandma is spraying the stable yard to keep down dust. She's wearing a pink bathrobe, pink mule slippers, white bath towel wrapped around her head. From where I'm kneeling, on the roof of the hay barn, I can see her white hands, bright red fingernails, holding the fat green hose snaked out behind her across the yard. We're fixing the roof over the hay barn. Jimmy says next time it rains hard we'll lose a couple of tons of good alfalfa hay if we don't fix the roof.

"I'm just goin' up to show Calvin how to hold a damned hammer," Jimmy says.

Jimmy's whispering loud, hoarse from yelling up at me in loud whispers all morning. His ribs hurt when he talks loud in a regular voice he says, and he'll run a pitchfork through anybody makes him laugh.

"You fall off that ladder you'll break more than three ribs," Grandma says.

"Ain't plannin' to fall off this ladder," Jimmy says.

"You fall off that ladder break that skinny neck of yours wouldn't exactly be a loss, Jimmy Root," Grandma says. "Besides, you're askin' too much of that boy, makin' him climb around that roof like a damned monkey—"

"Gimme a damned monkey any day," Jimmy says. "Monkey's got somethin' between his ears besides daydreams and excuses."

I'm at the top of the ladder, shirt off, hot morning sun baking sweat out of every pore in my body. My knuckles are skinned and bloody from handling the heavy rolls of roofing asphalt, green crushed stone on one side coarser than sandpaper. When I look down sweat runs off my forehead and into my eyes.

"Damned fool," Grandma says.

I look down. Jimmy's half way up the ladder. He's climbing with one hand, holding his other elbow tight against his ribs. He takes a step, pushes himself up, winces. I see white bandage wrapped around his chest under his half-opened shirt.

"You can just tell me from down there, Jimmy," I say.

"Well you're holding that damned hammer like a damned girl," Jimmy says. "I got to show you how to hold it right."

"I can do it," I say.

"Well I don't want you hammerin' holes in that damned new roofing asphalt," Jimmy say.

"I'm not," I say.

"Well let's see just what you're doin' up here," Jimmy says, pulling himself up above the eaves of the roof. "I don't want you jackin' off up here on my time."

"I'm not jackin' off," I say, holding back anger and frustration I've been feeling all morning. Jimmy's been yelling at me from the ground, criticizing everything, ever since we started.

Jimmy takes a long slow look at the courses of green roofing asphalt running across the roof of the barn. He leans around the ladder, looks closely at the seam of roofing nails running along the edge of the roof. Jimmy has a way of looking at my work that makes me nervous. I've only got one more run to finish.

"Well I guess you ain't jackin' off at that," Jimmy says, scowl fading into a nod and a smile. "Looks like you're doin' a pretty damned respectable job up here after all. From down where I was sittin' it looked like you was screwin' up this roofin' job somethin' royal."

It's the first word of praise I've heard all morning.

"Well help me swing around off this ladder," Jimmy says. "It ain't easy climbin' one handed."

I help Jimmy swing around the top of the ladder. I can tell that he hurts more than he's letting on.

"Well I brung you this," Jimmy says, pulling a bottle of Dr. Pepper out from under his sling.

"Thanks, Jimmy," I say, holding the bottle, looking at it.

"Well ain't you goin' to open it, son?"

"I gotta climb down get a bottle opener," I say.

"Judas Priest. Don't they teach you kids nothin' useful these days?" Jimmy says. He hooks the top of the bottle on the edge of the roof.

"Tap the top with your hammer there— Gentle now or you'll bust the neck."

I tap the top gently with the hammer.

"You hit the top with your heel of your hand there usually," Jimmy says. "But it'd hurt to Jesus if I tried that now."

The top pops off. Jimmy takes the first swig, then hands me the bottle. I press the cool bottle to my forehead.

"Nice up here," Jimmy says. "Better than down in the yard with all them damned jabberin' women."

"It's hot," I say.

"Yeah, but you get used to it," Jimmy says. "Down in Texas it was always hotter'n this. You just get used to it."

"How hot was it down in Texas?"

"Hunnert ten in the shade wasn't unusual. Colder'n a witch's titties in the winter."

"Didn't you like it down in Texas?" I ask.

"Like it down in Texas?" he says. "What do you think?"

"I don't know," I say.

"Wouldn't be sittin' here if I liked it down in Texas now, would I?"

"What didn't you like about Texas?" I ask.

"Know how to find Texas?" Jimmy asks. "Anyone ever tell you that?"

"How do you find Texas?" I ask.

"Walk east 'til you smell it— south 'til you step in it."

I grin.

"Know how to find California?" Jimmy says.

"How do you find California?"

"Walk west 'til your shit don't smell."

"What didn't you like about Texas, Jimmy?" I ask.

"Texas is all right," Jimmy says. He looks out over the stable yard. "Don't get me wrong, son. Any old place is all right if you got people there that love you."

"Didn't you have people down there in Texas that loved you?"

"I sure didn't think so at the time. But thinkin' back I ain't so sure no more—"

"What do you mean you ain't so sure?"

"At that age, I'm thinkin' now 16— 17 years old, I'm not really sure you know what love is, real love. I was just a hot young cock then, lived at the center of the world thinkin' I knew better'n anybody else around."

"What do you mean?" I ask.

"When I was 16— 17 I could ride faster, rope better, fight meaner, piss further than anybody else in the county, and the next county over. Thought I could, anyway. I figured people just had to love me I was such a mean son of a bitch. Couldn't figure out why nobody let me walk on 'em like door mats the way I thought they oughta. So I just beat the shit out of every poor fool crossed my path, men with my fists, women with my pecker."

"What about your parents? Didn't they love you?"

"Not the way I was thinkin' they oughta. All I saw was their drinkin' and fightin'. I was thinkin' love is people givin' you everything you wanted, lettin' you do every fool thing. That'n pussy."

"So what is it then—"

"What is what?"

"Love—"

"Love? You're askin' the wrong hombre, partner. But I know one thing for certain—"

"What's that?" I ask.

"Lovin' don't come free— You got to earn it."

"Earn it? What are you talkin' about?"

"By treatin' people with your own love— love and respect."

"Well I don't love nobody," I say. "And I'm never going to, neither."

Jimmy looks at me, strangely.

"Why do you say that, son?" he asks.

"I'm just not," I say.

"You never loved nobody?" Jimmy asks.

"I loved Dutchess— That's all."

"You love your mama?"

"Maybe— Used to."

"Didn't it feel good? Love your mama?"

"No, it just hurts—"

"Even when you were a little tucker? Didn't it feel good sometimes, just to be close to your mama?"

"Maybe— sometimes. But it just hurts too much."

"You afraid of a little hurt?" Jimmy says.

"I'm not afraid," I say. "But it's just not worth it."

"So what are you goin' to do then?"

"What do you mean?"

"What're you fixin' to do— got your whole life ahead of you?"

"Don't know, be a scientist I guess. Don't need nobody to discover things and stuff."

Jimmy lies down on his back, pulls his hat down over his eyes, stretches out, crosses his boots.

"I been hurt plenty of times," Jimmy says. "I been hurt in my body and I been hurt in my heart. My daddy used to beat me real bad. First time I busted my arm it was my daddy that busted it. People lived hard lives back then. Grew up hard. Raised their kids hard. My daddy was drunker'n a skunk. Meant to break my arm. I don't know what hurt me more— my arm or the fact that my daddy meant to break it. He hurt me so much for such a long time— switches and belts and sticks and fists— that time I was your age I didn't know what hurtin' was no more.

"I spent a whole winter in that Ardennes Forest hurtin' every minute I was there. Man that was somethin'. Rain, fog, black ice and snow. My feet and hands and nose hurt from the frost bite. My back hurt from sleepin' on the ice on the bottom of my foxhole. My stomach hurt from the food they give us which wasn't bad but didn't agree with me. And my head hurt from all the drinkin' we was doin'. I hurt most of all when I tried to shit out in the snow. Just knew Jerry was gonna come rollin' in just when I had my pants down tryin' to pass a turd out there in the snow. I thought at the time that it was my asshole that hurt. That something was wrong with my shitter. But I know now it was sheer scared shitless gripping my soul that sent that hurt piercin' down through my nether parts—

"And I hurt in the hospital when they brung me back, when they tried to patch my flesh and bones back together. Lordy did I hurt then. And I hurt even more because I didn't have nobody around who really gave a rat's ass whether I lived or died."

"What about when you were riding bulls?" I ask.

"Gettin' hurt ridin' bulls was nothin'. I'd break somethin', fill myself up with booze and pills, and break somethin' else again two days later. Doctors said I oughta be locked up I was such a menace to myself. When I broke my hip it was bad though. I knew then that I couldn't go on breakin' stuff without breakin' somethin' that just wouldn't grow back together again. So I just got shit blind drunk."

"Then what'd you do, Jimmy?" I ask.

"That's when China took me in. Now there's a lady got more love in her body than Texas got armadillos."

"You in love with China?"

"Not in the way you're thinkin', son. But I'd jump off this roof into fire for that lady, that's for damned sure."

"How are you in love with her then?"

"Well one thing you gotta know is that love ain't just about your dick. I've had that kind of love more times than a dog got fleas. And I been hurt in my heart think I'd die too, but I'd do it again in a minute."

"What do you mean 'love ain't about your dick'?"

"That's what I used to think when I was a young stud— Love was findin' some pretty young thing and puttin' it to her. That kind of love's real nice while it lasts. But she don't last long— Least in my experience.

"Real love's somethin' more than that. China taught me that. When China first took me in I thought that was all she had in mind, fat old maid lady runnin' a stable starved for dick. But she set me straight right off. First thing I found out was that China didn't need me for that. China has her fun, I can tell you that. But China's somethin' different, to me at least. She's like a sister— No. More than a sister. She's like that sun up there. Silent, but you feel her shinin' down even when it's all clouded up. That sun ever goes out, you just know it's gonna be night for ever and ever."

I finish the Dr. Pepper, wipe the sweat off my forehead. I look toward the show ring. Dixie and Alaska are working their horses, flashes of red and brown behind the fence posts. Shorty Hollister leads his gelding across the stable yard. I watch Shorty lead his gelding to the big green watering tank, watch the gelding's head disappear into the shadow of the peaked roof over the watering tank. I imagine the cool shadow under the roof of the watering tank, the gelding's lips sucking water, the two big goldfish in the tank darting here, there. I look toward the pond, over the top of my house, and see two white ducks drifting on the pond.

"Look, ducks," I say.

"Yeah. Mrs. Levinson bought herself couple more of them Pekins," Jimmy says. "Cops'll just pop 'em off again."

"Why do they do that, Jimmy?"

"Beats me," Jimmy says. "Cops is cops. I think they just see too much— fellow man at his cussed worst. So they get pissed off wanta kill somethin'. Ain't nice to kill people 'less you got to so they kill ducks. I used to feel that way myself more often than not. Shot a guy's car to shit in Waco one time, tryin' to kill him."

"Why'd you do that?" I ask.

"Just pissed off about some fool thing, I guess— Shit blind drunk when I did it."

I look past my house and up the road. Two cars, a Nash and a Pontiac station wagon, drive down the road and through the gate into the stable yard.

"Polliwogs," Jimmy says.

"What do you mean?" I ask.

"Just you watch," he says.

Six kids, four girls and two boys, spill out of the cars.

"Every year this time, parents start dumpin' their kids off to hang out at the stable. I call 'em polliwogs. Ones're still around at the end of the summer I call 'em frogs."

"You mean like Dixie, Alaska, Pooh and them? Are they frogs?"

"Yeah, they're frogs, but that Pooh's more like a horny toad," Jimmy laughs. "He's gonna get himself more than he bargained for rate he's goin'."

"I gotta put that last run of asphalt down," I say.

"What's your hurry," Jimmy says. "Barn ain't goin' nowhere."

Stuie Kramer drives into the stable yard. I hear his truck door slam behind the club house.

"Hi, Grandma. Waterin' the flowers?" Stuie says, walking around the corner of the clubhouse. Stuie's dog, Stormtrooper, trots around the corner behind him.

"You finish this up for me, Stuie, dear," Grandma says. "I gotta do my laundry."

Stuie takes the hose. The stable yard is dark where grandma's watered, bone white where the silvery spray kicks up spurts of dust.

"When you're done," Grandma yells from her porch, "the back yard could use a good hosin' too."

Boots climbs the ladder.

"What're you screw offs doin' up here?"

"Holdin' the roof down," Jimmy says. "Go down get us a couple of them Dr. Peppers and come back give us a hand—"

When Boots climbs back up, holding three Dr. Peppers, he's wet, water dripping from his chin.

"Son of a bitch Kramer just squirted me! Said it was an accident."

"I'll bet it was an accident—" Jimmy says.

"Feels pretty good, though, this heat, wanta know the truth—" Boots says.

"Stuie!" China bellows.

We look down. China's carrying a saddle over her forearm, wiping her eyes with her free hand.

"You cut that shit out now, you hear!"

"Old Kramer's havin' himself a good old time with that hose," Boots says.

"Watch this one," Jimmy says.

We watch the polliwogs walk from the rental barn and around the corner of the club house then squeal, throw their arms up as the spray hits them hard. Stormtrooper barks.

"Hey!"

"Cut it out, you!"

"I'm dripping—"

Stuie Kramer's grinning, holding the nozzle of the hose at his hip. The polliwogs retreat back toward the rental barn, Stormtrooper chasing them. There's something maniacal in Stuie's grin.

"Here comes Pooh. Let's see if Kramer's got the balls to squirt Pooh."

Pooh walks across the stable yard.

"Hey, Kramer, how's it hangin'?"

Kramer turns his back, squirts the hose the other way.

"Chicken shit," Boots says.

Pooh climbs the ladder.

"What're you fine gentlemen doin' up here on the roof?" Pooh asks.

"Poundin' pud?"

"Holdin' a prayer meetin'," Jimmy says. "Go down get us a couple more of them Dr. Peppers, come back up an' join the choir."

Pooh climbs back down.

"Hey, I got me an idea," Jimmy says.

"What's that?" Boots says.

"See them two buckets over there down by Rona's stall?"

"What about them buckets?"

"Kramer's gotta pull the hose through the box stalls there to spray down the back yard."

"I like what you're thinkin' if you're thinkin' what I think you're thinkin'," Boots grins.

"That's what I'm thinkin'," Jimmy says.

We climb down the ladder. I move the ladder to the box stalls. Boots waits for Stuie to turn his back, snatches the buckets, fills them up at the spigot behind the box stalls. We haul the buckets up the ladder.

Pooh climbs the ladder.

"What'cha guys doin' over here now with them buckets?"

Jimmy nods his chin toward the buckets then nods toward Stuie. Pooh grins.

We wait.

"Okay," Boots whispers. "Stay down, don't let him see you now."

Stuie drags the hose toward the box stalls.

"Ready," Pooh whispers.

"Aim—" Jimmy whispers.

"Bombs away!" Boots yells.

"You fuckers!"

Stuie looks like a drowned cat. His shirt's sticking to his skin, his face is red with anger, water streaming off the crown of his black hat.

"Bulls eye!" Jimmy whispers, trying hard not to laugh.

"You fuckers, I'll get you for this!" Stuie's trying to untangle the hose to get a clear shot with the nozzle.

"Let's throw his ass in the waterin' tank," Pooh says.

Kramer starts spraying us with the hose. Boots and Pooh bounce down the ladder, two rungs at a time.

"You shits!"

I follow.

Boots and Pooh are trying to grab Stuie. He's flailing his arms and kicking. Stormtrooper runs out of the shade of the clubhouse, barking.

"Pants him!" Pooh says.

"Don't get too rough now," Jimmy says. He's standing behind me, trying hard not to laugh.

The polliwogs come running. One of them grabs the hose and starts spraying Stuie in the face.

"You peckerwoods!" Stuie sputters.

"I got his belt," Pooh says. "Grab his legs there and pull his pants down." Stormtrooper nips Pooh's pant leg, pulling and snarling.

Dixie and Alaska come running, laughing.

Stuie's white underpants and white legs turn black with mud.

"Son of a bitch kicked me in the balls!" Boots says, turning red.

Boots grabs Stuie by the waist and hoists him over his shoulder. Stuie pounds on Boots' back with his fists, but Pooh's got him by the legs and the polliwogs are still spraying him in the face, drowning out his curses.

"In you go!" Boots heaves.

The water splashes up out of the watering tank and the hard iron rings like a bell as Stuie's boots hit the side.

Pooh picks Stuie's Levis up out of the mud—throws them in the tank.

Dixie and Alaska laugh.

Stuie comes up out of the water.

He stares at Dixie; face filled with blackness. She's still laughing.

He stares at Jimmy.

"I thought you was my friend," he says.

"I am your friend," Jimmy says, wincing, trying hard not to laugh. "Thought you'd like a little cool off is all—"

Standing in the tank, Stuie's dick looks pink under his wet underpants. The polliwogs are staring now. He steps awkwardly into his Levi's. Water pours over the waist band.

Stuie stares at Dixie then back at Jimmy.

"You ain't no more—" Stuie says, fumbling with the buttons on his Levi's.

"Sure I'm your friend," Jimmy says. "We just having us a little fun."

Now Shorty Hollister's standing, watching.

"Calm down, son," Shorty says.

Stuie's face is cold mean now, gray in the shadow of the roof of the watering tank.

"Some fun," Stuie says, glaring at Dixie.

"Stuie—" Dixie says.

"You pukes," Stuie says.

"Handsome—" It's China, pushing the polliwogs aside. "Climb out of there now, I need you to do something for me—"

"He can dish it out but he sure can't take it," Pooh says.

China glares at Pooh.

"Climb out of there now—" China says. "I need you to take my truck down to Hank's there on 98th Avenue, tell him to look at my clutch. You're the only one can get him to do it right."

Stuie's face softens.

"Hank never listens to me," China says. "But he listens to you alright, handsome. You got the right touch."

Stuie climbs out of the watering tank clutching his Levi's, China giving him a hand. Water streams out of the tops of his alligator boots.

China hands Stuie her keys then turns to Boots and Pooh.

"I got some box stalls need muckin' out, you two got nothin' better to do than waste my good water."

Stuie moves toward the clubhouse, squishing water. Stormtrooper trots beside him, licking his hand.

The polliwogs start backing away. China looks at Dixie, glaring. Then she glares at me.

"That roof fixed yet?"

"Almost—" I say.

"Well get it done," she says. "I need you to saddle up some rent string horses for a party comin' in this afternoon."

"He can dish it out but he sure can't take it," Pooh says again.

China turns on Pooh.

"What do you know about it, mister?" she says. I've never seen her so angry.

Pooh stares at the ground.

"What do you know about that boy? What he's had to take and what he ain't?"

Pooh's quiet now, exposed to her fury.

"Just what do you know, mister?  Maybe he's had to take more'n you'll ever know!"

# The Raid

POOH'S riding behind Alaska. His hair is black under the shadows of the towering laurels, then mahogany red again passing through the patches of bright sunlight. Sparks spray in the shadows of the trail when Alaska's sorrel mare strikes a rock with her shod hoof. The trail is narrow, winding down through the canyon along the bank above the slow creek. I reach out and touch the big moss-covered rock outcroppings overhanging the narrow trail. Sun bounces fiercely off the dry grass further up the canyon wall. Down in the creek I see silvery glints of reflected light in the shallow pools. I see deep shadows and moss under the overhanging ferns. It's been a scorcher of a day, but it's cooler in the canyon. The clack and clatter of our horses' shod hooves echo back and forth across the canyon walls.

Boots and Singer are riding ahead of Alaska, Boots on Shorty Hollister's gelding, Singer on Elvis. I'm riding Tululla, bringing up the rear. Tululla's the most spirited of the rent string horses, but she has a way of coming down stiffly with each step, jarring my teeth and bones. I think it's something she's learned to protect herself from the weekend cowboys, the steady renters, who have a way of abusing the rent string horses the minute they're out of sight of the stable. Renters usually have their favorite horses, but nobody ever wants to rent Tululla a second time. She was my horse, I'd get her over it. Dutchess had a way of dragging her feet whenever we rode away from the barn, stumbling over every pebble like she was on her last legs. But riding home, after a hard ride, she had a fast, sure-footed pace. She'd put her head down, nose near dragging in the dust, and she'd step out well ahead of the other horses, her brown and black ears flopping like they were on hinges. I never got her over that. I never even tried.

I'm thinking about China. This morning I was raking the yard in front of the rent string office when China rode up in a shiny black Buick. A man with a droopy face in a blue suit and a wide maroon tie was driving. China was wearing a dress with blue and white flowers. She was wearing white shoes with high heels. I've never seen China in a dress before. And I've never seen her in dress-up shoes. China was twisting white gloves in her callused red hands like she didn't know what to do with them. "Some people comin' later to ask about that girl with the broken back, sunshine," China said. "They ask questions don't tell 'em nothin'. Just tell 'em to come to the house, you hear?"

The people never came, but the shiny black Buick was parked all day outside China's house until it was gray with dust, China inside with the man with the droopy face and the wide maroon tie.

I'm wondering what it would be like without the China Seas. I couldn't stand it, I think. I know I'd run away if I had to stay around the house every day. When China drove up Boots just stared at the man with the droopy face. "Who's that driving China?" I asked as the Buick rolled toward the house, but Boots just walked away. He's been touchy silent ever since— thoughtful, edgy.

A loud explosion echoes through the canyon. The horses shy, fighting for footing on the narrow trail. Pooh cackles.

"Pooh! You stupid!" Alaska yells, calming her horse.

"Smooth move, Pooh!" I yell.

Pooh grins— flips me the bird. His pockets are filled with firecrackers and cherry bombs he bought down in Chinatown with Singer and Singer's brother Kirk. Just before we left for Dixie's house Shorty Hollister had run Pooh out of the stable for throwing firecrackers into the rent string corral. We picked him up at the top of the hill, walking toward Dixie's.

"Fuckin' little Napoleon," Pooh said.

"Been Jimmy Root seen you throwin' firecrackers into the rent string corral like that," Boots told him, "He'd tan your hide six ways to Sunday for sure and nail it to the barn. Or China."

"You want to walk?" Alaska says.

"Just puttin' some life into this funeral," Pooh says.

"Well you pop off another of them things and it'll be your funeral," Alaska says.

"Yes, Ma'am!" Pooh says, looking back at me, winking, making a jack off motion with his right hand.

"You heard Alaska—" Boots yells, "Pop another and I'll jam them damned poppers down your throat."

We see Dixie's house from the top of the hill, white fences, red barn, low ranch-style house nestled in the golden grass, turquoise pool. Out of the canyon, on the black top road down to Dixie's, it's hot again. I can't wait to get into the pool.

Dixie meets us at the gate. She's wearing a bikini, top slightly puckered so we see an outline of white against golden brown. She's eating toast, sucking strawberry jam off her fingertips. I watch a bead of sweat run down between her breasts. She sees me watching, thrusts her hip forward and gives me a smile. Her feet are caked with white dust.

"Hello, baby," Pooh says. Pooh slides off Alaska's mare, pulls Dixie close, and kisses her long on the mouth. He slides his hand under the pink elastic band stretched tight across her hips.

"Pooh!"

Dixie pulls away.

We tie the horses.

Pooh's the only one without a bathing suit. He charges out of the pool house in his underpants.

"Pooh! Go back in that cabana and try one of my daddy's swim suits," Dixie says.

Pooh comes back again with a baggy boxer suit dragging around his knees."

"Well no one's home," Dixie says. "Maybe it's okay."

Pooh lets the boxer suit drop to the pool tile and jumps into the pool naked.

"Pooh!" Dixie says, suppressing a laugh with her hand. "Put something back on!"

Pooh ignores her, swims a lap.

"I mean it, Pooh!"

June's lying back on a pool chair in the shadow of the house.

"Hello, Calvin," she says. "Want a Coke?"

"Sure," I say.

"How's your summer?" she says.

"Okay," I say. "I haven't seen you at the stable—"

"I've been away," June says. "On vacation."

June's wearing a red one-piece suit with a white lace flower over her left breast.

"Where'd you go?" I ask.

"Italy," June says. "Rome."

June's hair is different somehow.

"I've never known anyone who's been to Rome," I say.

"It's okay," June says. "It's real different. The guys on the street are really crude."

Singer's sitting at the edge of the pool at the shallow end.

"Going in, Singer?" Dixie says.

"Sucker can't swim," Pooh says, splashing water.

"You dork," Singer says, kicking water back with his foot.

Pooh splashes Singer again and kicks on his back into the deep end.

"Where's Alaska?" Dixie says.

"In the cabana," June says.

"Alaska girl! You fall in or something?" Dixie yells.

"Hold your horses," Alaska says, her voice muffled.

Alaska comes out in a black one-piece suit, tiptoeing across the hot flagstones, arms folded across her breasts. Her legs are as white as vanilla ice cream. Alaska pulls up a chair beside June.

"Going in?" June asks.

"No," Alaska says. "I hate the water."

I see a large mole, tufted with hair, inside Alaska's thigh. She sits, hides her legs under a towel.

Dixie enters the house, puts a stack of records on the hi-fi. Elvis Presley—*That's All Right Mama*—blasts out of an outdoor speaker under the eaves of the house.

Dixie comes back smoking a cigarette.

"When did you start smoking?" June says.

"Fifth grade," Dixie says.

"I've never seen you smoke before," Alaska says.

"I only do it when Mommy and Daddy aren't home—"

"Where're your mommy and daddy?" Boots asks.

"Who knows—" Dixie says, throat stretched, exhaling smoke in the air. "And frankly I don't give a damn."

Pooh lifts himself out of the deep end of the pool. His sleek wet body is covered with freckles, dark red hair curled around his cock.

"Pooh, cover yourself," Dixie says.

"Showing off," Alaska says.

"Ain't much to show, ask me," Boots says.

"And why aren't you in the water?" Dixie asks Boots.

"I'll go in, you do," Boots says. "Got another of them coffin nails?"

I do a racing dive off the deep end of the pool. The water's warm, oily almost. The dive takes me the full length of the pool. I try a racing turn at the shallow end, but scrape the bottom coming out. I swim two laps and stop beside Singer, breathing hard even though the pool isn't very long.

"Wish I could swim like that," Singer says.

"I'm not much of a swimmer," I say.

"Better'n me," Singer says.

"The most important thing is breathing," I say. "Want me to show you?"

Singer pulls away. "Kirk locked me in an old refrigerator when I was a kid," Singer says. "It was dark and hard to breathe and I thought I was goin' to die. That's all I can think about when I'm in the water— chokin' for air in that refrigerator. But sure looks like fun."

"Your body'll float if you let it," I say. "All you really got to know is how to relax and breathe."

June jumps into the pool. She swims underwater and grabs my legs. We wrestle underwater, splashing each other when we come up for air.

"I missed you," June says.

"I missed you too," I say.

June grabs my face, kisses me, then swims to the deep end of the pool.

"That one's hot to trot," Singer says.

"Who's that up there on the hill?" Alaska says, "Up there on the road—"

We look.

"Stuie Kramer's Jimmie looks like," Boots says. "Where's Dixie?"

"Inside, I think," Alaska says.

We push into the house looking for Pooh and Dixie, our wet feet leaving tracks on the white carpet. We call but get no answer.

The house is shiny clean— low furniture in pale wood and white swans on the end tables. The kitchen is larger than half my house and all gleaming and white except for dishes in the sink, strawberry jam streaked on the counter. We find Dixie's room, everything pale blue, clean and simple, a cross over the head of her bed, horse pictures, but she's not there. We try a door at the end of the hall. It's Dixie's parents' room, dark with the drapes drawn. Dixie and Pooh are making out on Dixie's parents' bed. We surprise them and Dixie's embarrassed, tying her bikini top behind her back.

Dixie pads into her daddy's den— returns with a pair of binoculars.

"Just what does he think he's lookin' at?" Dixie asks, standing in the shadow of the house and looking up through the binoculars.

"What's he doing?" Alaska says.

"Just sittin' in the truck lookin' down this way,"

"Spooky," June says.

"I'll give him something to look at," Pooh says.

"No, Pooh—" Dixie says. "Leave him be—"

"Seen him up there before?" Boots asks.

"No," Dixie says. "But we've been getting phone calls at two in the morning then no one says anything when we pick up the phone. Probably him—"

Pooh runs into the cabana, comes out, scuffed and dusty boots under his arm, hopping on one foot, shoving his other foot into his Levi's. He stumbles, sits on the grass beside the pool to pull on his boots. He runs into the house, comes out with a potato in his hand.

"And just what are you doing, Pooh?" Dixie asks.

"Givin' old Kramer cunt somethin' to look at," Pooh says and jumps across the rose garden and slips through the white fence.

"What's he doing?" Dixie asks.

"Gonna shove that potato up Kramer's tail pipe, I'd guess," Singer says. "That's what we used to do to people park up on Skyline—"

"Why?" June asks. "That sounds pretty stupid."

"Sometimes the car won't start. Sometimes it just makes a big bang. Sometimes it blows a hole in the muffler."

"That's childish," Alaska says.

"It's a blast," Singer says.

We watch Pooh slip through the grass, sneak up the hill toward Stuie Kramer's truck.

"Stuie's going to see him," Dixie says.

"Not from that angle," Boots says.

"Poor Stuie," Dixie says. "What's wrong with him?"

"Shit for brains," Singer says.

"He first come up the stable," Boots says, "He was always talkin' shit— Always wantin' someone to go nigger knockin' with him."

"That's ugly," June says. "Don't say that word."

"One time, at his house," Dixie says, "He showed me all these books he got from someplace down in Mississippi? It was horrible. I wanted to cry. That's why I stopped going out with him."

"Shit for brains," Singer says. "He's just trying to get people to think he's some bad dude. Don't know he's just a fuckin' weenie— stupid dork."

"He's cute," Dixie says. "Kind of. But something's wrong with him. I feel sorry for him—"

"Something's wrong he calls you up at two in the morning and don't say nothin'," Boots says.

"Nothin' a ball bat up side the head won't cure," Singer says.

"You don't know it's him," Alaska says.

"I think it's spooky," June says. "I think you should call the police."

We watch Pooh sneak up behind the truck. Pooh kneels down under the back of the truck, seems to stay for a very long time. Then we see him slip around behind the truck. Suddenly Stuie's dog starts barking and we see red flashes and smoke inside the truck and hear the rattle of firecrackers and Stuie's loud air horns.

"Son of a bitch Pooh threw a pack of firecrackers into the truck!" Singer shrieks.

The truck door flies open and Stuie spills out, jumping up and down, slapping his body. Stormtrooper jumps out, runs into the grass yipping.

"You peckerwood!" Stuie yells. "You want a fight? I'll fight you!"

We're grabbing the binoculars back and forth. Stuie stumbles around the truck, yelling. Then he climbs back in. We hear the starter growl, then hear an even louder explosion, and see white smoke billowing out from under Stuie's truck. Stuie gets the truck started and fish tails down the road.

"Poor Stuie," Dixie says.

"Poor truck," Singer laughs. "That truck was cherry."

Pooh slips back through the fence and cannonballs into the pool, Levi's, boots and all. He comes back up yelling like a banshee, splashing water at us.

"You moron," Boots says.

"Should've seen his face," Pooh giggles.

"Boots is right," Dixie says. "That was stupid, Pooh. He wasn't doing any harm."

"He's been asking for it—" Pooh says.

Suddenly we hear Stuie's truck screech into the driveway.

Pooh, Singer, and Boots run toward the driveway, Singer and Boots without shoes, hopping gingerly over stones.

We hear a loud pop and another, thinking it's more firecrackers. Stuie's truck screeches out of the driveway. Singer, Boots and Pooh come running back.

"That mother had a gun!" Pooh says.

Dixie turns white.

Boots face is torn, anger I've never seen. "He's gonna need more'n that little pop gun," he says, "Pull a gun on me."

"Stop it!" Alaska screams. I see she's crying.

"Wait'll I tell my brother," Singer says.

"You started it, Pooh," Dixie says. "You just get out of here, now."

"Baby—" Pooh says.

"I want you out of here, now!"

"I think we should call the police," June says.

Pooh is pissed, riding behind Singer on Elvis. "Why'd she run me off?" he says. We're riding, I don't know where, down the asphalt road past the fancy Chabot houses.

"Bitch!"

"You had it comin', Pooh," Boots says. He's been riding silent, face in thought.

"How'd I know the sucker had a gun?" Pooh says.

The sun is slipping down behind the hills in the West. Our shadows are soft and long on the pale asphalt.

"Where we goin'?" I say.

"Ridin'," Singer says.

"Stuck up bitch," Pooh says.

Boots is drawn into himself again, body swaying with the gait of his horse.

"Let's raid!" Singer says.

"Fuckin' A!" Pooh says.

Boots is far away.

"Come on, Boots," Singer says. "It'll be dark soon."

"I'm tired of this shit," Boots says.

"Come on, Boots, you pussy," Pooh says. "We ain't pulled a raid in a long time."

"What's a raid?" I ask.

"You'll dig it, Calvin," Singer says.

"Let's just give it up," Boots says.

"Chicken shit, Boots," Singer says. "Losin' your nerve."

"You comin', Calvin?" Pooh asks.

"Sure," I say.

"Infantile shit," Boots says, turning his horse.

"Chicken shit," Singer says. "Losin' your nerve because some pussy shoots at you with a pistol."

We watch Boots ride away, body slumped, bobbing with the gait of his horse.

"What're we going to raid?" I ask.

"Gotta wait until it's good and dark," Singer says.

"I'm hungry," I say.

"You won't die," Pooh says. "We'll scarf up at Jerry's after the raid. Want some gum?"

We ride down the hill, stop and dismount in the high grass beside Chabot road, bleached paper and flattened Budweiser cans hung up in the roots. Pooh starts to light a cherry bomb.

"Not here, stupid shit," Singer says. "You'll start a grass fire."

Pooh blows out the match. Throws it at Singer. Singer bats it away.

"I'd like to shove this cherry bomb right up Kramer's ass," Pooh says.

"My brother once broke a guy's arm in two places, pulled a gun on him," Singer says.

"I'll bust more'n an arm," Pooh says. "Kramer pulls a gun on me again."

We wait until dark, the horses grazing in the high dry grass. Cars pass on Chabot Road, blowing hot dusty air in their wakes.

"Let's go," Singer says.

"Still too early," Pooh says.

"We'll take it slow."

"What's up on Skyline?" I ask.

"You'll see," Singer says. "It's a blast."

We ride single file up Green Valley Road toward Skyline, hogging the narrow shoulder between pavement and dense greasewood. Traffic is light, but the few cars pass us fast and close, throwing up hot air and fumes, making the horses skittish. Skyline follows the crest of the hills from Oakland to Berkeley, shaded by tall shaggy eucalyptus trees. A narrow dirt road runs beside Skyline most of the way. We ride down the dark dirt road, looking out through the trees at the vast carpet of light spread around the bay.

"Hold up," Singer whispers.

Ahead I can just make out in the shadows the dark shape of a car parked under the trees.

"They're gettin' it on early tonight," Pooh whispers.

"We're Indians," Singer whispers. "You go first, Calvin."

"What do I do?"

"Ride down hard on 'em, pound the top of the car."

"What if they catch me?"

"You kidding?" Singer says. "You'd be dog meat—"

"One bozo chased us around up here for four hours," Pooh says. "Thought I'd never get home. It was a blast—"

"What if he has a gun?" I say.

"He gets out of the car," Singer says, "We'll ride him down from behind."

"Road's dark. He'll never see you," Pooh says.

My heart is pounding now. The car starts rocking on the springs. They're doing it.

"Ready, chicken shit?" Singer says.

"Yeah," I say.

"Go!" Singer yells.

I kick Tululla hard. At first she's surprised, then she bolts out. I'm screeching, riding down hard on the car, pounding on the roof, racing away.

The headlights snap on. I catch a glimpse of my moving shadow in the harsh light. Then I hear Singer and Pooh. Their screeches reach me over Tululla's hard pounding hooves. I look back over my shoulder and see Singer and Pooh silhouetted in the harsh headlights. Suddenly I see a flash of red in the car and hear the crackling report of firecrackers. I hear a woman scream.

Singer and Pooh pull up beside me, laughing like hyenas.

"You could have hurt them bad," I say.

"Don't worry about it now," Pooh says.

I hear a car door slam, a man screaming curses. I hear the car start behind us.

"Run, you sucker," Singer laughs. "That son of a bitch is hotter than a hornet!"

I'm hanging on for dear life, Tululla pounding down the dirt road—deep ruts from water runoff. I'm worrying about the ruts, seeing myself splattered on the road, Tululla dead with a broken leg. I hear Pooh and Singer peel off and clatter across Skyline. I hear the car peeling down the dirt behind me, see glare from its headlights bounce in the trees, throw my shadow long down the road. Tululla senses the car gaining behind us and surges out with renewed speed. I'm thinking about how we could cut off into the trees, lose 'em, when suddenly Tululla stumbles, almost throwing me. I'm hanging onto mane and loose flesh under Tululla's throat, but Tululla recovers. I pull her over to the side of the road, sensing the car pulling up beside us. I jerk Tululla into a skid and wheel her around in the opposite direction, catching the glimpse of a dark and distorted face hanging out of the car. I kick Tululla for all I'm worth and Tululla responds with speed I'd never thought she had in her. Suddenly I'm aware of the air in my face, the night, the intoxicating freedom of pure speed. We pound down the road into the darkness and I yell. I yell from someplace I've never touched before, the pure animal yell of freedom and release.

"Catch me, you dork!" I'm thinking. "I'm mercury through your fingers!"

"Where's Pooh?" I ask later, riding up on Singer.

"Fuck if I know," Singer says, walking his winded horse.

"You don't know?" I ask.

"And I don't much give a flyin' fuck," Singer says.

"Well what happened?" I ask.

"Little fucker's crazy," Singer says. "He wanted to stop and fight the sucker."

"He wanted to fight?"

"Called me a chicken shit, hit me on the ear, so I pushed him off—"

"Well maybe we should go back," I say.

"Let the fucker walk," Singer says. "He hit me hard— on the ear."

"You left him up there?"

"Fuckin' A," Singer says.

"Singer," I say.

"Stuff it, Moore," Singer says. "Let the crazy fucker walk for all I care."

"What if the guy catches him?" I ask.

"Hope he does," Singer says.

"Singer—" I say.

"Sit on it, Moore—" Singer says.

I ride back to Skyline looking for Pooh. I ride to the crossroad and back, hiding in the trees every time I see the lights of a car. I ride until I can't keep my eyes open, but all I see are deep shadows in the trees, an occasional car parked in the shadows, and overhead a cold black sky littered with stars. I shiver and feel like I'm going to cry, but I don't. I turn Tululla toward home. She puts her head down and steps out sure and fast, pacing down the dark road just as smooth and sure-footed as you please.

# The Sawdust Run

I'M playing with the last few Cheerios in my bowl, pushing them around the arena of milk with my spoon, swirling the milk, imagining fat palominos clashing in a wild gymkhana. Curly's sleeping warm under my feet and Mom's sitting across from me at the kitchen table making a leather belt. I glance up, see the top of her head, wisps of gray in her chestnut hair, flaky skin showing through her careless part. She's tapping tapping tapping with her leather carving tools, tapping out swirls of leaves and flowers. Every minute or so she stops, takes a long drag from her cigarette, holds it in her lungs as she swabs down the belt with a wet sponge, then exhales, silvery smoke swirling over her tools. Then she sips her coffee, black, and sits back, staring out the window while the water soaks into the leather to her satisfaction. Her skin is pale, puffy almost. It drives me nuts, the endless tapping tapping tapping, but I'm glad she's doing leather work again.

Mom does beautiful hand-tooled leather work. Everyone wants her to make something with their name on it, a wallet, a belt, a purse, or something, wants her to immortalize them in leather, but usually they don't want to pay enough to buy the skins and dyes and expensive lacing. But the sound of tapping tapping tapping and the acrid smell of leather dye filled the house before Teddy's business went bad. Mom made me a belt when I started showing China's horses, silver buckle and white lacing, "Calvin" carved on the back. Shorty Hollister wanted her to carve a saddle, but Mom said that you need special tools to make a saddle; said you had to be strong like a man to stretch the leather across the tree and if it didn't come out right it would be a crying shame in wasted materials. But I know Mom really wanted to make that saddle, as much for the challenge as the money. Given a choice she'd take

129

challenge any day over money. But she needed the money. Saving out enough to buy skins and lacing, she'd buy things for the house with whatever she made carving leather. Teddy refused to let mom take a real job, even though he spent money she needed to run the house at The Road House or the 296 Club, so Mom often used her leather money to pay the PG&E and the truck payment and, most weeks, groceries at the end of the week. But she always said that her leather money was hers to spend in any way she pleased, her mad money, and she hid it under the skins in her leather cabinet even though everybody in the house knew where she kept it.

When Teddy's business went bad this guy started calling every night asking for money. Sometimes the guy called very late when Teddy was at the 296 Club and yelled at Mom until Mom decided to pay the guy out of her own leather money. But Teddy had thought of the leather money first and when Mom opened the gray cash box that she kept hidden back under her skins, and rustled under the dye-stained receipts, she found nothing but pennies.

At first Mom thought that me or Sis had taken the money. But when she found out that Teddy had taken her leather money without asking, and then had lied, saying at first that he didn't know anything about it, and had laid into me about it, she stared at him, not like she was mad or anything, but like she was seeing something dead and oozing rot. She stared at him until he cursed. I thought he was going to hit her. But Mom backed away, closed the door to her room. She was sick for days, sleeping, feverish, her breath smelling like mouse guts. I could hear her retching in the bathroom at night, shuffling back and forth between her bed and the bathroom in her broken down sheepskin slippers. Teddy tried to make dinner one night, but he burned it and Sis cried. Teddy slept on the short love seat in the living room all the while, saying he wanted Mom to get a good rest. But then, when Mom was able to sit up again and eat milk toast, they had a real fight, shouts and thumps and bangs rattling things on the shelves, and Teddy moved back into Mom's room. Mom gave up leather work after that, but now she's working on something again. Even though it drives me nuts, it's nice to hear her tapping out leaves and flowers again.

"Mom," I ask.

"Damn! I slipped," she says.

"What're you working on?" I ask.

Mom keeps tapping, but I can tell she's thinking.

"You said you'd never do it again— carve leather," I say.

Mom looks up at me. I can't tell if she's mad at me or just thinking.

"How much does China pay you?" she asks.

"Fifty cents an hour," I say.

"Don't you think you should contribute something around here— pay for your room and board now that you're working?"

"China hasn't paid me nothing yet. She says she'll pay me at the end of the summer."

It isn't true exactly, but China's paid me just enough to buy a Dr. Pepper sometimes when it gets too hot at the stable or a cheeseburger when the guys drive down to Jerry's in Jimmy Root's convertible.

Mom sips her coffee without taking her eyes off me. But I don't think she's angry.

"Don't get your hopes up," Mom says. "China's having a hard time right now. I'm glad that you can help her out, but maybe you should get a job down at the drugstore or something."

"She'll pay me," I say.

"Well don't get your hopes up—"

"She'll pay me."

"And if she does pay you, what'll you do with the money?

"Buy a ham radio set," I say.

"What about school clothes?"

"Maybe I won't go back to school—"

Now Mom really is angry. She points her leather mallet at me, nails me with her eyes.

"Don't you even think about it, young man. You'll go back to school— get your damned grades back up. And you'll go to college too."

Mom puts the mallet down and takes a fierce puff off her cigarette.

"You don't need a ham radio set. You need to save your money for school clothes and college," she says.

"Tell Teddy that," I say. "He already stole my college money."

"He needed that money for his business," Mom says. "He told you that. And he'll pay you back."

"He needed it for his drinking business—"

"Calvin!"

The phone rings. Curly stirs and I feel his lungs heave with air under my bare feet.

"For you," Mom says.

It's June.

"Calvin! Am I glad!"

"Why?" I ask.

"Hear about Pooh?"

"What about him," I ask.

"Got arrested for stealing a car!"

"Stealing a car?"

Mom stops tapping. Her eyes bore into me.

"He called Dixie from the police station at two a.m. this morning and Dixie called China. China went down to get him."

"When did China go down to get him?" I ask.

"He called Dixie. It was two a.m.— At first Dixie's dad thought it was that guy who's been calling without saying nothing and started screaming into the telephone so that he woke up the whole house. Now Dixie's dad says he doesn't want Dixie to see Pooh ever again. Dixie's grounded. She called me to ask you to see if Pooh is all right."

"Where is he now?" I ask.

"I don't know, the stable I guess, but I was afraid you were with him last night. Were you with him last night when he got into trouble, Calvin?"

"Of course not," I say. "I wasn't with him."

"You were with him when you left Dixie's—"

"We split up after that. I came home."

"But it was late when I called you— ten o'clock— and you weren't at home when I called you at ten."

"Mom didn't tell me—"

"Junie called—" Mom says around the cigarette in her mouth, tapping again, but lightly so I can hear on the telephone. "I was asleep when she called. But you weren't at home anyway. Seems you never are anymore—"

"You sure you're not in trouble or anything, stealing cars?" June asks. "I don't know what Dixie sees in Pooh."

"Of course not!"

"Thank God!" June says. "Calvin—"

"Yes—" I say.

"Ride over to my house?"

"How can I ride over to your house if you want me to find out about Pooh?"

"Later this afternoon. I've got something to tell you—"

"I've got to clean box stalls this afternoon—"

"Yeah, well, tonight?"

"What time tonight?"

"Around seven maybe. I've got to baby sit my little brother."

"Okay—" I say.

"Calvin—" June says, and something else, quiet like, that I can't make out, just before she hangs up.

"What's that about?" Mom asks.

"Nothing—" I say.

"It's something," Mom says.

"Pooh—" I say. "Pooh got arrested."

"That's no surprise," Mom says. "I don't want you hanging around that kid. He's beneath you— he's trouble that kid."

"Pooh's all right," I say. "Sometimes he just doesn't think straight."

"Hear about Pooh?" Boots asks first thing when I walk into the club-house.

"I'm looking for him," I say.

"Up there," Boots nods, over his shoulder.

"Up where?"

"The spring."

"What's he doing up at the spring?"

"Been up there since China brought him back this morning. Just walked up there when he got out of China's pickup first thing this morning. China says to leave him be."

"What's he doing up there?"

"Pounding pud— How should I know? You see him, tell him to get his ass down here. We need to do a sawdust run for China and that's the least he can do after China bailed his ass out of jail."

I climb the fence behind the show ring, whack my way through the weeds and thistles, then start up the hill. It's a tough walk up to the spring. The hill is so steep I have to walk on the sides of my boots. The grass is sparse, flat, dry, and slippery on the fine gravel talus of the hill. Prairie dog holes and rutted horse trails cut into the side of the hill make it easier. The spring has cut a dark green notch in the side of the hill. From the spring you get a good view of the stable, Stella Street, my house and the pond. You're even high enough to see the bay and across the bay and, on a clear day, the cross-hatched streets climbing the hills of San Mateo. When I was little I used to catch blue-belly lizards on the rocks above the spring.

Pooh is lying on his side in the green grass where the water seeps out of the pool, head on his hand, sprig of grass in his mouth, looking up at me with blank eyes as I climb nearer. His face is streaked— lines of dirt running down through his rusty freckles.

"You fucker, Moore— " Pooh says. "Where the fuck did you disappear to last night?"

"I rode all over Skyline lookin' for you."

"Last I saw you was a cloud of dust disappearing down Skyline— I thought you'd run home and hid under your bed or somethin'."

"I rode all over Skyline lookin' for you after Singer told me what happened—"

"Singer, that fuck—"

"What happened? Why did Singer get so pissed off?"

"He thought that guy in the car was gaining on us so he pushed me off and took off down Skyline like the chicken shit he is. Guy would have been all over me, except I took off down the hill. Racked my leg good on a goddamned barbed wire fence. Lookee here."

Pooh lifts his leg. I see a long L-shaped tear in his Levi's exposing his white thigh, angry torn flesh, brown smudges of dried blood.

"You should clean that up, " I say, "You'll get lockjaw."

"It's nothing—" he says. "Cop looked at it, said it didn't need no stitches. But hurt like a mother when I did it."

"Singer said you wanted to fight the guy—"

"Why should I want to fight the guy? I just wanted to get the hell out of there—"

"What happened later— with the cops?"

"Shit, I just needed to get home. I racked up my leg on that goddamned barbed wire fence— bleedin' like a mother— and there was no way I was goin' to make it five miles back to my house on foot without bleedin' to death."

"So you stole a car?"

"I was just goin' to borrow the sucker and bring it back. Besides, it was just a shit box old Nash."

"So how'd the cops get you?"

"I had the door open so I could get down under the dash to hot wire the sucker when I saw the lights come over the hill. I tried to pull the door shut but just as the car come over the hill the wind blew the door open and the overhead light popped on."

"Shit—"

"Still, I could have got away easy, slipped between the houses, if I wasn't all gimped up."

"And then what happened?"

"Know who was drivin' the cop car?"

"Sorenson?"

"Yeah, old elephant nuts—"

"No shit! What'd he do?"

"Just shoved his flashlight in my face and told me to get into his car— He gave me some stuff to put on my leg that stung like a mother and looked at me real sad like I'd been hit by a truck or something. Said if I hadn't cut the ignition wires he'd of let me go. The fucker—"

"But that's his job. What could he do?"

"It wasn't like I was a thief or nothin'. He knows me. I just needed to get home. I'd have brought the car back."

"But you can't just steal a car—"

"I wasn't stealing it. I was just borrowing it. Nobody was using it anyway. I'd have brought the sucker back in the morning."

"But you didn't ask. That's stealing, Pooh—"

"Stealing, shit. I wasn't stealing. The guy was asleep. How am I goin' to ask if I can borrow his car if he's asleep? I didn't even know the guy. Wasn't worth stealing anyway, shit box old Nash. Things just don't work out for me."

"What happened then?"

"Sorenson drove me down to 73th Street there. Said he was supposed to cuff me, but he never did. He just run on about his daughter gettin' married. Says she's four months pregnant but the guy she's marryin' is an asshole and probably a homo he'd like to ream his ass with his riot stick."

"Did they throw you in the can?"

"They said I could call my dad—"

"Did you call your dad?"

"I called him—"

"And?"

"Fucker was three sheets to the wind. Said they could throw me in San Quintin for all he cared."

"Your dad said that?"

"Sergeant got kind of pissed and yelled at Sorenson. They let me call Dixie. I told them that she'd get me out. But her old man said who the fuck was I to call."

"Yeah, so I heard. And what happened next?"

"The sergeant wanted to throw me in with the drunks, but Sorenson talked him into letting me sit in the canteen where the cops drink coffee. One cop even bought me a cup of chicken soup. It was kind of cool listenin' to the cops come in tellin' their bullshit stories. One cop come in with blood all over his blues from bustin' up a colored bar. His eyes was really scary and he kept talking about how he really pinched some heads that night and he couldn't wait to get home and climb onto his old lady. And the guy he was with says what ya plannin' to use, your riot stick?,' and then tells me in a loud whisper like the guy can't hear him, right, that the guy can't get it up since he got the clap from some Mexican whore named Rim Job Rosy. You think we talk dirty! You oughta hear them cops when they get at it! Then the sergeant comes in at the end of his shift and says someone come down to get me out."

"China?"

"Yeah. China. I never thought she liked me much, but she come right down when Dixie called no questions asked."

I see Pooh's eyes glistening up, flashes of sun in his dark red lashes.

"She say anything about you stealing the car?"

"No. She asked if I wanted to go home, but I couldn't go home. My old man would've killed me."

"So what then?"

"She drove me back to the China Seas. Sun was just comin' up over the hill red as blood. Ever notice how sunrises are different from sunsets— more luminous like, that what you call it? I think it's because the sun's comin' at you instead of goin' away. China said I could stay with her until I got things worked out. Asked me to come in for a plate of eggs and beans but I didn't want none."

"But what about the car?"

"Shit if I know. I think China talked 'em out of really booking me or anything. I think she knew that I spent time in juvie. I think she knew that I'd really get fucked if they booked me what with my record."

"June says that China bailed you out—"

"Yeah, whatever—"

"So did she?"

"Did she what?"

"Bail you out? How much did it cost her?"

"So what do you care?"

"I care—"

"It was too early. I never saw a judge or nothin'—"

"So they just let you go?"

"I think she just slipped something to the sergeant or something."

"That's weird—"

"What's weird. Happen's all the time."

"Can they do that?"

"Cops can do anything they want."

"You mean she bribed the sergeant to get you out?"

"Happens all the time. Why do you think Sorenson's always hangin' out at the China Seas jawin' around with Grandma? Because he likes her coffee? Why do you think he's always talkin' about the city crackin' down on horses— special licenses— shit like that?"

"I never thought about it—"

"Lots of things go on that you never thought about, did you?"

"Well Boots says you gotta come down. He needs you to help make a sawdust run."

"Boots thinks I'm his slave or something— just because China got me out of the can."

"You think she really bribed a guy? She doesn't have enough money to fix the barn or pay the vet. And she's got that lawsuit to think about. She might lose the stable. She can't go around— throw money around bribin' people."

"Well fuck you too, Bozeroo. I can't help it if the fuckin' wind blew the fuckin' door open just when Sorenson's drivin' over the hill. And I can't help it if China can't afford this shit or that. I never asked her for no money. She didn't have to do shit for me if she didn't want to— So fuck you, fuck head!" Pooh's eyes are flashing murder.

"I'm sorry, Pooh," I say. "I didn't mean it the way you think."

"Yeah, I guess you didn't mean it. I just didn't get me no sleep last night. Know what I've been thinkin'?"

"What's that? What've you been thinking?"

"See them polliwogs swimming around in the spring down there? I feel like one of them polliwogs trapped in the spring— bumping my nose against weeds and rocks and shit like that, then swimmin' around like I'm blind or something and bumpin' my nose again."

"I used to catch polliwogs up here when I was a little kid—"

"But then I was thinking that maybe one of them polliwogs would turn into a frog— a super frog that could jump out of the pond and down into the pond behind your house. And then maybe he could jump over the hill into the bay. And then maybe he could jump right over San Mateo into the Pacific Ocean. A super frog like and maybe I could be that frog—"

"You could be that frog—"

"I could be that frog—"

"You're a crazy mother, Pooh. You know that?"

"Yeah, that's what they say, man. Shit, maybe I'll jump all the way to China."

"You're already there," I say.

"What do you mean?"

"The China Seas."

"Yeah, I guess—" Pooh says, pushing himself up off the ground. Now he's smiling. "China Seas—" He throws a shoulder block, pushing me down the slope. "You're a pretty smart ass fucker for a little prick," he says. "You wasn't but 14 years old I'd kick your ass all the way down the hill."

"Fifteen," I say. "I'm fifteen."

"Yeah, whatever."

The Chevy flatbed is backed up behind the clubhouse, Jimmy Root hanging over the left fender into the cavernous engine compartment. He's banging on something with a silver crescent wrench. I see a wad of gum stuck to the bottom of his left boot, a penny stuck in the gum.

"You're a rich man, Jimmy," I say, but he doesn't hear me.

Legs are sticking out from behind the front tire. Pooh jumps up on the running board, hangs out the open window, and starts rocking the Chevy on it's springs.

"Son of a bitch!" Boots yells. "Who the fucks doin' that? Gettin' rust in my eyes!"

Pooh cackles and Boots comes sliding out on a dolly.

"You son of a bitch, Pooh! I'm goin' to bust your nuts!"

"Thought we was goin' after sawdust—" Pooh says.

"Fuckin' sawdust in the head," Boots says.

"What're you doing?" I ask.

"Well at least make yourself useful, Pooh," Boots says, "And put the sides on the damn truck."

"So what're you doing?" I ask again.

"Puttin' a patch on the damned manifold exhaust— Really need a whole new exhaust system."

"Doin' a real good job, though," Jimmy Root says. "Be good enough to get the old bucket of bolts down the shaving mill and back."

"Balin' wire and bubble gum—" Boots says. "China really needs a new truck."

I help Pooh lift the plywood sides, slip the stakes into the rectangular iron slots on the sides of the flatbed. The stakes are worn hard and shiny from slipping in and out of the iron slots. When we're done Boots hands me the keys.

"Want to drive, kid?" he asks.

"All the way down to the shaving mill?" I ask.

"Why not?" Boots says. "You're gettin' good enough. Besides you need more practice in traffic and I need a snooze."

"Lordy me," Jimmy says.

"Well he's got to do it sometime," Boots says.

"Nobody's goin' to argue with him behind the wheel of that truck," Pooh says.

"Well jump in and say your prayers, mother—" Boots says to Pooh, slamming the hood down on the truck.

"Ain't you goin'?" Pooh says.

"Sure I'm goin'" Boots says. "But I already made my peace."

"Glad I ain't goin'," Jimmy says.

"Jimmy, look at the bottom of your boot," I say.

"Lordy me," Jimmy says, picking the penny out of the gum.

"You take this here penny, son," Jimmy says. "Maybe it'll bring you luck."

The windows are stuck open in the truck and the wind blows sawdust and straw around in the cab and into my eyes. I can't hear myself think over the roar of the engine. The exhaust comes up through holes in the floorboards and makes me choke, makes my eyes sting and water. But I feel so great sitting up high and driving the truck. Boots is sitting next to me, ready to grab the wheel in case I fuck up or we see a cop. I can't see over the right fender very well. Only thing that scares me— I keep thinking I'm going to hit mailboxes or cars parked on the side of the road.

"Get over on your own side," Boots says, "You're takin' your half in the middle."

"Should I shift now?" I ask.

"Better rev it up a bit. Don't ride the clutch."

"Watch out!" Pooh says, "A dog!"

"Ten points!" Boots says.

I hit the brake, but it don't do no good. The truck keeps rolling. I can't see the dog anyway. My foot's almost on the floorboard.

"Missed him by a mile," Boots says. "Better luck next time—"

"Mile, shit!" Pooh says. "That puppy shit a mile of dog shit he come so close."

"Maybe you better take it, Boots," I say.

"You're doin' fine," Boots says. "Just slow down for that stop sign up there."

I run the stop sign and then clash the gears trying to shift down in the middle of the intersection.

"Don't worry about it," Boots says. "Just relax and let the engine tell you when to shift."

"We're comin' to the freeway," Pooh says. "Maybe you should take over, Boots."

"He's doin' fine," Boots says.

"I don't know—" I say. "Really, maybe you should take it, Boots."

"Come on, Boots—" Pooh says.

"You can do it," Boots says. "Just stay in the right lane."

My knee is shaking when I pull onto the freeway, but pretty soon it's easier. Cars and trucks pass me like I'm standing still, but there's really nothing to do but steer.

"Holy shit, I'm goin' to kiss the earth," Pooh says when we pull into the shaving mill.

"You want to back her in?" Boots asks.

"Why not," I say.

"Just go easy," Boots says. "And line up those posts through your side view mirrors."

"Let me out first," Pooh says.

I can see the big sawdust hopper up on six-by-six stilts through the side view mirrors.

"Easy now," Boots says. "Let the clutch out slow and easy— Careful now—"

"Watch it!" Pooh yells.

Suddenly the truck comes to a hard stop, jarring my body, throwing my head back against the rear window, making me bite my tongue.

"Well you almost made it," Boots laughs. "Want me to back it in?"

"No!" I say.

"Well just don't knock that hopper down," Boots says.

I'm shaking hard, tasting blood in my mouth, but I pull forward and back in again, this time slipping between the six-by-six uprights and right under the canvas shoot.

"Slick as snot!" Pooh says.

"Way to go, kid!" Boots says. "You get to pull the rope."

I feel a kind of pride that I've never felt before, even when I won my first blue ribbon on Dutchess.

Boots and Pooh run well clear and I pull the rope and the yellow wood shavings flood down out of the hopper and onto the bed of the truck, piling up between the plywood sides and engulfing me in a cloud of suffocating dust. I wipe my eyes and laugh and climb up the back of the truck and jump down into the mountain of shavings. Boots and Pooh jump right in behind me, Pooh grabbing my legs, Boots burying me in shavings, the sharp clean smell of newly shaved cedar filling me with joy. Then, all the way home I itch so bad I can hardly drive, squirming all over the hard seat of the Chevy, trying to relieve the maddening itch jumping around under my clothes like an army of ants, attacking now under my collar, and now between my shoulder blades, spreading up under my arms, and now jumping most maddeningly of all into the sweaty folds of my crotch.

"Itches like a mother, don't it?" says Pooh.

We answer. "Like a bitch!"

Later, crossing Stella Street for a quick shower before riding over to June's, I see Smitty Walsh's pickup parked in our front yard. Shit, I think. Smitty Walsh is Teddy's friend, a lumberjack at least nine feet tall and built like King Kong. Smitty Walsh has seven kids with IQs in the single digits and a skinny wife with stringy gray hair who smokes one cigarette after another and wears dresses that look like feed sacks. When Smitty Walsh comes down from the woods he gets roaring drunk first thing then comes to our house and always wants to give me boxing lessons. Once he cut my lip so bad I couldn't eat for a week and another time he hit my ear, knocking me over onto the coffee table and I heard trains running through my head.

"Got to learn how to duck," he said. "Most important lesson in life."

I think about going back to the stable, but decide that I'm not going to let Smitty Walsh run me out of my own house. I'll run him through with a pitch fork before I'll let him hit me again. Just the same I try to sneak through to my room without being seen.

"There's the whipper snapper," Teddy yells and Smitty Walsh charges out of the kitchen and grabs me in a bear hug, his foul breath hitting me harder than any fist.

"Someone grab you like this, kick him in the nuts," Smitty Walsh says.

I twist and turn, bring up my knee.

"That's it," he says as I struggle, "But I'm expecting it, see, so I could snap your neck easy or stomp on your foot like this and push you backward, see, gimp you up for life."

I try to hold back, but tears fill my eyes when I break free, or rather when he chooses to let me go. I turn to push past him into my room but Smitty Walsh grabs me by the shirt collar, pulling the top button up into my throat, nearly lifting me off the floor.

"Gotta get some meat on this boy. Let me take him up to the camp with me and we'll turn him into a man in no time at all and if not we'll fuck him like a woman. Want to come up to the camp with me, my boy?"

I struggle and pull free.

"What're you raisin' here, Teddy-o," Smitty Walsh says, staring hard into my eyes, "A cry baby? Let me bring him up to the camp and we'll kick the baby shit out of this one quick enough."

Then his voice softens. He throws his arm around my shoulders and kisses me on the top of the head.

"Never let 'em see that they're gettin' to you, kid," he says. "No matter how much you're hurtin', never give 'em that edge, see? Piss in their eye—"

"Piss in your own eye, you fucker!" I say, pulling away.

"That's the way now, but listen kid, you've got to help me load that fleabag of yours into my truck now. I've got things to do."

I stop. "Fleabag?"

"Sure, kid. Glad to take the ol' mutt off your hands."

I look at Teddy. Teddy's looking down at the floor. He reaches into the change pocket of the Levi's hanging down over his skinny ass and pulls out a five dollar bill all crumpled up. "Here, you can keep the money— buy yourself a toy or something."

"You sold my dog?" I say, "Curly—"

"You know we have too many mouths around here—" Teddy says. "You can buy yourself one of those radio gadgets or something we don't have to feed—"

"We'll give him a real good home," Smitty Walsh says. "My kids love that old pooch. They need a dog real bad I'm away so much."

"You can't take my dog!" I say, but suddenly I can't talk any more. I feel like I could make the whole house explode. I throw a punch, but Smitty Walsh pushes me aside like a gnat.

"Well suit yourself," Smitty Walsh says. "Guess I can load the ol' hound without your help. Got a rope, Teddy my boy?"

I rush into the kitchen. Mom's sitting at the table, staring out the window. I hear Curly yelp and whine. I hear a curse.

"Mom—" I say.

"We just can't afford to keep him, hon," Mom says. "You never feed him anyway. I'm the one who feeds him—"

"But, Mom—" I say.

"I'm sorry, honey," Mom says. "It's just the way it's gotta be."

# Dad

I can't make my teeth stop chattering. I hug my knees tightly against my chest. I slammed out of the house without my jacket, just my Levi's shirt with the sleeves ripped out at the shoulders. The front of my Levi's shirt is soggy and cold with snot and tears. I feel the wetness drying on the back of my arm, pulling the hair and cedar dust on the back of my arm into hard crust. I explore the crust with my tongue, feel it dissolve warm and salty on my tongue, lingering taste of turpentine. I wonder if turtle shells are made of dried tears, God's frozen tears protecting naked lizards too slow and soft to make it on their own. I think of my sleeping bag rolled tightly under my bed. I think of stealing horse blankets from China's tack room, rolling up into a warm cocoon. I think of Dutchess' hot breath warming my hands, the heat of her side as I lean against her in her box stall. I think of lighting a fire in the hay barn, dying in flames.

It's black, a kind of velvet blackness, on the top tier of bales in the far dark corner of the hay barn. It's silent too, except for rustling mice, a soft nicker from the horse barn, the clank of halter hardware on water buckets and wood rubbed smooth as the back of a shovel. I stretch out on my back, imagine hard polished wood enveloping me, warming me, but I can't stop shivering. I reach up, thinking to touch wood, but my hand touches nothing, reaches up into the cold darkness touching nothing but cold black space. I let my arm drop back onto the prickly bale. The exquisite pain of prickly hay on the underside of my arm feels good kind of so I slam my naked arm down again and again onto the hard unyielding bale.

Now I walk up Stella street holding my arms wrapped tightly around me, at first from cold, but then from something else, and finally because

145

I want to. It's hard to walk like this, without arms swinging for balance, especially on the rutted shoulder of the road, but my arms feel like sheets wrapped around me and I feel like I can't unwrap them for anything. I think of dried leather wrapped around me like a mummy skin, I think of what it's like to be born with stumps for arms, and I think about walking across the country like this, no arms, from California to Pennsylvania, wondering how long it would take. I try to walk softly, Indian style with my toes touching the ground before my heels. But it's hard in cowboy boots. So I try walking hard, like I'm twenty feet tall, heels crushing stone, smashing into the earth, until my heels ache from the pounding. I see yellow lights in windows, halos of pale light around bushes and trees. I imagine fire, raging bushes and trees and forests of flame.

I turn toward the hills at the end of Stella, following the rutted fire road. I let my arms drop. They're tingling with restricted circulation. I turn off the road, scrambling up the bank and into the dried grass and thistles. I climb, swishing through the dried grass, until my breath is short and my heart is pounding but I push harder up the steep hill. At the top I stop and look toward the city, lights stretched from horizon to horizon. I imagine God pouring lighter fluid across the sky and lighting a match and the lights flaring up and blazing out into the glow of embers and then fading to blackness deeper than a pit.

I push on over the crest of the hill and down toward the ravine, picking up a narrow horse trail, half walking, half sliding down the eroded trail. It's black in the canyon. There may be sound, insects or night animals maybe, but my breath is all I hear, rushing through my ears like a pulsating waterfall, my breath and the grinding of leather on stone as I slide down the hill. Near the bottom the ground levels onto a meadow deep with grass, now tinder dry, but in the spring lush and green. In the center of the meadow is a lone oak, from here a shade of black against black. I trudge through the grass to the tree, stooping under the drooping branches, feeling the spiny leaves rake my face and bare arms. I slump against the gnarled trunk, slide down, sit with my legs thrust out. I listen to my heart, pounding pounding, until night sounds return, bugs and frogs, strange stirrings in the black ravine at the edge of the meadow. I stare across the silvery grass into the blackness of the ravine, so still, so alive.

This is where I killed her. I'd unsnapped the lead rope and tied one end of the stake rope to her broken halter. The nose strap that connects to the brass ring at the end of the cheek strap had rotted out over the winter. It was now little more than a noose around her neck. I'd pushed my shoulder up under her neck, holding her soft warm sinewy neck against my head, murmuring, indecisive about the broken halter, groping under the chin strap with my fingers to comb a cocklebur from the long hair under her jowls. She was flicking her head against my chest, reaching for grass, blowing air through her nostrils. Then I'd tightened the neck strap and released her, tied the other end of the stake rope to this tree. But rather than graze she had stood there, head low, watching me. I'd smacked her on the rump and watched her skitter into the belly-high grass, watched the stake rope pay out through the grass. I'd leaned against this tree and watched her graze in the early morning light, midway between me and the morning mist rising out of the space beyond. I'd watched her head plunge into the deep green grass, disappear, snap up, ears forward, alert to morning sounds coming up out of the deep ravine. I'd listened to her breath, her teeth tearing grass out of the earth, chewing, chewing. And then I'd left her, climbing the hill for school. The ground was slick and muddy and I had to hobble across islands of grass to keep my school shoes clean.

I rise, picturing the iron-hard rope stretched across the silvery grass into the blackness. I duck under the spiny leaves of the tree that should have yielded and follow the ghost rope, stumbling through the tangled grass toward the blackness. Stars glitter overhead like hard ice, but I walk on toward the precipice, imagining the faint smell of rot, then more than imagining, knowing that I'm near the edge of the drop off, hard now, but that day muddy and loose after a night of rain. When all is blackness before me, I feel my way along the edge until I sense the place where the grass is torn out still. The smell is real now, faint like you wouldn't notice if you didn't know it was here, lingeringly sweet like, sensed deep down in a place that is at once revolted and straining to take it in. I slip over the edge, find purchase with my heels against the eroded bank and lean back against the cold crumbling earth. I could leap forward into the blackness from here, but it would do no good. I'd simply slide into a dense thicket of greasewood and poison oak far above the trickling creek. I look down, straining to see, but it's so black my boots are in blackness. But I know she's here, somewhere just below— an unspeakable pile of rotting hide and bones lodged in a muddy bier of shattered poison oak and greasewood. I breathe, aware of her, seeing her scramble for footing, hooves rooting in mud until the edge crumbles away, then falling hard, jerking with a sharp crack to slam against the mossy bank. Teddy had wanted to soak her in gasoline, burn her, but the risk of a brush fire was too great even after the rains and China had talked him out of it. I had wanted to drag her out and bury her but Boots had told me that the earth was too loose to bring in a tractor. Best to cut her free and let her slide.

It's too dark and steep to see from where I am, spread-eagled against the steep earth, but her presence fills me. I see clear as noon a broken halter around my neck, strained to near breaking against an iron-hard rope stretched across the silvery grass to the stunted oak tree that should have yielded. I imagine horse weight snapping horse bone, twisting horse head to an angle that, more than anything, has stayed in my mind from that late afternoon after school, later than usual because I'd found some foolish thing to delay me, that late afternoon when I'd first found her, until now, this moment, here, clinging to the edge of this ravine.

I hear the creek trickling far below and frogs chorusing up and down the depths of the ravine. Across the black space I see the crest of the hill black against the black sky. Above I see stars hard and cold splashed across the sky. I imagine my body empty against this cold clay, rotting, while my soul flies faster than light into the stars. I try to imagine the distances, years, centuries, time longer than time from here to the faintest stars, and wonder how the edges of my grief can be out there farther still when I'm so small, so nothing, here, clinging to the edge of this beckoning ravine.

Somehow it comes to me that I have a choice. The pain is so deep— I could cast my being into the stars, so far, so remote, or I could leap into this ravine, plunge into the blackness to take my place beside the frogs and other night things. But I don't know how to do either and I can see no other way, no choice of human scale, no warm place where I can fill this ravine in my chest, this hole that's deeper than the farthest star, with forgetfulness. I can see no welcoming spaces where I can be forgiven.

I feel a tingling in my legs, a stone jabbing my back. I try to reach down to scratch my leg, but my footing is too precarious. The tingling moves up my legs like ants or other live things. I imagine the hoards of life feasting on the decaying carcass just below me, the worms and maggots and flies and meat wasps and busy ants. I wonder if the ants work at night, crawling in and out of the holes in the festering hide. The tingling in my legs becomes unbearable, my knees shake. I feel pressure in my bladder. I inch toward firmer footing, turn, then hoist myself back up over the edge of the ravine. I walk toward the oak, stoop under the spiny leaves, unbutton my fly with wooden fingers, and piss and piss on the gnarled black trunk, surprised by the sudden unbearable pressure in my bladder, the warmth of release, realizing that this too nourishes the tree and the beetles and the worms living under the dead leaves.

I walk through the dark canyons and over the bleak hills. Once I stumble, falling hard against rutted gravel and stone. But I walk through the pain, following the fire road through the shadows and moonless dark. Once, cresting a hill, I look back and see the city again, but I turn and continue on down the distant slope into a canyon again, under oak and laurels and across a muddy creek reflecting stars.

There's a rim of light in the eastern sky as I climb through the board fence into June's lower pasture. The house is dark, but one light casts a harsh cone on the corner of the barn. I think about curling up in the barn but I'm too tired and too cold and sore so I continue on up to the house, making my way around the swimming pool and up the stone stairs and down the flagstone walk. I pause under June's window, not knowing what to do. But I'm shivering uncontrollably and my shoulder is sticky with blood so I squeeze through the shrubs and tap gently on the glass, calling softly, whispering June's name.

"Calvin? What are you doing here— so late? I waited, then didn't think you were coming. I was so mad! Look at you— you're freezing!"

June helps me through her window, holding me as I crawl stiffly over her desk, scattering pencils, a cloth doll and a Kleenex box, and slump to the floor inside. I feel her warm nightgown against my skin, smell her sleepy breath as she stares into my eyes.

"What are you doing here— so late?" she asks again, but then seems to realize that I'm incapable of speech. She scans my face, touching my cheek in the dim light, then rises. "Come," she says, pulling me toward the bed, "We've got to get you warm."

I shake my head, no, resist, but she pulls me firmly in behind her. "It's OK," she says. "I know you'll behave. We've got to get you warm."

"Son— Maisie says it's time to wake you for dinner."

I look up, disoriented. The room is pink and blue. Mr. Rogers, June's father is hovering over me.

"I— I'm sorry—" I say, startled, then embarrassed.

"It's OK. Junie told us everything. We thought it best to let you sleep. I've brought you a towel and these— your clothes. Maisie washed 'em for you this morning. You can shower, but better hurry because Maisie says that the dinner she's fixing ain't very good when it gets cold."

I look around when he leaves. I'm in June's bedroom, in June's bed, under a thick down comforter. I've never been in a bed that's so comfortable. I'm floating in warmth, can't tell where my body ends and the world begins.

"Hello, Calvin," June's mom says as I walk into the dining room. "Sit yourself down. I hope you're hungry because I made extra and Junie's made an apple pie."

"I— Ma'am—" I stammer, unable to walk further into the room. June's father motions to the place next to him and Mrs. Rogers is dishing out a large serving of mashed potatoes on top of the roast beef and vegetables heaping the plate in front of the empty place. June's little brother is staring at me and June is looking down into her plate, trying not to smile.

"Hurry up now, dinner's gittin' cold. You know, I've got a bone to pick with you, Calvin—"

I look up, expecting—

"The next time you call on my daughter I'll ask you to come through the front door. Even if you take it into your head to see her in the middle of the night, I don't mind. I'm a light sleeper. You like roast beef don't you? I've never known a man that don't."

"Give the boy a chance, Mais—" Mr. Rogers says turning to me. "She'd sleep through a tornado in a gong shop so you might just as well use the window."

"Daddy!" June says, then looks at me, smiling.

"Well sit down, Calvin. We don't bite or anything you know."

The food looks good but I can't taste it. They talk. I try to smile, nod. I look down, my plate is clean. Mrs. Rogers gives me more. I try to eat it. "Calvin—" Mr. Rogers says as we're finishing June's apple pie, "Junie and me got some differences of opinion about this new Arab mare of hers. We need advice from a real horseman—"

"Me?" I say, "I'm not— anymore."

"Well all them ribbons and trophies make you a better horseman than me. Show me a leaky water pipe and I'm your man but I didn't know which end of a horse goes over a fence last until Junie got this horsie bug. Come on down to the barn with me, help me feed the horses— help me decide a few things."

Now I see June and her mom looking down at their plates. For a moment I'm frightened, but Mr. Rogers is smiling, moving behind me, waiting to help me slide back my chair. June's little brother starts to slip out of his chair, but Mr. Rogers says, "No— Help your sister with the dishes."

The dogs follow us down to the barn. Mr. Rogers walks ahead, long loping walk. He's wearing town pants and town shoes and a lime green windbreaker. The horses nicker, push their heads over the half doors of their box stalls. Mr. Rogers checks the water in each box stall, pours grain, talking softly to his horses and to me, showing me by his movements that he knows a lot more about horses than he says. When the horses are fed he walks out, looks out at the yard, then walks back, sits on a five-wire bale, motioning me to sit beside him.

"Son, I don't want to know more than you want to tell me, but I know you've got trouble at home and I want you to know that you've got a place to stay as long as you need to sort things out."

I'm silent but Mr. Rogers is quieter still, twirling a hay stalk between his fingers.

"I— don't know what to do," I say, feeling tightness in my face.

"Not many of us do," he says.

"What do you mean?"

"I mean that life throws us doozies and all we can do is fumble around until we can get a grip on up from down."

"I can't go back— now," I say.

"Maybe not," he says. "You got somewhere else— to go, I mean?"

"Maybe my dad's."

"Where's your dad?"

"In Philadelphia."

"Philadelphia?"

"Yeah," I say.

"That's a long way— Philadelphia. How'd you get there from here?"

"My dad works for the airline. He could get me a ticket."

"He keep horses?"

"No. He lives in an apartment."

"By himself?"

"No— He's got a family. I mean, there's my stepmother and I got two half sisters."

"That's a big family— For an apartment, I mean."

"It's one of those big ones. In a big building."

"He a well-to-do man?"

"Well enough I guess. And I could get a job."

"So then, what are you going to do?"

"Call him, I guess—"

"Yeah," he says.

"Can I use your phone?" I ask.

"Sure. But I've got a suggestion— You know, for what it's worth."

"What's that?"

"Wait until tomorrow before you call— maybe tomorrow night. You an' Junie can take it easy around the pool tomorrow— Or maybe I could take you down if you're interested, show you my shop and stuff."

"I don't want to put you to no trouble," I say, "I can call tonight—"

"Sure, if you want. But sometimes— sometimes it's best to let things sit a bit before you make a big decision like that."

"But I've decided—"

"Then a day or two won't make no difference."

"You don't think I should do it, do you—"

"You're the one who knows best what you've got to do in a situation like this, Calvin."

"But—"

"What?"

"You want to tell me something else, don't you—"

"No, not really. I was just thinkin'."

"Thinkin' what?"

"You make a big decision like this— leave everything behind that you know—"

"And—"

"Well what if it don't work out there in Philadelphia? What then?"

"What do you mean?"

"I mean, where would you go then?"

I look into the dark eaves of the barn, wishing that I could fly into that darkness. "What do you mean?" I say.

"Damned if I know. I'm just a guy who knows how to fix pipes. It's probably the best thing. Listen, it's pretty late there back east now. What's say we go up and see what's on the boob tube. You can call your dad tomorrow."

It's dark. The house settles. I'm on the couch in the rec room, hunkered down in a sleeping bag that smells of must and wood smoke. Mrs. Rogers had fussed over me, bringing me a toothbrush, a fat pillow. "I hope you'll be comfortable here—" she says. "This was supposed to be our guest room but Ben says we need it for the ping pong table and one thing and another."

Now I hear bare feet on the stairs. It's June in her nightgown. She settles down on the couch beside me.

"What did my daddy say?" she asks.

"He thinks I should stay."

"Here?"

"He thinks I should wait to I call my dad."

"I'd miss you," she says.

"I can't stay here anymore," I say. "In California, I mean."

"Will you remember me?"

"Yes—" I say.

June touches my cheek and pads back up the stairs.

"Dad?"

"Yes?"

"It's me, Calvin—"

"Hello, son."

"Can you hear me?"

"Yes. How are you?"

"OK."

"That's good."

"Dad—"

"Yes?"

"Can I come live with you? There— In Philadelphia?"

"Well— Yes. You're sure everything's OK?"

"Yes. But I need—"

"You know we don't have much room, son. I need to talk to Alicia."

"Yes. Well—"

"I mean, you're welcome here. We might have to fix up a room is all."

"I—"

"Calvin— You're sure everything's OK?"

"I—"

"Do you need money or anything?"

"Can you get me a ticket?"

"Sure. But let me talk to Alicia first. We can put Cynthia in Dot's room."

"I won't be no trouble. I can get a job back there."

"That's OK, son. Let me talk to Alicia. We'll work something out. I'll call you, OK? Next week?"

"Yes," I say. "Next week."

"I'll call you next week. So take care, son."

"Yes," I say listening to the hollow silence long after the click of the phone.

# Shorty Hollister

FIRST there's a flare of light against the juniper bushes, then Shorty Hollister's Cadillac bounces into the driveway, its headlights stabbing my eyes, the sound of its motor deep as the purring of a mountain cat. I step around and see Boots in shadow, sprawled back in the shotgun seat, the bill of his baseball cap pulled low over his eyes. The rear door handle is nippy cold but car-warmth and new car smell envelope me as I swing the heavy door open then close it behind me with the thud of heavy silk on silk.

"How's it hangin', Man—" Pooh says from the seat beside me, his face a yellow flicker as the dome light plunges to black.

"Got somethin' for you in the trunk," Shorty Hollister says. "Want it now or wait 'til we get back?"

"Somethin' for me?" I say.

"Stuff your mama give me to give you—" he says.

"What stuff?" I ask. "When did you see my mom?"

"Last night— After I talked to you. Says if you ain't comin' home again you can at least take some clean underwear and stuff."

"You really ain't goin' home again?" Pooh says.

"You really ought to talk to her—" Shorty says.

I'm silent.

"You ought to let her know what you're thinkin', at least. She told me to tell you she's sorry about what happened and all—"

I see the curved brim of Shorty's Stetson over the seat, tufts of salt-and-pepper hair, fat neck on bulldog shoulders.

"You still with me back there, son?"

I'm still silent.

"Says she got your dog back—"

155

I catch the flash of his eyes glancing at me in the rear view mirror as he backs into the road, swings the wheel. I feel the velvet seat press around me, see a few lights in sprawling houses at the end of dark drives, inky blackness in pastures and fields as he accelerates down the hill.

"Mornin' Calvin," Boots says, low from under his cap.

"Thought you was sleepin'—" Shorty says.

"Was—" Boots says.

"So what you goin' to do?" Pooh says, "Stay at June's from now on out?"

"Head back to Philadelphia, I guess—"

"No shit!" Pooh says. "That's way back East, ain't it— near Chicago or something?"

"Or something," Boots snickers.

"I thought you was just stayin' at June's for awhile." Pooh says. "So when you goin'?"

"Soon— " I say. "Soon as my dad sends a ticket— few days maybe."

"Shit, Calvin—" Pooh says.

"I been to Philadelphia," Shorty says. "Ain't like here, that's for sure."

"What do you mean it ain't like here?" I say.

"Just ain't—"

"What's it like then?" I say.

"They got some real hoity toities in Philadelphia, that's for sure."

"You mean like rich people?"

"Rich ain't the word. But most people live cheek by jowl in Philadelphia, worse'n west Oakland."

"Don't listen to him, kid," Boots says. "Philadelphia's probably got its good points like everywhere else."

"I'm just sayin' he oughta talk to his mama before he decides to go to Philadelphia— Hate to see him makin' some damned fool mistake."

"We all make mistakes—" Boots says.

"Life's a mistake," Pooh says.

"Yeah, but some mistakes we don't need to make—" Shorty says.

"You talk to your mama before you split from home Shorty?"

"That was different—"

"Different how?"

"Depression for one thing—"

"Yeah, but you talk to her? I mean really talk to her before you split from home?"

"That's the point—" Shorty says. "I never did."

"So what's with this Calvin talkin' to his mama?"

"I just think maybe he should, is all—"

"Maybe he should and maybe he shouldn't talk to his mama. But the kid's got a right to decide for himself!"

I see Shorty's head turn, look at Boots, turn back to the road. The headlights pick up reflective road signs like startled deer. Hanging bushes cast shifting shadows along the red road cuts as the Caddie takes the curves. "I just don't want him makin' a mistake, is all—"

"What mistake is that?"

"Just a mistake, is all."

"So what mistake, I want to know?"

"Forget it—" Shorty says.

"No, tell me—" Boots says.

"Well, you're so nosy— I run away from home and my mama died the very next winter— "

"Maybe she would have died anyway," Boots says. "My mama died ironing my Cub Scout uniform— Never got a chance to tell her jack all."

"You never told me that," Pooh says.

"Never told no one," Boots says.

"Told me," I say.

"Yeah, I forgot—"

"Yeah, but this was different," Shorty says.

"Different how?"

"Different's all—"

"So, different how?"

"Well, Mr. Nosy Parker— The night my mama died, she kept askin' for me— right up to her last breath. Died with my name on her lips."

"So—"

"She was dyin' there, askin' for me— Know what I was doin'?"

"Dyin' to know—"

"I was down in some pig hole south of the border layin' with a woman— My first time—"

"You mean you was off getting your cherry popped the night your mama kicked off?"

"No call to be crude about it—"

"Your mama would have gone to heaven with a smile on her face," Boots says, "She knew what you was doing."

"Ain't no laughing matter—" Shorty says. "The night she died askin' for me I was down in Tijuana gettin' humped and rolled by some two dollar Tijuana fancy woman—"

"No shit!" Pooh says.

"Goes to show—"

"Coincidence," Boots says. "Could of happened to anybody."

"Coincidence my foot. I still think about things I should have told my mama before she up and left this earthly pale. So I just think maybe Calvin should talk to his mama before it's too late is all."

"Well nobody talks to their mamas before they split from home," Boots says.

"Some do—"

"They able to talk to their mamas they wouldn't split from home in the first place."

"Maybe, maybe not," Shorty says.

You talk to your mama, Pooh?"

"Ain't split from home yet, 'less you count juvie."

"But still, you talk to your mama?"

"Not if she don't catch me first."

"See—" Boots says.

"So how old was you, Shorty?" I ask. "When you split from home?"

"Not much older'n you. Sixteen maybe. Was in nineteen hundred and thirty seven— thirty eight, maybe— Lived nineteen miles from town. Sick of milkin' cows sun up and sun down and muckin' cow plop. Was goin' to lie about my age and join the submarines."

"You was in the submarines?" Pooh asks.

"Heck no— Turns out I couldn't hack livin' in a broom closet— you ever been in a submarine, that's what it's like. Turns out I'm a wide-open-spaces sort of guy. So they put me in a motor pool. Drove big brass around San Diego until the war ended. Blessing in disguise."

"Shit, Calvin," Pooh says. "So you really goin' to Philadelphia?"

"He just told you he's goin' to Philadelphia, numb nuts—" Boots says. "Can't we talk about this shit later or something? I got a bitch of a headache— throbbin' like a mother."

"Out drinkin' with Singer again?" Pooh asks.

"Shit no, drinkin' with my old man—"

"Drinkin' with your old man? Thought you wasn't talkin' to your old man—"

"Wasn't, 'til we started drinkin' last night. Now I am again. He wants me back in the business."

"I thought you was in the business already," Pooh says.

"Was— then I wasn't after I rolled that D9 last winter."

"You never told me that—"

"Never told nobody."

"So you goin' back into the business then?"

"Maybe— Maybe not. But I got to help out old China first. By the way, China asked about you, kid—" Boots says to me, his voice soft in the darkness up near the glowing dash.

"It's been kind of hard to get over there," I say.

"No, she just wanted to know that you was OK is all. Says she knows you gotta do what you gotta do."

"Is everything OK?" I ask. "At the stable and all?"

"Shit—" Boots says. "You really don't want to know—"

"I want to know," I say.

"Bad to worse."

"Insurance won't cover that girl broke her back—" Pooh says.

"Never heard that," Shorty says.

"Jimmy Root told me—" Pooh says.

"That's a shame," Shorty says. "That's a gall darned shame."

We glide past my old elementary school then over the last hill. The streets are red with morning light as we roll down 98th Street and into the flats of Oakland.

"Shorty—" Pooh says, "I gotta get me a job—"

"Got you a job, didn't I?" Shorty says.

"I mean a real job— somethin' steady. I gotta make me some serious bread— fast."

"Stay in school," Shorty says. "You boys hungry? I know a place that whips up some mean pancakes, sausages, and eggs."

We pull in between two big Peterbilt semis. The sun is glinting hard over the Piedmont hills, wispy fog in the canyons tinged with red.

"Sure you want to park here, Shorty?" Boots says. "These rigs could roll over your Caddie like a Budweiser can."

"Caddie's insured," Shorty says.

"Your Caddie," Boots says.

We enter the diner, have to wait crowded in a narrow doorway behind three drivers. The drivers are horsing around, laughing, pushing us back out the door. The tall one is wearing a leather belt with his name carved on the back.

"Hey, Walt," Boots says.

The tall one turns, looks at Boots up and down, glances at Pooh.

"Give us some elbow room here, will you cowboy?"

"Shit, Boots," Pooh says. "You're really on the rag today, ain't you?"

"Sure thing, darlin'—" the driver laughs, stepping further into the diner. "That do you?"

"Been thinkin'," Shorty says.

"What you thinkin'?" Boots answers.

"China's gonna need money."

"You tellin' me? She ain't got but four boarders and that rent string don't bring in beans."

"And that stallion's pastern still ain't healed up way it's supposed to," Pooh says. "Least that's what Jimmy Root told me."

"China's gonna need serious coin what with legal bills and all."

"So, what you thinkin'?" Boots says. "You got money to bail her out?"

"I'm thinkin' maybe we can help her organize some kind of fundraiser. A dance or something—"

"Or a barbecue—" Pooh says.

"Or maybe an overnight ride," Boots says.

"Or why not all three?" Shorty says.

"Shit, why the fuck not!" Boots says.

"What do you think, Calvin—" Shorty says. "Think you can get your step dad to donate steaks for a barbecue?"

"Shorty—" Boots says.

"Yeah, sorry son," Shorty says. "Wasn't thinkin'."

"Table for four?" a waitress says and leads us to a table behind the bubbling orange and red Wurlitzer playing Hank Snow— *I'm movin' on, I'll soon be gone—*

"Not there, Darlene," a burly man yells from behind the counter.

"Give 'em that table by the window. New girl—" the man mouths, smiling at Shorty.

"That panel van still runnin' OK, Harold?" Shorty yells back.

"Like a top—"

"Well gives you any trouble you bring it right in, you hear? Come here all the time—" Shorty says.

"Early for you, ain't it Shorty?" a waitress says, not Darlene. "The usual?"

"Howdy, sugar. The usual for me. What about you, Calvin? Anything you want."

I order a cheese omelet, side of ham.

"Want some joe to go with that"? Shorty asks.

"Milk is OK," I say.

"And what about you boys?"

Boots orders pancakes, eggs on the side. Pooh's reading the menu.

"Pooh?"

"Can't decide—"

"Can't decide?"

"Can't decide—"

"Need a minute, honey?" the waitress says.

"No. Give me toast."

"Toast is all?"

"Yeah, toast."

"This is on me, son—" Shorty says.

Pooh looks up.

"Go ahead— get whatever you want, son."

"No shit?" Pooh says.

"Fringe benefit—" Shorty says.

"Well then give me the Lumberjack Special!"

"Want some juice or somethin'?" Shorty asks.

Pooh looks up again.

"Put some orange juice on there, sugar," Shorty says. "Big glass."

Pooh looks at Shorty.

Shorty's flipping through the juke box selections. "Gonna be a hard day— Gotta fuel up."

Boots stretches back in his chair. "Nice place," he says.

Pooh pours sugar into his palm, licks it.

"Shit, Pooh!" Boots says. "Can't you wait for your eggs and shit?"

Pooh looks up, embarrassed.

"Miss your supper last night, son?" Shorty asks.

Pooh looks away.

"I missed a meal or two in my time—"

"Wasn't much in the house—"

"Went three days one time, nothing to eat—" Shorty says. "'Til in the end I ate a cat."

"A cat!" Pooh says.

"Was a big old orange tabby— tomcat. Tasted like possum. Only gamier."

"When was this?" Boots asks.

"After I left home before the Navy took me."

"So'd you eat it raw or cook it?"

"Was up in Nashua, New Hampshire—"

"New Hampshire?"

"You see, we was from way up state Vermont— near the border. Was on my way to Boston. Never before been but twenty miles from home—"

"Why Boston?"

"Man at the Navy recruiting office in Burlington told me that Boston was the only place you could enlist for the submarines. Weren't true, but I think he suspected I was under age— wanted to get me out of his hair."

"And you believed him?"

"Course I believed him. Was discouraged at first. Thought about givin' it up, goin' back to the farm. But then I saw this beautiful Hohner Harmonica all silver in the window of a music store, had my name written all over it. So I bought the sucker. Had just enough coin left over for the bus to Boston. I grabbed that harmonica, run to the station, spent my last penny on a one-way ticket to Boston."

"So how'd you end up in Nashua?"

"My head was so filled with that harmonica I jumped on the first bus I saw. Only it wasn't the bus to Boston. Was the bus to Nashua. Driver must of been half asleep or somethin'. Never noticed I give him the wrong ticket."

"So what'd you do when you got to Nashua?"

"Was rainin' cats and dogs. Wettest spring on record they told me. I looked for work but there weren't none. But I found this old barn where I could hole up, get myself out of the rain. Only thing was I didn't have no food and didn't have no money to buy none."

"So what'd you do?"

"The first couple of days nothin' but play my harmonica. I looked around in the box stalls and the hayloft and up in the rafters but I couldn't even find a pigeon egg to satisfy my hunger. Every day this big orange tabbie come in through a hole in the foundation, soakin' wet, and rubbed himself up against me."

"So you fuckin' ate him?" Boots says.

"Had no choice. Was either him or me—"

"What do you mean, 'him or me—'"

"Don't you think he wouldn't a dug in and had himself a feast if I keeled over from hunger there in that barn? This was no house cat. This was a big ol' wild barn cat."

"Still—" Boots says.

"Finally I was seeing pictures in my head— that kitty begin to look more and more like a grain-fattened heifer. So the last day there I kneeled beside that hole in the foundation there with an old shovel over my shoulder and when that tabbie come through that hole there I let him have it with everything I had."

"And you ate him?"

"Sure I ate him."

"Cook him first?"

"Sure I cooked him first."

"So what'd you use for fire?" Pooh asks.

"Built a fire in a bucket. Lit it with this old merchant marine lighter my uncle give me."

"Shorty, this true?" Boots says.

"Well, could of been," Shorty says, showing his gold tooth.

I see houses boarded up, garbage on the streets, a few people on the sidewalk moving like swimmers under water. An old black man in white shirt and black tie slides open a black iron gate in front of a liquor store. We pull into the alley behind the Tastee Market early, sit in the Caddie listening to country music, waiting for the truck.

"So how'd you make all your money, man?" Pooh asks Shorty.

"What money?"

"You got this Caddie, a bitchin' house, bitchin' horses—"

"Bank owns most of it," Shorty says.

"Bank wouldn't give me the time of day," Pooh says.

"Well you gotta do this and that," Shorty says. "Started with the car lot down on East 14th. Bought a couple of trucks."

"But how'd you get started?" Pooh asks.

"Like it says on those cement trucks you see around town— 'Find a need and fill it.'"

"Simple as that, huh?"

"Well this skipper I used to jockey around San Diego pointed me in the right direction."

"What's his name," Pooh asks. "I need me a few pointers."

"He was a good man," Shorty says. "Down with his ship off Midway."

"This another story?" Boots asks.

"No this is a true story— This old skipper told me that the only way to get ahead in life is to own your own business."

"That's what Teddy said—" I say. "Then he went bust and the rest of us ate spoiled meat until we wanted to puke."

"Well— Teddy—" Shorty says.

"—used to sit around all day in the damned bar next to his shop drinking with the meat salesmen. The drunker he got the more meat he bought until he had meat piled up and rotting in the freezer."

"Well your step daddy—" Shorty says.

"What?" I say.

"He just never looked under the surface of things is all—"

"What do you mean?" I say.

"Never looked under the surface of ownin' a business— learned about the hard part that goes on underneath."

"So you really think we can do it, Shorty?" Boots asks.

"Do what—" Shorty says.

"Make enough money with these dances and shit to save China's ass?"

"Maybe not that much," Shorty says. "But maybe we can buy her a month or two— buck up her fightin' spirit. Well looks like the party's over, boys— truck's comin' around the bend."

The big Dodge stake truck pulls in groaning under a mountain of watermelons. Shorty jumps out of the Caddie, walks backward across the alley, guiding the truck in past a pile of wooden pallets.

"This here's Danny," Shorty says, waving toward the driver. He bangs on the back door of the Tastee, skips back to the truck, hoists himself up on the tailgate.

"Now here's the first thing you gotta know about unloadin' water-melons." Shorty stands on his tiptoes, hoists a large striped melon up over the stakes, tosses it down to Boots who staggers under the weight.

"Drop that melon down in the road there—"

Boots looks at Shorty, starts to stoop.

"No! Just drop it— on the road there."

"You kiddin'?" Boots says.

"Said it, didn't I?" Shorty says. "Go ahead, drop it now."

Finally, Boots lets slip and the melon explodes with a plop on the asphalt, splattering our boots with watermelon juice, black seeds, and rind. Shorty jumps off the tailgate, kneels down, pulls out a red shard from the largest piece of rind.

"Now this here is the heart, see—" he says, taking a bite and handing the rest to Pooh. "Now it's goin' to get hot as blazes later today and these melon's is goin' to get heavier'n stone. So you feel like you need a breather, any time, just go ahead and do like I showed you, sacrifice a melon to the cause. But just eat the heart, see, because the rest ain't worth the trouble. Besides— your time's worth more than these melons. Don't want you wastin' time spittin' seeds."

Shorty sucks his fingers, wipes his hands on his Levi's. "Be back around noon," he says. Shorty heads toward his Cadillac, then pauses, turns—

"Second thought— don't drop 'em all over the road," he says. "Wait'll the truck is near empty. Drop 'em in the bed of the truck. That way, we can feed the leavings to the horses."

"Calvin," Pooh says watching Shorty drive away, "Philadelphia— think your old man can get me a ticket too?"

# The Overnight Ride

W E'RE 47 riders saddled up and restless, bunched in the yard between the clubhouse and the watering tank, the box stalls and
China's back porch. *Release Me, Darlin'* bawls full-volume out of the
clubhouse, but we're louder, friendly insults, voices and laughter, dancing hooves and nickering, jangling roller bits and creaking leather. We're
sprawled across our saddles, knees hooked on saddle horns, scuffed
and dusty boots, polished boots, tennis shoes and beaded moccasins
pivoting into stirrups, dangling free, swinging over curried haunches.

"Somethin', huh?" Boots says, shying back into me, then nudging his
horse, Tullula, back through the whirl of faded jeans and peddle pushers, fancy chaps with fringe and tight leather shotguns chafing carved
leather pommels.

"Never thought you'd see this many riders in China's yard, did you
Calvin?" Boots yells over his shoulder.

"No," I think. "Never did—"

We're stretching in our stirrups and slumping back, twisting and
squirming to secure slickers and ponchos and heavy mackinaws, bedrolls, canteens, lead ropes and lariats, hoof picks, curry combs and wire
cutters. We're gentling down our skittish paints and bays and buck-
skins, piebalds, chestnuts, roans and palominos, patting muscled rumps
and glistening withers, flicking leather reins black with sweat.

I see Singer, bow-taut in his rent-string saddle, arc a beer can onto
the roof of the horse barn.

China's friend, Rhona, snaps her mare with the tasseled end of a
horse hair lead rope then snubs it's head up hard against its chest when
it dances out. "You bitch!" Rhona yells, jerking the tightly braided rawhide reins, contorting the confused horse's jaw unnaturally in the bite

167

of the steel-hard hackamore.

I feel part of this, then oddly apart, cut off, drifting in a kind of silence. I'm here but not here, a beetle stuck in pitch, an icy stone orbiting distant worlds. Boots had driven us, getting the word out about this ride.

I scan the roof line above the horse barn, the dark judging stand looming behind the barn, follow a swirl of black birds across the hill above. The hill is parched and dry, veined with meandering horse trails and pocked with prairie dog burrows. I drop my eyes, follow the green asphalt eaves of the horse barn, the flat roof of the clubhouse, the rise of China's shingled roof, dusty dry on the side where the sun bakes it, moldy damp on the other side under the black shadow of the shedding eucalyptus that fills China's side yard. China's house was white once, but now it's streaked rusty yellow where rain washes summer dust over the eaves, cracked and peeling around the upstairs windows from too many summers of relentless sun.

"Calvin, where's Junie?" Dixie shouts, threading toward me through the maze of riders on her buckskin mare. I nod toward the watering tank where June is letting her Arab drink.

"Calvin, seen Dixie?" Pooh yells from across the yard. I point and Pooh jostles his rent-string gelding through the crowd, waving to catch Dixie's attention.

"When we movin' out, Shorty?" someone yells.

"Gittin' saddle sore just sittin' here," yells another.

"Singer," Alaska says from somewhere behind me, "Leave me alone!"

I turn, see Shorty Hollister near the front gate, small on his rangy roan, leathery face beer flushed, nudge his roan into motion. I feel the current of motion ripple back through the riders, sweep us out through the gate. We contract like a gas through the narrow gate, horse heads shaking over swaying haunches, flashes of hats and hands, turquoise and rawhide, silver conchos and oiled leather. Once out, we turn left, expand out across the road, the staccato sound of hooves echoing between my old house that's no longer my home on the one side of the road and China's hay barn on the other.

I'm swept near the falling fence in front of my old house as we ride by. I look, seeing it anew as though moving in rather than moving out. I see the rusty horse trailer, tires flat, on one side, the fake yellow brick asphalt siding, crooked window frames. I see the dark and empty windows, the shriveled shrubs. I see the front door, closed but probably not locked, an empty milk bottle on the step, the tree that was once our Christmas tree climbing up the living room window, towering over the sagging roof. I see the naked gash in the siding where I once backed Teddy's truck into it. Mom's car, Teddy's truck are gone. The driveway is empty, oil stained, cracked where Teddy once tried to pour concrete, rutted gravel leading in. I'm struck how small the house is, compared with June's house where I've been staying. It was once a double-stall horse barn, but Teddy had converted it, added on. I remember playing with the disk-shaped knockouts from the electrical boxes, pretending they were coins.

I'm riding Peaches, Mr. Rogers' new paint mare. She wants to move out, take the lead, but I slow her up, let the crowd clatter on ahead. Stella Street is a ribbon of pot-holed asphalt with gravel-bottomed ruts on either shoulder carved deep by the winter runoff that torrents down from the eroded hills. I slow her up even more, almost stop, in front of Harris' pasture. It's empty now and has been since the Fourth of July when the glue truck man had pulled into China's yard and told us the news. Harris had hit an oil slick on the downgrade out of Truckee. His rig had bucked the abutment and plunged down blasted talus into the Truckee River. Harris used to pay me two silver dollars every Saturday morning for feeding his horses. The day I quit he'd looked hard at me, shoved his hands into the pockets of his scuffed leather flight jacket, and leaned into the rusty barbed wire fence. "Maybe when I retire I'll have time to ride these crowbaits, take care of 'em right," he'd said. I remember his horses, balking at the ramp even with four of us from China's helping the glue truck man drive them in. They were good horses, a little soft with no one riding them, but now there's a for-sale sign on the gate and weeds growing in the corner where they used to wait for me every morning, nickering. I wonder if they'll build houses on the pasture now. Currier and Sundown— ghosts now, nothing but names.

I wave to Sammy Burwin, across the road, nailing shingles on the roof of his new red barn. He shades his eyes with his hand, waves back, and takes up his hammer again. Sammy is always building, fixing, tearing down and rebuilding. His house and yard and barns are the neatest on Stella street. China says he knows more about sick and injured horses than any vet alive. But I've never seen him ride. I remember him, little more than a shadow in the rain, one boot wedged in above the other on the treacherous slope, staring down at me sprawled in the mud beside Dutchess, shaking his head slowly, telling me with a gentle nod that some things were even beyond his power to heal. I remember the flood of hatred then as I'd realized the futility of my last hope, taste some of it still.

"Calvin! You comin'!" I look up. One of the polliwogs has dropped back to ride with me. He's wearing tennis shoes, yellowed rubber puckered and peeling away from frayed canvas once black but now gray, thrust too far into the stirrup.

"Somethin' the matter?" he asks.

I nod, try to smile, look away. His back is slumped, all wrong, a half-empty feed sack rather than proud straight. His jaw is slack, bobbing with the movement of his horse.

"Is it true they goin' to build houses all the way up to the pond?" he says.

"Probably," I say.

"They ain't goin' to leave no place to ride," he says.

I shrug.

"Calvin," he says, "When you leavin'?"

"Soon—" I say. "Was supposed to leave yesterday—"

"So why didn't you leave?" he says. "The overnight ride?"

"Airplane ticket never come."

"Never come, why?" he says.

"Just never come."

"Well maybe you ain't supposed to go—"

"Why's that?" I say.

"Well you never got the ticket— so maybe you ain't supposed to go."

"I'm goin'—" I say.

"My mama says when something bad happens it was probably meant to be—"

"Meant to be by whom?"

"I don't know— God or someone. Calvin—"

"Yeah," I say.

"When you leave, think China would give me your job?"

Boots is waiting as I lag last up the hill.

"You're lookin' like you lost your brother, kid," he says.

I shrug.

"Glad you got to make this ride," he says. "Maybe the last time I get to see you. Calvin's last ride—"

"Boots—" I say.

"Yeah," he says. He tries to joke with me, but he's too excited about the success of the ride, and I'm too quiet, so mostly I ride alone after he jogs out to catch up with the others. I have a lot to think about.

Peaches is skittish when we get to Chabot Road. She breathes hard and dances as cars and trucks whoosh by. She demands all my concentration as we ride the mile down the shoulder littered with beer cans and broken glass and cigarette butts and a mud-caked teddy bear with stuffing bulging out of its split belly. She's winded by the time we cut up toward the watershed, hit Skyline, so I climb down and walk her for awhile. She seems to like this, nuzzling me on the shoulder. Inside the gate into the watershed I remount, let her step out to catch up with the others. I'm thinking again, but don't seem to get anywhere. The shadows grow in the canyons and I see bats and night birds swoop across the brush, then, for a long time, nothing except the faint trail ahead of me and black hills against the sky. Now and again I hear plodding hooves of other riders echoing down the canyons. I'm hypnotized, then awakened.

First I hear the riders up ahead, shouting, and spurring their tired horses, then I hear the scratchy whine of country music and see the red glow of the barbecue pits down through the trees. We've been riding for an hour or more in darkness, the boisterousness of the first few hours long since given way to long silences and quiet conversations among riders bunched out in groups of twos and threes over a mile or more of trail. The ride has been longer than anyone expected. Some of the polliwogs are hurting bad and complaining and even I'm a little saddle sore. The trail diagonals down into the canyon, into the blackness under the trees where we cross a creek. I hear the singing and laughter swell louder still in the damp air of the canyon bottom and feel Peaches perking up under me as she realizes that the end is near.

"My ass feels like I been sittin' on a belt sander!" someone bellows down through the trees.

"I'm so hungry my stomach thinks my throat is cut!" rises above laughter.

Peaches slips on a rock in the middle of the creek, clatters for footing, almost goin' down, but she recovers just as my boot starts to fill with water. The faint wind rolls down a whiff of charcoal and sizzling meat and Peaches whinnies and a horse, maybe June's Arab, answers from the high bank up ahead. I lean forward in the saddle as Peaches clambers up the muddy bank beyond the creek and feel like shouting myself as we break out into the meadow.

"Calvin— Over here!" June shouts. Coleman lanterns hang under trees on the far side of the meadow. Riders are throwing bedrolls and saddles onto the ground, casting long shadows across the trampled grass, walking their lathered horses to cool them down. I see June and Dixie waving from the circle of light.

"We thought we'd lost you way back," June says.

"You oughta see Rhona," Dixie says. "Three sheets to the wind already, lusting after poor Boots' bod."

I dismount, pat Peaches on her sweaty neck and withers.

"Peaches here is going to be a real good horse," I say. "She started out a bit skittish and green, but she come through like a champ."

"Well cool her off and bed her down," June says. "We found a good spot down under the trees."

"I should have watered her down at the creek before we come up," I say. "I don't like the idea of sliding back down that bank in the dark."

"Daddy hauled up some buckets of water," June says.

"Your dad's here?" I ask.

"He hauled in the grill for the barbecue," she says, "but he had to drive out again. Some big emergency at one of his job sites."

"Well whatever," Dixie says. "You don't do something quick, we'll miss the steaks, won't be nothing but hot dogs burned to a crisp."

I'm hungry and saddle weary as we walk out of the darkness toward the barbecue pit. Riders are hunkered around the circle of Coleman light eating rib eyes bigger than paper plates and corn-on-the-cob and baked potatoes wrapped in foil. Someone has hung a speaker from a tree limb and hooked a record player up to a car battery, and a few are dancing, and others are jostling in around the barbecue pit for firsts and seconds or just to keep warm. I see China, face glowing, handing out paper plates and utensils from behind a table made up of planks balanced on beer kegs.

"There you are, sunshine," she says. "I thought you was lost down in one of them side canyons."

"Just dawdlin'," I say.

"Well take some salad here, and get yourself a steak. Want a beer—wash the trail dust out of your teeth?"

I move in closer to the barbecue pit and then see Teddy telling some kind of story, weaving in and out of the rippling hot air and smoke above the barbecue pit. He's flipping steaks with a blackened fork, waving a beer can in his free hand, cigarette dangling from his knuckles, face smudged with soot.

"There he is," Teddy says. "The Yacob Strauss. Good enough to eat my steaks, but too good to live under the same roof with his mother and me."

Shorty Hollister moves in, but I step away, walk out into the darkness under the trees.

"Goody two shoes whipper snapper," Teddy yells. "I got somethin' to say to you!"

I'm cold, sitting alone on a damp log well out in the darkness. I hear Junie crashing around, calling me, but I can't bring myself to answer.

"There you are," she says, stumbling into me. "I brought you a steak, but it's probably cold by now."

"I don't want it," I say.

"Calvin," she says, "You can't let him win."

"He can do anything he wants," I say.

"Well so can you," she says. "You think you can run away, but he's still pulling your strings. You can't let him do that."

Junie pulls at me, pulls me back into the light. We hunker down against a tree at the edge of light, sharing cold steak. More people are dancing now, voices growing louder. Jimmy Root is strumming his guitar, singing to himself in his low raspy voice. Dixie and Pooh are wrapped around each other, supposedly dancing, but hardly moving to the beat.

"Calvin—"

I turn. Mother is sitting beside me, her hair haloed against the fire.

"I'm going to get a Coke," June says. "Want one?"

"Yes—" I say.

"Can I get you something, Mrs. Moore?"

"She's a nice girl," Mother says.

"How'd you get here?" I say.

"We brought the steaks."

"Oh—" I say.

"I brought you these," she says, handing me an envelope. "From your father. Came to the house."

"My ticket?" I say.

"I guess—" she says. "He wrote you a note— and there's some money. I put some in too."

"I've got money," I say.

"Yes, but you'll need more—"

"I'm— I'm sorry, mom— But—"

"Yes," she says. "It's probably for the best."

"I didn't—" I say.

"I understand, honey," she says.

"Well— why do you stay with him then?" I ask.

"Your stepfather?"

"Yes," I say.

"He's my husband—"

"But I'm your son—"

"Yes," she says. "No matter what."

"But don't you even care?" I say.

She stares at the ground, searching. "Care? Calvin, I—"

I see tears, but can't be sure. I fight my tears.

Mom turns, stares into the fire, turns back.

"Calvin, honey," she whispers, "I care more than you'll ever know."

"But why do you stay with him?" I say.

"It's— it's what you do," she says. "You can't always run away from your troubles."

"I'm not running!" I say. "He's the one kicked me out. He gave me no choice!"

"I know, honey," she says. "But, you know, I love you both."

I look away.

"I need you both."

I can't answer.

"Don't you understand that?" she says. "I need you both!"

I study the darkness under the trees.

"Calvin—" she says.

I still can't answer.

"Before you leave— I mean before you fly back East— come an' see me, hon. I know you got to leave and all. But I can't bear it like this."

I'm still looking into the trees.

"I'm cold," mother says. "I'm going up to get my jacket."

Later I'm sitting in a small circle with Boots and Shorty and China. Rhona is sleeping, sprawled out in the dirt, mouth open, snoring softly, head framed in hair tangled up in Boots' lap. Some are still dancing, but most have trundled off into the darkness, snuggled into sleeping bags.

China is drunk and crying, something that I've never seen before.

"Where will they all go?" she says. "This is where they belong—"

"It won't happen," Shorty says, "You'll see—"

"I'm so scared," China says.

"China—" Boots says.

"I don't give a tinker's damn about me, don't you see?" China says. "They can take the whole damned pile of manure if they want it— just take it to hell for all I care. But these kids still need some place to go— some place that really wants 'em. I've seen what the streets do to babies. I grew up on the streets, remember, and I swore that I'd never ever let it happen to my babies. I can't let it happen, don't you see?"

"It won't happen," Boots says.

"You're a love, Boots," China says, "And you too, sunshine. But what do you know, damn it all! I'm really tired of fightin'—"

"You'll fight it," Shorty says.

"Well I'm really really tired of fightin'—"

"Singer!"

We all turn. Alaska is screaming out in the darkness.

"What's the matter, hon?" Shorty yells.

Alaska stomps in out of the darkness.

"That damned Singer poured a bucket of water on my sleeping bag!"

We hear Singer, cackling.

"Singer!" China bellows.

The woods are suddenly quiet, even the horses.

"Singer, you jackass!" China yells. She's standing now.

Singer comes in, head hanging, Pooh right behind him.

"Get your sleeping bag—"

"What—" he says.

"Bring me your damn sleeping bag. Right now!"

"I didn't—" he says.

"Now!" she says.

Singer trudges into the darkness.

"It's alright, sugar," China says to Alaska.

Singer trudges back in, dragging his sleeping bag.

"Here you go, sugar," China says, grabbing the bag from Singer and handing it to Alaska.

"That's one way of getting her into your sack," Boots laughs.

China glares.

"But what am I—"

"You'll figure it out," China says. "Shorty, get me another beer."

"Calvin," Junie calls to me from across the clearing. I see that something's wrong.

"What," I say, standing, walking toward her.

"Dixie thinks she's seen Stuie Kramer's dog, Stormtrooper."

"Stormtrooper? What's he doing up here?" I ask.

"She's sure it was him, sniffing around the horses."

"She see Stuie Kramer?"

"No, but that's the thing—"

"Where's Pooh," I say.

"Last time she saw Stuie Kramer he said some really scary things—"

"So where's Pooh?" I ask.

"Getting his sleeping bag for Singer."

"So where's Pooh going to sleep?"

"I don't know— with Dixie, I guess."

"So where they now?"

"Down near the horses— Down where we put the bed rolls. What if he's out there, Calvin? Remember that day at Dixie's?"

"It's probably nothing," I say. "Probably some dog looks the same—"

"But what if he's out there?" Junie says. "Stuie's really weird. What if he's out there watching us?"

"He's not," I say. "Probably some stray dog smelled the meat."

"But what if he's out there? Calvin, move your sleeping bag closer to mine— I'm kind of scared. Stuie scares me—"

I'm sleeping, dreaming about endless streets, brambles, when someone shakes me hard.

"Calvin!" It's Junie.

"Junie?" I say.

"What are they doing?" Junie screams. "Stop them!"

I hear hard thumps and breathy screaming.

"You whore bitch motherfucker!"

I hear hard, hollow thuds in the darkness.

"Junie!" I say.

It's cold and damp and shadowy under the trees. I see violent movement down near where Dixie and Pooh had bedded down.

A horse screams and horses clamor in the darkness. I hear the clatter of hooves across the meadow.

"Hey! Hey!" Shorty Hollister comes running, his yellow flashlight bouncing in the darkness, illuminating tree trunks and branches and leaves.

And then it's silent. I'm standing in my underpants looking down as Shorty zips back the sleeping bag, green fabric shredded with cotton batting fluttering in the jittery light. Then I see black stains spreading up through the lumpy bag. Then, in the light, see the spreading stains looking like shiny red plastic.

"They're breathing," Shorty says. "We need help here quick."

June is crying hard, hand to her mouth, staring down at Pooh's mangled face, Dixie's blood-matted hair.

Alaska pushes into the circle.

Alaska lets out a scary moan.

Singer pushes in behind her, bobbing shadow outside the light.

"Stuie Kramer—" Singer says, "That crazy fuck!"

# Trackin'

So why can't we let the police do it?" I ask.

"Police no good— this kind of shit," Boots says.

"So what we going to do if we find him?" I say.

"We'll figure it out," Boots says.

We're in Jimmy Root's Chevy convertible, bombing down to Stuie Kramer's house, coming from the emergency. My body aches from no sleep and the long ride in and out of the watershed. The August sun is overhead and glare off the cars and the busy street feels like someone is pounding me above the eyes with a two-by-four. Boots is squinting hard, big callused hands beating time on the top of the amber steering wheel, face twisted in a way that scares me. Something has come out in Boots that I've never seen before, especially since we left the emergency. He's singing to himself, singing in a monotonous way, face twisted, hands beating time on the steering wheel. Sweat rolls down his shaggy sideburns. The taut denim under his arm is black with stains, ringed with dried sweat.

"Ever been to Kramer's house?" Boots says suddenly.

"No," I say.

"Down by the salt flats— little piss ant cracker box?"

"You were at Stuie Kramer's house?" I say.

"A party once— Fucker had this party not long after he started comin' up to China's— before we knew what kind of dumb shit he really was."

"What kind of party?"

"Wasn't much— Sittin' around eatin' potato chips. He made out it was goin' to be this wild make-out party— like he knew these swingin' chicks that really liked to do it and shit."

"And what happened?"

"Jack all— Turned out the chicks were his cousins or somethin'— still wearing braces, not much more than twelve years old, skinny as rats. Kept popping their gum and staring at me like I was King Kong or somethin'. Kramer kept wanting to play grab ass or spin the bottle or somethin' but I wouldn't have touched 'em with a 10-foot pole. Kramer's mama kept comin' in every twenty seconds to see if we was havin' a good time. Said she was soooo glad little Stewart had such lovely friends— wasn't but four of us there includin' little Stewart, and two of 'em his cousins. Fuckin' Kramer." Boots' voice starts out tight, gets tighter as he tells the story. He's beating time on the steering wheel again.

"Pooh tell you anything?" I ask. "At the emergency?"

We'd borrowed Jimmy Root's convertible and bombed down to the emergency as soon as we'd cooled off the horses at China's. The horses had been hard lathered from the ride back, Boots pushing us at a kidney-bustin' jog all the way. I'd put Peaches up in a spare box stall with a shock of hay and a couple of coffee cans of rolled oats, but she was too winded to do more than push the grain around with her nose. It wasn't visiting hours or anything, but Boots had snuck in anyway while I watched the car in a no-parking zone. Says he almost got into a fist-fight with Dixie's old man trying to get in to see her.

"That Pooh—" Boots says. "Keep a secret?"

"Sure," I say. "What?"

"I mean like not tell anyone— China or anybody or I bust your ass?"

"Yeah," I say.

"Little darlin' Dixie's knocked up."

"What do you mean?" I say.

"You know— she's pregnant."

"She's not married—" I say.

Boots looks at me. "Don't have to be married, didn't your mama teach you that? You know, the old in and out thing?"

"Like— Pooh?" I say.

"Who do you think? He told me the day we was roustin' watermelons, piss-pants scared as a cat on the Fourth of July. Dumb shit little fucker—" I see Boots shaking his head, rubbing his eyes.

I'm silent, watching the brown lawns, squat houses zip by, one no different from the next.

"They in totally different wings of the hospital," Boots says. "Dixie in a private room. Pooh in the charity ward."

"But they OK?" I ask.

"No they ain't OK—'" Boots says. "Dixie's got a busted nose, bunch of stitches, maybe more— concussion maybe. She ain't goin' to be as button cute as she used to be she get out of that place, that's for sure." Boots' head is bobbing to some song I can't follow.

"And what about Pooh?" I ask.

"Pooh— He was breathin' when I looked in on him, but out like a light, maybe in a coma. All hooked up on blood and stuff and one of those heart beat things. Shorty was there and Pooh's mother, cryin' like a spigot. I couldn't find his chart."

"His chart—"

"You know, where they report his condition."

"So what do you know about charts?"

"Spent more'n a year in and outa hospital when I was younger'n you— ought to know somethin' about charts."

"From what?" I say.

"Some kind of blood infection or something. Kept coming back and wouldn't go away— finally went away by itself. Wasn't much I didn't know about hospitals time they let me out of that place, that's for sure."

"So why ain't you goin' to medical school?" I say, looking out of the corner of my eyes, hoping to see the old Boots.

"Thought about it," Boots says, still beating time on the steering wheel. "Really did. But then I thought it was more fun digging holes in the ground with a D9."

Boots is silent for a moment, hands resting on the steering wheel. He shakes his head, rubs his eye, starts beating time again.

"Chip off the old block, I guess. Diesel fuel in the blood— earth movers on the brain. Take a look at that brown paper sack on the seat there. I wrote that Kramer fuck's address on it there somewhere."

The shriveled lawn in front of Stuie Kramer's house runs ten feet from the sidewalk to the bare foundation, no shrubs. I see a faded "For Sale" sign hanging upside down on a splayed stake, corner nibbled out like a giant rat bite. A narrow walkway—cracked concrete—runs up to a narrow porch cut in beside a front window not much wider than a door. The house is jammed in on the street with other houses that look like they were all painted against the sky with the same stencil, most painted soft blue and tan, some newly painted, with green lawns, but most fading to one color with flecks of paint shedding onto burnt grass, yellow dandelion heads.

"You believe this shit hole?" Boots says, waving his arm to take in the street and the houses on it. "Built less than ten years ago. Fuckin' developer oughta be strung up from a telephone pole "

We walk to the door, knock. At first there's no answer and then the door cracks open. It's black at first and then I see Boots and me reflected in pink lenses surrounded by pink frames studded with rhinestones.

"Yes?" the voice says in a throaty whisper.

"Stuie Kramer home, ma'am?" Boots says.

"Do you mean Stewart?"

"Yes, ma'am. Stewart—"

"No," the voice whispers. "I'm his mother."

"Can we come in, ma'am?" Boots asks.

"What do you want?"

"Just want to talk to Stuie is all—" Boots says, pushing the door. "Remember me, ma'am? I come here to a party once?"

"You Stewart's friend?"

"Sort of—" Boots says.

The door opens wider. Cigarette smoke hits us, pushes us back. Stuie's mother is shorter than me, dressed in pink with big white clown buttons down the front. She's wearing purple slippers with pointed toes, beads and sequins flashing in a triangle of light.

She tilts her head back, looks Boots up and down, glances at me. She sucks a cigarette fiercely, holding it between us like a knife. "You young men in the agricultural field too? Stewart's in the agricultural field, you know."

Boots looks at me.

"We just like to talk to him," Boots says. "Know where we might find him?"

"Well he's not here—" Stuie's mom says.

"Mind if we look in his room?"

"Well he's not in his room either," she says. "That's what I told the police already— Don't know what they want with my Stewart. Can you tell me why every Tom, Dick, and Harry is looking for my Stewart?"

Boots edges around Stuie's mother. "Back here, ma'am?" he says.

"Well I'd know if he was in his room wouldn't I? I'm his mother."

"Just want to take a look," Boots says.

Suddenly I notice someone sprawled on the couch. At first I think it's Stuie, but then I see it's an old man, mouth open, pepper stubbled chin.

"Don't wake Mr. Kramer," Stuie's mother whispers. "He works hard, you know— He's in the security field."

The man is watching me, eyes black under white eyebrows. I nod. He keeps watching. The air in the room stinks of stale cigarette smoke. Dying plants in ceramic pots drape over grinning porcelain dwarves on the mantle.

"Back here, ma'am?" Boots says.

Stuie's room is filled with books, no shelves, but books stacked on the desk, the puke green carpet, on every horizontal surface.

"Wouldn't have figured Kramer for a reader," Boots says.

I'm staring at the poster over Stuie's bed. "Southern Christian Redemption." It shows a flaming cross, dark figures hunched at the bottom, hauntingly terrified eyes.

"Well he's not here, the chicken shit—" Boots says, kicking over piles of books, sorting through them with the scuffed and dusty toe of his motorcycle boot.

We're bombing down Skyline again, headed toward Boots' house in Piedmont.

"Maybe we should go back to China's," I say.

"Got to get somethin' I told you."

"Get what?" I say.

"Just somethin'. Won't take but a minute."

"But maybe we ought to let the police find him."

"Police ain't goin' to find him."

"Why ain't the police going to find him?" I say.

"Just ain't," Boots says. "Watch the turnouts. Keep your eye out for his Jimmie."

"Think he's still down in the watershed?"

"Betcha anything— Down in some canyon fuckin' Rhona's mare. We looked everyplace else he could be."

"Maybe he's leaving the state or something—"

"He ain't that smart I told you— He's still down in the watershed thinkin' he's some kind of outlaw. Holed up with Rhona's mare— "

"Maybe Rhona's mare just tore loose," I say.

"And Santa Claus flies down chimneys and diddles canaries. He's down there and Rhona's mare too. Rhona says she give me a big C note I find her mare."

"Then how'd he get down to the camping area?"

"Nearest gate ain't but two miles over the ridge. Even Kramer fuck can walk two miles long as he ain't chewin' gum."

"Then why didn't they find his Jimmie?"

"How the fuck do I know why they didn't find his Jimmie? Hid it in the brush or something."

"Did you see those books?" I ask. "Think he reads 'em all?"

"Heavy shit," Boots says. "Nietzsche—"

"Who's that?" I say.

"Some crazy German fuck—"

"Everybody says he's stupid," I say. "But he reads lots of books."

"Ain't books make you smart," Boots says, beating on the steering wheel again. "That horse thievin' fucker's gonna learn somethin' he'd never learn from books time I get through with him—"

We wind down the hill into Piedmont— houses set back on big lawns. Big houses with columns and stone lions. I've never been to Boots' house before. He pulls into a narrow drive between tall flowering shrubs, winds back through the trees.

"Boots—" I say when I see his house through the trees. "I didn't know you were rich."

"Who says I'm rich?"

"This—" I say, waving toward the house.

"My daddy's rich, but don't mean jack shit to him."

"Why?" I say.

"Just don't. And it don't mean jack shit to me. Rich meant a lot to my mama though."

"What do you mean?" I say.

"My mama wanted this house real bad, so my daddy bought it for her. Year before she died. Thought maybe this house would keep her alive a little longer than the doctors said, but it didn't do jack all."

"What do you mean 'didn't do jack all'?"

"Just didn't. Died anyway. Rich ain't for shit and don't let 'em tell you different, kid."

We pull around to a side door behind a silver Cadillac, streaked with mud and dust.

"Just be a minute," Boots says, rubbing his eyes. "Got to get somethin' from my room. You can come in or sit here— suit yourself."

I follow Boots into a narrow hallway stacked with newspapers, boxes of empty liquor bottles.

"Edwin? That you?"

I hear a shuffle and a clatter. An old black woman bulging out of a stiffly starched nurse uniform big as a tent appears in a doorway lit with fluorescent light. She's breathing hard, leaning on a walker.

"Well Master Edwin, aren't you goin' to come in for a minute, pay your respects? Aren't you goin' to introduce me to your friend?"

"This is Calvin," Boots says. "We just here for a minute—"

"Well Calvin, you come in with the civilized folks. I'm Mrs. Carter. Edwin ought to be ashamed bringing you in the back door like you aren't company. Edwin, where's your manners."

"Edwin?" I say.

Boots leans over and kisses Mrs. Carter on the cheek.

"How's your leg today?"

"Old. Like the rest of me. And I can see you aren't eating enough to keep a Pekinese scratching fleas."

"I'm eatin' plenty," Boots says.

"Well you finish your business and come down to my kitchen. I knew you were coming so I baked your favorite kind of pineapple upside down cake."

"How'd you know I was coming? I ain't been here for a week."

"Well you know I always know when you're coming, where you're goin', and what you're thinking. Now you finish your business and come down to my kitchen before I eat that cake all to myself. I don't like that devilment I'm seeing on your face one little bit—"

"What devilment is that?" Boots says as we step into a hallway— dark wood, fancy black Chinese tables, tall Chinese vases.

"Can't hide nothin' from that one," he says to me. "Devilment. She got that one right."

"She likes you," I say.

"Come in to take care of my mom. Then took care of me. Now she's more like a mama than my mom ever was."

We pass a wide door that leads into a room that looks like something out of a movie— deep purple carpet, more dark wood, polished brass, tapestries, and a crystal chandelier, quiet as a tomb. Boots pushes me up a wide set of stairs, gleaming with wax, then holds me back outside a heavy walnut door.

"Meet my dad," Boots says, knocking softly.

"Howdy, son," Boots' dad says, half rising then sinking back into a black leather chair. The room is dark with the draperies drawn and all I see at first is a small TV with a round screen and fuzzy picture sitting on a rickety TV table and a shadow in the chair. Then I see construction boots, one resting on the muddy laces of the other, Levi's with muddy cuffs, brown workman's shirt open at the neck, curly gray hair spilling out. His heavy hand drops down into an ashtray overflowing with butts, spilling butts onto the carpet. He leans over, picks up the butts one by one, puts them back into the ashtray.

"Why don't you get rid of that piece of shit, get somethin' with a half decent picture?" Boots says, nodding toward the TV.

"Nothin' worth watchin'," Boots' dad says. "Bunch of faggot shit."

"This is Calvin," Boots says.

"The rider, eh?" Boots' dad says. "Won all those ribbons? Way Boots talks, I thought you'd be ten feet tall."

I don't know what to say, nod.

"How's it goin'— down at the site?" Boots asks.

"Same shit. One day like the next. You get your ass down there, get to work, it'd go better."

"You do all right without me," Boots says. "Maybe better—"

"Better with you."

"Well, Pops, we got to make it—"

"What's the hurry? Have a cool one with me."

"Stuff to do—" Boots says. "Bad shit. Fuckin' Kramer creamed Pooh an' Dixie real bad with a tree limb— put 'em in the emergency."

"So what are you goin' to do about it?"

"Go find that fuckin' Kramer— He stole a horse. Think he's holed up in the watershed."

"Then what— you find him?"

"We'll think of something—"

"You and the rider there?"

"Yeah, and Singer—"

"Uh huh. And Singer's brother?"

"No. Just us."

"That's a blessing. Better think before you do something stupid, son. Didn't I teach you that?"

"Yeah, Pops. You did."

"Well, think about it."

"I will."

"Yeah, but you'll do what you damned well please now, won't you?"

"Probably—"

"Always have. But think about it. You gotta slap him around a little, slap him. But don't break nothin' can't mend. See you around, Mr. Rider," Boots' dad says. "Want a job diggin' or shit, just give me a call. Boots got the number."

"Wouldn't know from lookin' at him but he was a hell raiser—" Boots says out on the landing. "Before my mama died. Now he just sits there when he ain't out on a job'. Got a good foreman now, so he's sittin' there more and more. Sittin' in the dark."

Boots' room is still a kid's room, yellow and white, late sun pouring through crimson flowers hanging on vines outside the window glass. I see his football trophies, model trucks and earth moving equipment on red lacquered shelves. Boots walks into his closet, pushing the folding door aside.

"This is the beauty I'm lookin' for," Boots says, reaching high on his tiptoes and pulling out a Winchester .30-30 from the top shelf. I'm startled, eyes held by the weathered walnut stock, dried up leather scabbard blotched with gray leather mold, but beautifully carved. Boots spits on his hand and rubs the mold off the scabbard then slowly slips the rifle out of the fleece-lined scabbard, slamming down the lever with a sharp metallic clack, looking into the breech.

"Gun that won the west," Boots says. "Belonged to my grandfather who got it from his father before him." He's humming again.

"What are you going to do with that?" I say.

"Nothin," Boots says, eyes going hard again. "Just bringin' it along for insurance."

"Against what?" I say.

"Never know," Boots says, polishing the deeply blued steel barrel with the edge of his bedspread. "This kind of shit. Reach down in that bottom drawer there— get me some of them boxes of shells and that can of gun oil."

"You really think we need that along?" I say.

"Just get the shells—"

"But I don't think—"

Boots looks at me, hard. "You ain't my damned mother now, are you?" he says. "Get me them damned shells, will you?"

We reach the gate into the watershed well before sun up, but the stars aren't so bright anymore and we're beginning to hear birds and see a glow through the eastern trees. Singer reaches down and slips the chain over the steel post. China had given Boots her Appaloosa stallion to ride and the stallion is still testing, skittish at everything, dancing around. The stallion slams into the steel post as they ride through the gate, dances sideways, rolls, and slams in again, crushing Boots' leg against the steel post.

Boots howls.

"You dog meat motherfucker!" Boots yells, cracking down hard with the end of his reins. The stallion snorts and dances into the grease-wood and poison oak beside the trail, startling a covey of sleeping quail, wings beating like sudden rain in the brush. The quail send the stallion into a frenzy.

I'm shivering, more asleep than awake. We're packing bedrolls and food for two days. We'd planned to ride into the watershed before dark but Singer had kept us waiting at China's until after midnight. Boots was ready to ride in without him, but he had sent Singer out shopping for food while we helped Jimmy feed the rent string. Singer was pissed that he was the one had to do the shopping. He drove off in Jimmy Root's convertible all bent out of shape. "Shit," Boots said. "Our sleeping bags are in the trunk." So we'd waited 'till late, sitting in the club-house, tossing cards, listening to Jimmy Root give us the same advice ten different ways.

"You see signs of Kramer, ride out and tell the police," Jimmy said.

"Fuck that," Boots answered. "He be long gone time the police get back in there."

"Well some things best left to the authorities," Jimmy said.

"Well we ain't goin' to lynch him," Boots said.

"Well I hope to hell you ain't," Jimmy said.

"Most likely—" Boots answered.

"Most likely what?" Jimmy said.

"Most likely we ain't goin' to lynch him."

Boots jumps off the dancing stallion and kicks him in the stomach. "Fuckin' leg," he says, rubbing his knee. "Football knee."

It was too late to ride when Singer pulled up in Jimmy Root's convertible. Boots had called him a fuck up, how long does it take to buy a few groceries anyway, almost ready to fight him, but Singer had looked at the ground, cupping his hand over his eye, rubbing the side of his head.

"Ran into my brother—" he said.

Boots had wanted to saddle up and ride out, but Singer had said, "Fuck that!" he hadn't slept for two days so Boots had let us sleep in the hay barn for two hours before rousting us out to saddle up and head out across the black fire roads into the watershed.

"Fuckin' brother," Singer'd mumbled a couple of times in the dark of the hay barn before we slept.

"Fuckin' brother what?" Boots had said.

"Fuck you!" Singer had answered.

"So how we goin' to do this?" Singer asks.

"Give me a sec," Boots says, limping up and down the trail.

"He's goin' to need food and water."

"Right on my fuckin' football knee—" Boots is leaning over, blowing hard. China's stallion is standing behind him, looking innocent.

"What do you think we ought do with that fucker, we catch him?" Singer says.

"I'm hungry," I say. "Maybe we oughta cook us some eggs."

"I think we oughta shoot the fucker and bury him down in some ravine somewhere," Singer says.

"Shut the fuck up," Boots says, limping now, trying to flex the pain out of his knee.

"Maybe we oughta eat something, " I say.

"Yeah, maybe—" Boots says. "I was hopin' we could see his fire, down in one of the canyons. But the sun's comin' up too fast."

"We don't even know he's here," I say.

"He's here—" Boots says. "Down in one of these side canyons—"

"And he's mine!" Singer says, leaning over and slipping the Winchester out of the scabbard strapped to Boots' saddle.

"Put that iron back, dinkweed," Boots says, wincing as he grabs his saddle horn, swings his boot up into the stirrup.

We ride the ridges first, following the fire roads, looking down into the long canyons, but the brush is heavy in the canyons and Kramer could be anywhere. By noon the sun is too hot on the ridges so we slide down a grassy hillside into the shade under the laurels and unsaddle our horses. The musty smell of horse sweat mingles with the sharp odor of bay from the laurel leaves. The horses snort and pull hard toward the smell of water further down the canyon, but we want them to cool off before we water them.

"Haven't even seen a fuckin' fresh track—" Singer says.

"Maybe we doin' this thing all wrong," Boots says, reaching into his saddle pack.

"What do you mean?" Singer says.

Boots tosses me a tin of sardines and another to Singer. He reaches back into the saddle pack, singing to himself. He becomes suddenly rigid. I think there's a snake in his saddle pack.

"Singer— You fuck!" Boots yells, pulling out three Hershey bars.

"Dipshit! Told you to get hard candy, didn't I? These Hershey bars are about as limp as my dick!"

"What do you mean doin' this thing all wrong?" Singer says.

"God was passin' out brains you must of been takin' a leak."

"But I like Hershey bars—"

"Any shit-for-brains knows you can't carry Hershey bars in a saddle pack— Not less you want chocolate soup."

"Then you be the mother next time," Singer says, "You do the shoppin' while I lay around the Seas next time you so fussy. So what we doin' that's so wrong?"

"And you didn't get crackers like I told you either, did you?"

"Get your own crackers next time. What we doin' so wrong?"

"Everything!" Boots says. "Didn't even get the fuckin' crackers—"

"Fuck the fuckin' crackers, will you! Just tell me what we're doin' that's so fuckin' wrong!"

Boots shakes his head, stomps over to the edge of the clearing to take a leak.

Now I see a bruise around Singer's eye— hadn't seen it in the dark last night.

"Your brother do that?" I say.

Singer moves his hand up to his eye. "Fuck my brother," he says, "And fuck that fuckin' Boots too."

Boots drives us on a forced ride all the way into the camping area.

"We ride right by him this rate, wouldn't even know it—" Singer says.

"Got to get to the camping area before dark so we can pick up his tracks," Boots says.

"Shoulda done that this morning we was goin' to do it that way—" Singer says.

"Didn't think of it," Boots says.

"Well why the fuck didn't you think of it?" Singer says. "You're the fuckin' Napoleon."

"Why didn't you think of it?" Boots asks.

"You the genius big bwana sir leader—" Singer says.

"Yeah, I'm the leader—" Boots says.

"We got to rest these horses," I say. "They're getting too lathered up."

"We'll rest 'em at the camping area," Boots says.

"We make it that far—" Singer says. "Bet we rode two hundred fuckin' miles or more in the last three days."

"So what we goin' to do if we find him?" I say.

"I can think of a bunch of things," Singer answers.

"Maybe we should give him to the police like Jimmy says," I say.

"Yeah, give him to the police," Singer says. "Right!"

"Shut the fuck up about the police, will you, Calvin?" Boots says.

It's too dark to look for tracks by the time we get to the camping area.

"We start early—" Boots says. "See if we can pick up a trail."

We build a fire, sizzle cube steaks in a frying pan, wrap potatoes in aluminum foil, bury them in the coals. Then, later, we slide down the bank to the creek, wash our plates with crick water and sand, scramble back. Singer takes a long time in the darkness, checking the horses.

"Singer," Boots says. "You pounding your pud?"

Singer comes weaving back with a pint of Canadian V.O. "Look what I found in my saddle pack, boys! Better than crackers—"

Boots takes the bottle. "Well, maybe you got somethin' right."

"Why the fuck are we here?" Boots asks.

We're lying in our sleeping bags beside the fire.

"Because that fuckin' Kramer knocked that fuckin' Pooh and Dixie up side the head with a stick and stole Rhona's horse—" Singer says.

"No— I mean, here.  And not somewhere else— China or some planet with beautiful women spinnin' around one of them stars up there."

"We got to be somewhere," Singer says. "Why not here?"

"Why?" I say.

"Why what?"

"Why do we have to be somewhere?"

"Because we do—" Singer says.

"Why?" I ask.

"Because we do. If we wasn't here or somewhere we'd be—" Singer's quiet for a moment.

"Where'd we be, Singer?" Boots asks.

"How the fuck should I know. Where's that Kramer? That's what I want to know."

"He's out there—" Boots says.

"Sneakin' up with a stick—" I say.

"A big fuckin' tree limb," Boots says.

I hear Singer rustle in his sleeping bag.

"Singer," Boots says.

"Hope the fuck he is," Singer says.  I hear the lever action on the Winchester.

"Singer, you fuck!"

I see the muzzle blast like a flash bulb, feel the report slam into my ears.

"You stupid shit, give me that rifle!" Boots says.

"Maybe he's nowhere," I say, ears ringing, heart pounding, muzzle flash echoing behind my eyes.

"Least he knows we're here now," Singer says.

"Give me that fuckin' iron," Boots says.

I hear the lever action again.

"Stop it!" I say.

"We're here and he's somewhere out there—" Singer says.

"Yeah," Boots says. "Maybe right over— there!"

The muzzle flash blinds me again.

"Stop!" I yell, sitting up in my sleeping bag, holding my hands over my ears. "This is so stupid!"

Singer and Boots take turns firing, pump, and fire, grabbing the rifle back and forth. A hot shell arcs out of the chamber, hits me in the forehead.

"Over there—" Singer says.

"We got to save up ammo," Boots says, but they bicker, grabbing the rifle back and forth, pumping and firing.

"Hey, Calvin—" Singer says, "this is a bitch! Sure you don't want to do some shootin'?"

"Fuckin' Calvin's in another world," Boots says. "He's goin' to Philadelphia."

I bury my head in my sleeping bag, shut my eyes hard, while they fire away again and again into the night.

# The Judging Stand

I WAS sleeping hard, but now I wake with a cotton mouth and a sharp rock in my back, at first wondering what I'd meant to remember, but now it comes back, and I know that I won't be able to sleep again, knowing what I have to do.

The moon is straight overhead, full and shimmering like a new silver dollar. The grass is white in the meadow and the shadows under the trees are black and soft, taking shapes, sometimes moving in the corner of my eye, but freezing when I stare straight at them. I hear frogs down by the creek, some kind of night bugs up in the meadow, the horses in the grass, Boots and Singer breathing long and slow in sleep beside me. I'm warm in my sleeping bag but know that I don't have much time so I slide out into the cool air, slip into my boots, reach for my saddle. But then realize I'll wake Boots and Singer if I saddle up, so I untie my lariat from the fender of my saddle and make my way quietly to the horses.

China's stallion challenges me, but I calm him, find Peaches tangled in her stake rope. I slip my head and arm through the coiled lariat to free my hands, unwind the prickly stake rope, and run my hand up and down her pastern, feeling for rope burns. Peaches nuzzles me and leans her weight into me, dragging the cold brass work dangling from her halter across my back. I flip a half hitch around her nose, grab her mane, and swing up onto her broad back.

I ride up the fire road, shivering now, seeing stars on the horizon. When I reach the top of the ridge I'm under a glowing bowl, with the moon straight overhead, stars on the horizons, blackness in the canyons. My lariat, hard as rock, is chaffing my neck, so I slip out of it, try carrying it with one hand or the other. But it's too tiring, so I slip my head and arm back through the coils again and try to ignore the chaffing pain in my neck.

Jimmy Root helped me build this lariat. He went with me to buy the right kind of rope at the tack store, showed me how to tie the honda, how to soak a rawhide patch in water and sew a chaffing sleeve tight around the bight of the honda while the leather was still wet. He showed me how to flip the noose over a fence post and tie the shank end to the bumper of the Chevy flatbed and how to stretch the rope out taut as a guitar string and how to melt beeswax and how to rub the molten beeswax into the hemp fiber with a scrap of sheep skin until the rope was hard as steel. Then he showed me how to coil the rope into a tight spiral of perfect circles and how to hold the coils in one hand and the noose just so in the other and how to flip the noose at an upside-down water bucket over and over again, paying out the coils with my left hand, until I could snap the noose out like a striking rattlesnake. But now, I think, without a saddle and a saddle horn to snub it off, my lariat won't do me much good even if I do get a chance to throw it.

I stop under a lone oak tree in the saddle between two ridges. I slide off Peaches, let the stake rope pay out so she can graze. My mouth is still cottony and I feel dizzy, want to vomit. It had come to me last night in the echoing rifle fire why I had to do this. The grass is long and dry and brittle. The air is soft, but has a nip when it moves so I stretch out in the grass to get under it, cold, taking in the powdery smell of the grass and earth, feeling the prickly stubble dig into my back. I remember other days, grazing Dutchess this way, the oat grass green and hip high so when I sank down into it all I could see was blue sky fringed with dangling bells of near-ripe grain. I would strip the grain from the stalks between my thumb and forefinger, suck on the succulent stalks, listen to insects sing, see black birds and butterflies flit across the sky, feel the drowsy summer heat roll across my chest. I was hidden in the grass, away from it all. You would have stumbled over me before you found me. You wouldn't have seen me from six feet away.

Now I'm cold and hold my arms tight around my chest. The sky is a kind of violet now, changing.

For a moment I feel like I'm in two places at once, one warm and summery and the other cold and shadowy. I remember Boots' question, "Why are we here?" and think how slippery the idea— Here. Am I Here, now, with Peaches, when I'm thinking of that time, in the grass, with Dutchess that seems so real, so immediate in my mind? Could I, with sheer will, squeeze myself through some kind of skin of time so that I'm There thinking about Here instead of Here thinking about There? What is it about Here that binds me, keeps me from passing through? This rope? This grass? This tree? Peaches? These hills? Am I Here by sheer accident, some kind of joke, or do I have a job to do? I think about Philadelphia, the crumpled ticket in my hip pocket, but I've never been there so I have little to hold onto in my mind. I think about my dad, but what is he to me now? I think about Stuie Kramer. Where is he? And what is he thinking about? Maybe he's lying in the grass not six feet away, yet hidden so I'd never see him in a million years. Wherever he is, I think, he deserves to tell his side. That's what I'd tried to tell Boots and Singer, but they'd kept firing into the night. If I don't do this, I think, how can I expect anyone else to do anything right? It's our fault too I'd tried to tell them. But they'd just kept firing and the sound deafened everything and the muzzle blasts just made the darkness seem darker— carved dark into black.

It's funny to be so alone knowing that someone equally lonely is out there, somewhere, maybe only six feet away. Maybe there are thousands of people— millions— out there, lonely, reaching, wishing that they were somewhere else, in some other time.

The western slopes are ablaze with pink light when I start riding the ridges again. I'm following the path of least resistance, the most likely path taken by a man in a hurry or a horse suddenly free. Of course a man in a hurry would cover the ground with deliberate speed, seeking to create distance, while there's no accounting for a horse on its own following its own notions of space and time. But both, I believe, together or separately, would follow the path of least resistance, in this country the ridges, because the canyons are deep and dark and the slopes down treacherously steep and thick with chaparral. But there's water in the deepest canyons and shade and by mid-day the sun on the ridges is unbearably hot. By mid-day I know that I'll have to drop down into the canyons which will make my search infinitely more difficult.

I hear distant rifle shots, three in succession, but press on, scanning the slopes and grassy meadows. We drop down under a ridge, follow a narrow rocky trail around a lichen-covered out-cropping. Suddenly Peaches spooks, blows wind through her nostrils and dances back, ears cocked for any rustle, eyes scanning all ahead. I calm her, listen too, examine the dark crevices under the slabs of fallen rock, imagine eyes peering out of the darkness. This is lion country, I think, imagining Pancho crouched tawny in the seared grass at the base of the rocks, stalking. I imagine myself placing one padded paw in front of the next, soundlessly, my eyes caressing my prey, my tail twitching, watching, waiting for the precise moment to spring. Mountain lions hunt alone.

I think of Emilio, face taut as a drum. "Who is to say the prey is not playing the cat?" he said. Cat and mouse. Stuie the mouse.

"Emilio," I say, *"Amigo."* And then it's like he's standing beside me. Then I'm looking through his eyes. Maybe I am him, gray work clothes sagging— I feel something clawing deep inside, something ferocious, like something eating me from the inside out. I see blazing eyes. Lion eyes. Then I step aside. I see Emilio smile.

I'm walking now, leading Peaches with the stake rope. The sun is starting to burn and heat is rising from the red gravel earth. I'm on the top of the world, on a high narrow hog back, seeing ridge upon ridge growing purple into the distant haze, Mount Diablo rising above the ridges. I'm hungry now, trying not to think about cheeseburgers and chocolate milk shakes, feeling a little faint even. My mouth is dry as dirt so I try sucking on a quartz pebble. I hear the sound of wind and the sound of the pebble clicking on my teeth and the sound of Peaches wheezing. Below me, on one side, almost a sheer drop, I see the blue depths of Lake Chabot, smooth as glass in the coves, rippled silver in the reaches. On the other side, clinging to the slope down into a bottomless canyon, I see a wall of dirty green greasewood, hard shadows under the brush canopy woven thick as carpet. I'm following tracks, but they're faint and few and far between. I zigzag through the scraggly stands of manzanita to follow them, plagued by deer flies thirsting for my sweat and blood. The tracks could be deer or anything, up here a hundred years old even. Maybe some old *vaquero* or some old sunburned and glassy-eyed settler staking out a ranch. But I know they're not. They disappear between two stunted oak trees clinging to the edge of the eroded summit— the last mark a blaze of scraped earth pointing down into a break in the greasewood. I sit in the shade of the tallest oak tree, taking a breather, thinking about Dixie's swimming pool, so sleepy, ready to doze, that I almost miss the furtive brown movement across an opening in the brush far down on the opposite slope. I watch, my eyes stalking shadow to shadow. I hold my breath, but see nothing more.

I grab mane and swing onto sweaty back, tap Peaches with my heels. Peaches balks at the brink of the slope, but I nudge her, startle her with my urgency. We plunge into the brush and I'm nearly swept off her back but I wrap my arms around her neck and bury my face in her thick mane and let the sun-brittle brush slide over my body. I think maybe it'd be better to walk, duck and dodge under the sharp branches, but Peaches seems to be following a trail of some sort, a deer trail maybe, so I just cling to her back, keeping my head low, letting the branches and leaves batter me from one side to the other. I'm drenched with sweat and the dry twigs and leaves working under my collar make me itch unbearably but I can't scratch and cling to Peaches' neck at the same time. We're angling down the slope, but still dropping so fast that I keep sliding up on Peaches' neck. Sometimes she stops abruptly, as though undecided which direction to take, and I'm pitched hard up on her neck, almost over her head, and once I'm swept off her back by a wrist-thick branch, landing hard in the twilight labyrinth of roots and vole trails at Peaches' feet, nearly strangled in the lariat noosed up around my neck. It happens a second time, but I'm better prepared, land with less pain, then, deeper in the canyon, we're plunging through clinging vines of poison oak and Peaches is snorting, moving fast, plunging straight down now, sliding on broken rock, stumbling, hard on the scent of water.

It's all I can do to keep Peaches from drinking too much too fast. We're in a narrow pool between two rocky banks— the water black and clear beyond the muddy swirls where we'd landed, and welcomely cold. My boots are filled with water, but it doesn't matter. I keep my shoulder under Peaches' neck, holding her satiny muzzle between my hands, talking to her softly, holding her back from the bloating water, then letting her sip, the slurping sound, next to my pounding heart, the loudest noise in the canyon. Further down the watercourse I find a patch of miner's lettuce, cool and tangy to eat, and cool silky mud to sooth the stinging scratches that have lacerated my face and neck and shoulders. Peaches is scratched up too, dotted arcs of blood, so I rub her down with mud and talk to her soothingly and lean up against her, taking in the smell of wet horse hair, enjoying the cool moist air in this dark canyon.

We pick up tracks again in a sand bar further down and follow them up to a deer trail cut into the side of the slope. Withered oak leaves have collected in deep composting piles along the deer trail, so we lose the tracks again. I take a guess and follow the deer trail still further down the canyon, riding Peaches again through an open oak forest, tensing and relaxing my toes in my soggy boots, feeling the mud drying on my face, puckering my skin. The canyon spreads out into a narrow meadow deep with grass. I see Rhona's mare across the meadow, grazing, still haltered, dragging her stake rope. The mare cocks her ears, glances at us, but keeps on grazing. I take my time scanning the meadow and the brush and the trees beyond. I sit still, listening, hearing only Rhona's mare and a few birds, so I dismount, tie Peaches to an oak tree just off the trail, and make my way slowly across the meadow. Rhona's mare stops grazing now, stares at me. I see twigs and leaves snarled in her mane and tail, mud splashed up on her flanks and hindquarters. Her eyes are bloodshot and wild. I talk softly and she backs away. I freeze, wait her out. She starts to graze again, so I move in closer. Suddenly she bolts and I do a stupid thing— I throw myself down on the stake rope, grab it in my hands. But she's moving fast now and the rope whips through my hands with me trying to hold it with all my strength and just before the end snaps across my wrists I feel the fierce fire of rope burn scorch across my palms and radiate out through my fingers. Feels like I'm holding a ball of molten steel.

"What in the world happened to you, sunshine?"

It's still light, but barely, when I ride into the China Seas, riding Rhona's mare bareback and leading Peaches. My hands are open blisters, black and clotted up, and I can't move my fingers out of a claw-like curl so I have Peaches' stake rope draped in front of me, holding it with my right knee. I'm guiding Rhona's mare with the other rope held between my wrists. My shoulders are burning from the unnatural pressure of holding the rope between my wrists, but I'd found that it was the only way I can hold it and maintain any sort of control. I'd tried water and mud and soft green leaves on my hands but everything had made the pain rage deeper until I wanted to curl up in the brush and scream like a wounded jackrabbit. I'd tried wrapping the stake rope around my wrist but that chaffed, threatened more burns.

Rhona's mare had teased me on a hard chase across the creek and up into the greasewood and back down the ravine into a steep and rocky water course slick with stringy moss, floating leaves and trickling water. I'd lost footing leading her out and slid down over a rocky bank back into the creek, ripping open the blisters on my hands. I'd fallen into the ferns and shadows under the bank, curled in slime and mud, lost in the pain throbbing through my hands, the stake rope snaked up the hill to Rhona's mare crooked through my elbow. I'm riding Rhona's mare now because I trust Peaches more at the end of the lead rope. I'd had to untie Peaches from the oak tree with my teeth.

"Let me help you off there, sunshine," China says. "You look like you been battlin' banshees."

"They find him yet?" I ask.

"We just found his truck," China says. "Jimmy found it backed into the hay barn when he went in to break out a couple of bales for the rent string."

"The hay barn?" I say. "How long has his truck been in the hay barn?"

"Nobody been in the barn since the overnight, Jimmy says."

"So where's Stuie?" I ask.

"We been lookin' everywhere, in all the stalls, high and low for the last hour."

"Boots and Singer back?" I ask.

"Since four o'clock. They took Jimmy's Chevy back up to the watershed to fetch your saddle— see if they could spot you on the road. You did the right thing, sunshine. I didn't know them two hotheads had that rifle with 'em."

"But I didn't see no sign of him—"

"Well you goin' to be a hero with Rhona, that's for sure."

"He's got to be around here somewhere—" I say.

"He'll turn up," China says. "Let's get a good look at them hands."

It's after ten when we hear it, a dog howling like it was caught in a steel trap.

We're sitting around China's kitchen table— me, China, Grandma, and Jimmy. We've looked everywhere without a sign, the clubhouse, the tack rooms, China's cellar, even in my barn across the street, and now it seems like we just need to be together, to sip coffee and to talk, to listen to one another's silence. The only thing keeping me awake is the pain in my hands.

"Will you listen to that!" Jimmy says.

China jumps up, pushes to the screen door, sloshing her coffee, toppling her chair in the movement of her large body, pauses with her ear to the rusted screen.

"It's up in the show ring," she says.

I grab the big six-cell flashlight in my bandaged hand, stumble with the pain of holding it, and push past, run ahead of the others, through a box stall, and up the steep wooden stairs into the judging stand that overlooks the show ring.

At first I don't see a thing in the harsh beam of my flashlight but dust and cobwebs and empty Coke bottles and crumpled show programs, but then I see the lariat rope stretched taut across the rafters. I follow it with the flashlight out through the wide viewing window of the judging stand and up where it makes a hard right angle over a roof beam, and follow it down, until I find Stuie Kramer, hanging outside the judging stand, face blue, eyes popping like big surpise, swaying. I almost drop the flashlight, but I catch it numb to pain, framing Stormtrooper on the ground below, howling up at the thing now far out of reach that had once been his master.

# Alaska

W<small>E'RE</small> silent mostly, riding in China's pickup, Jimmy driving, China in the middle, her heavy shoulder crowding me up against the passenger door. China's reading off directions, giving turn directions too late, making Jimmy slow down to read street signs. Finally Jimmy pulls into the curb, throws the truck into neutral. My hands are bandaged up like boxing gloves, stinging like the devil.

"Let me see them directions, Missy," he says. He studies them, pulls away, and two minutes later we pull into the deserted parking lot beside the funeral home. China looks at herself in the rear-view mirror, pats her blonde hair, studies her eyes, rubs a smudge of lipstick with the tip of her little finger. Her face is white and dry, eyes puffy.

"Not many here," Jimmy says.

"Ready, sunshine?" China says.

"Let's get her done," Jimmy says and we climb out onto the hot asphalt.

Jimmy's wearing a black western shirt and string tie. China's wearing a black dress that's so tight she has trouble swinging down out of the high pickup. Jimmy stops her on the sidewalk, brushes wood shavings off her hip with the brim of his hat. He still moves with deliberate care, face anticipating stabs of pain. China takes my arm as we start up the walk, one hand under my elbow, the other resting on my forearm. I see the sign over the dried up hedge, "Franklyn Funerals," and look away. Jimmy opens the heavy walnut door with one hand and herds us in with the other, touching my back. It's cool and dark inside, deserted, just a small table with a vase brimming over with flowers. We stand, disoriented, then Jimmy pushes us toward a door next to the vase, pointing to a small typewritten sign in a brass frame, "Stewart

Martin Kramer."

We're in a tiny chapel, also deserted, thick yellowish light pouring
through a bottle glass window, with canned organ music so soft that
I'm not aware of it at first. At the end of the aisle there's a narrow stage
framed in wine-colored curtains, a small table with a silver candelabra,
a podium.

"We must be early," China says.

"Ten minutes late," Jimmy says.

"We got the day right?" China asks.

"I wouldn't expect too many," Jimmy says and nudges us into a pew
not too close, but not too far back.

We wait, looking around, and then a young boy, awkward in a black
suit, pushes through the curtains at the back of the stage. He's carrying two vases of white flowers. He arranges them on either side of
the podium without looking up, then pushes his way back through the
curtains and we're alone again. China is fingering a balled up tissue,
working it like dough.

At last the door behind us opens and I see Stuie's mom, dressed in
black and white with big white buttons up the front, and Stuie's dad,
older than I'd thought, shuffling. An usher guides them in, seats them
across the aisle from us and up a couple of pews. This seems to sig-
nal the minister, or whatever he is. He walks out of the side wings,
slowly, studying notes. He glances up, down again, then asks us to rise
in silent prayer. He stares at the empty pew in front of the podium, his
face tired and gray, his black suit flecked with dandruff, his fingers self-
consciously dancing from his notes to his tie to his hair and back to his
notes again, and then starting over. He motions us to sit.

"We're here to share these few moments in memory of Stewart Martin Kramer, an only son, with Susan Elizabeth Kramer and Martin Drew
Kramer, Stewart's loving mother and father."

China grips my hand. I glance over, see the flush on her cheeks, but
can't see her eyes.

"I did not know the deceased, Stewart. He was not a member of
my congregation. Nor are his parents, Susan and Martin. But when
Stewart's mother asked me to say these few words I looked into her eyes
and into her heart. I saw the depth of love and loss that she bore. And I
knew that I had to do what I could to get to know her son, Stewart, and

to convey to you the meaning of his life, and his departure, to the best of my ability.

"I have talked with Stewart's mother. She tells me that Stewart was a loving son, obedient. He made her a birdhouse, nursed her when she was ill, read to her when she was indisposed.

"I have talked with Stewart's father. He tells me that Stewart was a deep thinker, a reader, but kept his own counsel.

"But, as you know, Stewart chose to terminate his own life before his natural time. In my faith that constitutes a sin. But a special kind of sin. A sin that leaves each one of us wondering, 'What did I do? Where did I fail? What could I have done?' A sin in which each one of us may well feel complicity. Perhaps a sin that casts harsh light on sins of our own.

"Terminating one's own life before one's natural time is a sin for two simple reasons. First, it creates an irreparable rent in God's own plan. God reserves for Himself the power of life and death and He guards His power jealously. As the story of Job teaches us, it is not for Man, you nor I, to question the trials that He thrusts upon us.

"But paradoxically, God leaves us free to choose. Why? Why does he give us this power to choose?

"And there's more— Taking one's own life creates an irreparable rent in the community of Man— family, friendship, neighborhood, nation. Human communities are all too fragile as it is, especially in our difficult times, and sometimes the loss of one, the least among us, is more than the fragile bonds that bind us, that make us more than beasts in the darkness, can endure. So taking one's own life violates our responsibility to others, the community, the ones who nurture us, depend upon our being.

"So looked at one way, terminating one's own life is an abuse of freedom.

"But why these lingering questions— 'What did I do? Where did I fail? What could I have done?' What does Stewart's life and death have to teach us about that?

"I have come to know more about Stewart by standing in his room, browsing through the books that fed his questing mind. I have come to know that Stewart flirted with hateful ideas. Stewart took on poses.

"Now why would a boy, with loving parents, a secure home, sufficient material means, seek out the dark ideologies of our time? Harden his heart against others? And, why, still in his minority, terminate his God-given life as though he'd hardened his heart against his very own body and soul?

"These are questions that discomfort us.

"I don't know the answers. Who can know what lies festering in another's troubled soul. But I know the questions. Was he accepted, loved? I know his parents loved him. But did we in the community make sufficient place for him? Did we seek to look behind his ugly but all too fashionable poses to forgive and accept the boy within— the little boy who made birdhouses for his mother? Read to her when she was indisposed?

"Unfortunately, only you, his friends and family, his community, can answer these questions— not, I might add, to revel in guilt. But to understand the meaning of his life and the meaning of your own. I never had the chance to know Stewart. But my prayers go with him now. May the Lord accept and forgive him, and may he rest in peace. Let's rise again in silent prayer."

Outside the chapel, in the vestibule, China hugs me, then Jimmy. She turns when Stuie's mom exits, offers her hand.

"Mrs. Kramer, I'm sorry—" she says.

Stuie's mom is sobbing. She reaches out, touches China's face. Then her hand freezes. Her face turns hard.

"You," she says. "It's because of you!"

China is stricken, turns red. Jimmy backs us through the front door. Outside the sun is so bright my vision narrows to a dark tunnel. I almost stumble over a black form slumped on the concrete step, clinging to the iron rail.

"Alaska, sugar!" China says.

Alaska looks up. She's wearing a mannish suit with square shoulders. Her face is streaked with tears.

"I couldn't come in," she says. "I wanted to, but I just couldn't. Was it nice?"

The Kramers spill out the door behind us. Mrs. Kramer glares. Mr. Kramer mumbles, apologetic, and pushes Mrs. Kramer on down the sidewalk.

Jimmy helps Alaska to her feet. She's wearing high heels. They look clumsy on her, like something from another time.

"How'd you get here, honey?" he asks. She points toward a Pontiac pulled carelessly into the curb, rusted out, with one headlight broken.

"I borrowed it from my neighbor."

Mr. Kramer shuffles back up the sidewalk, alone.

"You must forgive her," he says. "She's not a well woman."

"Yes," China says. "I am sorry—"

"She couldn't let go. She suffocated him. Her prejudices became his obsessions. She blamed you when Stuie started spending so much time up at your establishment."

Mr. Kramer reaches into his side pocket, palms something into China's hand.

"We found this when we were goin' through his effects. She wanted to burn it. But I thought you should have it. You meant a lot to him. Without you, this— might have happened sooner. You probably didn't know, but some of his teachers, counselors, said his mind wasn't quite right. The Mrs. denied it, refused to take him to a specialist."

He looks at us, his face soft and mournful.

"Thank you for coming," he says. "All of you. Stewart didn't have many friends."

We watch him walk away.

"What is it?" Jimmy says.

"A letter," China says. "Something Stuie wrote— to me. But he never sent it to me."

Alaska's staring at the letter in China's hand.

"About that girl broke her back— says it was his fault—"

"No one's fault—" Jimmy says. "I was there—"

"I should have been there—" China says, staring at the letter.

"We talked about that," Jimmy says. "Wouldn't have made no difference."

"You want to follow us up to the Seas?" China asks Alaska.

"I promised I would bring the car back right away, " she says.

"You goin' to be all right, sugar?" China asks.

Alaska nods, her eyes following the Kramer's car out of the parking lot.

"It's good that you came," China says. "It would have meant a lot to him."

Alaska watches the Kramer car disappear in traffic. Her face is puffy red.

"Maybe you oughta ride with her," Jimmy says to me. And the four of us hug, fiercely, my bandaged hand squeezed in agony between the warm bodies.

"Was it nice?" Alaska asks. "The service—"

I nod.

"Do you like my chariot?"

"Cherry—" I say.

"I've got to stop for oil," she says. "Would you believe that this thing goes through a quart of oil every ten miles? Seems like it, anyway."

Alaska's squeezing the steering wheel too hard. Her eyes are filled again, and I don't know what to say. I offer to drive, but she waves me away.

"Come to my house," she says. "I'll drive you home later."

Alaska lives up a dirt road in a redwood canyon. Her house is hand-built, beautiful really. We enter through a door with many small glass panes framed in rough-hewn redwood.

"I want you to meet my dad," she says. "Daddy!"

"Still here, Tootsie. Just where you plopped me— How was the funeral?"

Alaska leads me by the hand through a narrow kitchen, iron stove, white enamel sink with rusty circle under the dripping spigot, and into a living room with no right angles, oak floors, redwood beams, huge stone fireplace.

"My daddy's blind," Alaska whispers. "Accident last year."

"He can see that for himself soon enough," a voice says from a deep overstuffed chair, back toward us. "Anyone with half a good eye can see that I'm blind." He thrusts his hand up over the back of the chair, not quite in my direction.

"So you get him good and planted?"

"Daddy!" Alaska says.

"Hear he killed himself— Noblest act of man. Who'd you bring home this time, Tootsie? Hope he's got more between his ears than that last one."

We move around the chair, sit in a deep leather couch.

"Funerals are a waste of good money— shameful superstitions. When my time comes, burn me up in an old barrel in the back yard, will you

Tootsie? What do you say, whatever your name is?"

"Calvin," Alaska says. "Daddy, don't be rude."

"Rude? Am I rude, Calvin? Get us some ice tea, Tootsie, while I talk with this boy. Calvin some kind of religious name?"

"So what makes you think he's a boy?" Alaska asks. "Maybe he's my married lover."

"Of course he's a boy. You're too young for real men, and Calvin ain't a girl's name now is it? You're a boy, ain't you, Calvin?"

I nod, then say, "Yes."

"Hear that other boy committed suicide—"

I nod. "Yes," I say.

"Well you ever think about suicide?"

"Yes," I say.

"Well that's the ticket. Suicide is the highest expression of protest and individuality. Last chance to spit in their eyes!"

"I don't know," I say.

"Don't know! Well what do you think about funerals, then? 'Do you think that the deceased would prefer the oak casket or the mahogany?' Funerals are a vicious scam perpetuated by the clerical class, don't you think?"

"I don't know," I say. "This is the first funeral I've ever been to."

"Well, what did you think?"

"It was— nice," I say.

"Nice. Tootsie, give your old man a kiss. I missed you today, honey. At your age you ought to be giving your time to the living, not the dead. But this boy is OK. A little misguided, but good material. You can bring him around any time. You play chess, Calvin?"

We're sitting on Alaska's bed, Alaska showing me her grandmother's embroidery on a yellowed linen pillowcase.

"Look at these tiny stitches. I could never do this with my big hands. Funny, though, she was a big woman too. I can't imagine that her hands were much smaller than mine."

Alaska's room is overstuffed with furniture, solid oak, side tables and dressers, a highboy filled with stuffed bears, and a heavily carved bedstead.

She has one yellow show ribbon hanging over her mirror. I remember when she won it. There were only three riders in her class.

"All this belonged to my grandmother," Alaska says. "Daddy wanted to give it to the Salvation Army, but I made him give it to me."

She slips off the bed and walks to the dresser. The top of the dresser is covered with perfumes, fancy bottles, an ornate table lamp. She opens a bottle of perfume and dabs a whiff behind her ear. "Smell this," Alaska says, offering me the bottle. "'Forbidden.' It belonged to my mother. She was a dancer."

Alaska is talking nonstop. She always seems so silent, so judgmental, but not now. She presses close to me and holds the bottle under my nose. "Like it?" she says. She dabs a little behind my ear.

"—my mother had the most beautiful legs."

"Stop it," I say.

"Sorrrry," she says, looking at me.

"Why did he do it?" I say. "Kill himself."

Alaska is crying again.

"He was so weird."

"But still—" I say.

"I had braces on my legs until I was nine," Alaska says. "Mother said I'd never be a dancer."

She lifts her dress over her knees.

"Do my legs look too skinny now? I don't like people looking at my legs. That's why they're so white. They're too white, aren't they?"

"No," I say. "They look OK."

"It was because of Dixie. He was really in love with Dixie, you know."

"I think it was something else," I say.

"A boy can kill himself over a girl—" Alaska says.

"Maybe," I say. "But still—"

"He can—"

"That letter was right," I say. "It was his fault that that girl broke her back."

"So?"

"So China might lose the stable— He knew that."

"She won't—"

"Boots told me— It was Kramer's fault."

"He used to call me sometimes," Alaska says.

"Kramer?"

"Yes, Stuie—"

"What did he say?"

"He came over once—"

"What did he want?"

"My mother died when I was five, then we moved to Alaska."

"Alaska— I thought that was just your name."

"Boots started calling me that."

"So what's your real name?"

"I don't like my real name."

"So what is it?"

"Alaska— Now."

"Isn't it cold in Alaska?"

"My mother's name was Ruth. These are the only things I have of hers. These perfumes. Don't you like perfume, Calvin?"

"So what did Stuie talk about?"

Alaska looks at the bandages on my hands. She reaches for them. "Let me see your hands, Calvin," she says.

"Why?" I ask.

"I just want to see them." She starts unraveling one of the bandages.

"Please don't," I say. "So what did Stuie talk about?

"What did Stuie talk about when?"

"When he came here."

"Maybe he just wanted to see me. Would you kill yourself over Junie?"

"So what did Kramer talk about?"

"No— You're not the type. You're so— intellectual."

"Come on, Alaska. Tell me."

"Dixie— We always talked about Dixie. What else. Until that last time."

"That last time?" I say.

"That last time he called me."

"The last time he called— When was the last time?"

"The day after—"

"The day after what."

"You know, after the swimming party at Dixie's. The day after—"

"After what?"

"Well he was hiding up in the haystack when I rode back up to my barn."

"You mean he drove up to your barn after the swimming party?"

"I didn't see his truck at first— it was around the back of the barn— like he didn't want me to see it."

"You mean he was hiding in your barn— hiding in the haystack? Did he have his gun? What did he do?"

"I didn't see him at first. Then— He was so— angry. He was pathetic. You should have seen him. He was so pathetic. I was afraid—"

"Afraid of what?"

"He was screaming at me. I was afraid he was going to—"

"What?"

"Rape me or something— 'You're like the rest of them—' He kept screaming at me. 'You're just like the rest of them.' He threw me across one of the hay bales."

"And what happened?"

"He tore my shirt and threw me across one of the hay bales."

"Alaska—" I say.

"And then— And then— He asked me to forgive him."

"What do you mean?" I say.

"He— kind of fell apart. He fell on the floor of the barn in front of me— on his knees— asked me to forgive him. Said that I was better than you guys. I could understand him, that he wasn't like everybody thought. He asked me to talk to Dixie."

"And what happened?"

"I screamed at him. Told him to leave."

"And then what happened?"

"Nothing. He called me the next night. Said some vile things. He talked about people being real sorry. He said that I'd be sorry too— I tried—"

Alaska's looking at me fiercely now.

"Maybe I should have let him!"

"Let him what?"

"I don't know— Rape me or something."

I'm holding Alaska now. She seems big in my arms, awkward, but so fragile. Suddenly she's kissing me, pressing me into the bed. I struggle. "Calvin—" she says.

"Hold me—"

I pull away. She stares at me, hard, then slaps me.

"You're no good!" she says.

"Don't—" I say.

"You're always so— above it all."

"Alaska—"

"You're leaving— Philadelphia or some stupid place like that? So what do you care?"

"Alaska—" I say. "Did you tell anybody? Don't you see? If somebody had known—"

Alaska's silent.

"How could I have known?" she says.

"But maybe—"

"Maybe what?" I say.

"Maybe I did."

"Did what?"

"Know what he was going to do— know that he was going to do something bad."

"When you used to talk to Stuie," I say, "Did you— like him?"

"Maybe—" Alaska says. "A little— He was more intelligent than people thought."

"Did you love him?"

"What do you think?" she yells. "What do you care? At least I talked to him. You guys tormented him! Everybody put him down! Now everything is falling apart."

I touch her cheek.

She lashes out, scratches me.

"Alaska!"

She falls into her pillow, sobbing. I try to comfort her, but she kicks at me, pushes me away.

I move away.

"Don't go," she says.

Alaska is looking at my hands, her eyes red. "You poor thing—"

I look away.

"We all did, you know—" she says

I'm silent.

"We did!"

"Did what?"

"Put Stuie down so we could feel superior."

"Maybe," I say. "But he was always asking for it."

"I remember when he first started hanging around the stable. He just wanted to be accepted."

"By pushing people around? Talking trash about the coloreds?"

"Maybe he didn't know any other way."

"Right. How to make friends and influence people."

Those books he talked about— They made him feel like he belonged to something."

"They made him sound like what he was— a bigot and a bully."

"We put Stuie down just like he put down the Negroes. All Stuie had, when Dixie dropped him— and everybody turned on him— was that stupid thing he had about Negroes. Hate. That was all he had left. We took away the one thing he really wanted— to be accepted."

"China says we all hang out at the China Seas lookin' for something," I say.

"And for Stuie maybe it was his last chance to find it."

"And soon there won't be no China Seas. Where will we go then?"

"I don't know," Alaska says.

"What are you looking for?" I ask.

Alaska is crying again. "I don't know," she whispers.

Light from the table lamp on Alaska's dresser casts glare across her window. A moth, outside, bangs against the window, attracted by the light.

"I just don't know."

I sit with Alaska through the night, listening to the moth, wondering about love and hate— wondering how easily hatred pours into our empty spaces, how hatred strikes us blind.

# Thistles

"YOU'RE welcome to stay longer if you need, you know," Junie's dad says, "If you need more time."

I nod, stare down at the plate of toast.

"We really like having you, hon—" Junie's mom says. "So don't worry about that or anything."

June is silent, nibbling on a strip of crisp bacon. June's little brother is squeezing egg yolk through the tines of his fork.

"That Peaches," I say. "She's going to be a real fine mare."

"Remember your tickets?" June's mom asks me. "They were on the pool table."

"Yes," I say.

Mr. Rogers drops me off at the top of the hill. He offers to drive me all the way, but I need to walk— feel the air— smell the grass.

"These are hard things to decide sometimes," he says. "The hardest. But you got a good head on your shoulders. Don't worry about your clothes or anything. Mais will get 'em to you."

I walk down through the canyons. The air is still cold under the laurel trees, but warm and dry higher up. I climb, stop to scan the city. I see flashes of gold and silver as sunlight glints off windshields, watch an airplane, maybe a DC-6, lift slowly, watch its shadow crawl down the bay.

I walk down the fire road, veer off, scramble up the eroded bank. The grass is dry and trampled, red with recent dust. Giant earth mover tracks crisscross the grass, following new-cut survey stakes aligned up the hill. Cats roaming the hills, but the wrong kind, I think. Should be mountain lions. But these are the kind that tear up the earth. I pull one of the stakes, run to pull another. But then I give it up, walk slowly up the hill, then half slide down the gravel ruts toward the meadow. The oak tree is olive green in the meadow, dry and dusty, the outer leaves curled and ready to drop. I swish through the brittle grass, stop to work cockle burrs and foxtails out of my socks, wish I was wearing my riding boots. I pause near the oak tree, watch a soft cloud blow up from behind the hill across the ravine, listen to birds, the late summer buzz of insects. I walk on, flushing grasshoppers before me, but stop before reaching the drop. A stand of thistles, dense and green, has grown up and over the edge of the slope. I push into them, but give it up, brush my tender palms against the jagged leaves under the purple crowns. Some are dry as bone, thorns sharp as knives.

"You're early, sunshine," China says. She's standing in the stable yard. Her trailer's all hooked up— ready to haul her Appaloosa over into the valley.

"Is it true?" I ask.

"Yes—" she says. "They give me thirty days to sell the place."

"All the horses?"

"Everything."

"What then?" I say.

"Don't know really," China says. "One step at a time."

"But where will you go?" I say.

"The Bay Area's too crowded for me. That's for sure. Maybe north somewhere, some quiet little valley where I can raise fine horses. You'll come, help me when I get settled, won't you, Calvin?"

"Yes—" I say.

"So you finally decide?" she says.

"Yes," I say.

China looks at me. "Well?" she says.

I pat my back pocket.

"Got my airplane ticket right here—"

"So you're headed back east?"

I'm silent.

"Kind of hard is it?"

I nod.

"Want to talk about it?"

"It's like everybody's saying, 'Don't go, Calvin.'"

"But what do you want to do, sugar?"

"What do you think I should do?"

"I can't tell you that. That's a choice you have to make for yourself."

"If I go— It's like Teddy kicked me out. But if I stay— It's maybe because I'm afraid of living with my real dad. Maybe it won't work out."

"Some choices are hard, Calvin. But no one else can make them for you."

"China— Why'd Stuie kill himself?"

"That I can't say, sunshine. For some reason it's the choice he made."

"And he can never come back—"

"He can never come back. Big choices are usually like that."

"That's what I'm afraid of."

"How's that?"

"My friends are here. The places I know are here. This is where I grew up."

"And?"

"Why should I let Teddy kick me out?"

"Good question."

"But if I stay— what if it still don't work out?"

"Calvin, whatever you choose, you'll work it out," China says.

"Will I?" I say.

"I know you'll do your best."

"So why are you leaving?"

China's silent— stares toward the old barns.

"You said you gotta stay and fight it out. That's what you told me."

"Did I, sunshine?"

"You said it," I say.

"Well sometimes you gotta know when to fold."

"But how do you know?" I ask. "The difference?"

"Sometimes there ain't much difference," China says. "You just do what you think is right and take what's comin' to you— Load this Appaloosa into the trailer for me, will you, sunshine? We best get this show on the road."

"So Rodney bought the Appaloosa back from you then?"

"Wanted to pay me extra— Training fee, he said."

"Did you take it?"

"Rodney's a dear friend," China says. "What do you think?"

It's dark when we return from the valley.

"Thank you," China says.

"For what?"

"For being you."

"And you—" I say.

"Well, I'll see you," she says, but we sit longer in the dark pickup, neither of us wanting to move.

We follow a light bouncing fast down Stella Street. Singer slides into the circle of China's headlights on a muddy dirt bike— walks the bike up to my window."

Calvin—" he says. "That you? Been lookin' all over for you—"

He twists, unclips a black box strapped awkwardly behind him, shoves it through the open window of the pickup. It's the ARC-5 communication receiver we'd left under the hedge.

"Brought you this," he says. "Been keeping it. Thought I'd forgot, didn't you? But I didn't."

I'm not sure what to say.

"China," Singer says, "Anything I can do?"

"No, sugar," China says. "You done enough. Just keep yourself well, you hear?"

"Got to go get my girl," Singer says.

"Your girl?" China says.

"Laurie," Singer says. "I'm movin' out on my brother."

China lets me off in front of my house. I watch China pull into the stable, Singer's red tail light bounce up the road. I turn, pause on the driveway, look through the front window, see Teddy sprawled on the love seat, mouth open, frail in the flickering light of the television. But for size he could be a baby sleeping in a crib. I look through the kitchen window, see mom back lighted, staring into the sink. I step up to the window, tap, and she looks up.

"Calvin," she mouths, "That you?"

# Pancho

MY first day of high school it rains most of the day, but slows to misty drizzle toward the end of sixth period. The road into the zoo is wet and slick. Large drops falling from the high palms that line the road make loud splashes on the asphalt. I hear the rifle shot, hurry, then have to jump aside as an ambulance careens by, headed toward the cougar cages.

They're pacing around the cage, pumped up, Mr. Winter in his safari jacket cradling his big game rifle.

I see them load the covered stretcher into the ambulance, flowers of blood spreading out from the white bulges.

"What happened?" I ask.

"Isn't pretty, son," the driver says. "Better step away."

I see Pancho sprawled on the wet concrete inside his cage like a tawny brush dipped in blood, a river of blood flooding from under his blind side.

"Poor bugger didn't have a chance," the cop says.

"That Emilio," Mr. Winter says. "I warned him and warned him—"

"But he loved that cat," the cop says. "He talked to it— fed it, watered it, cleaned its cage. What would set it off like that? And why didn't he know better?"

"It's their nature," Mr. Winter says, wiping water spots off his big game rifle. "Cage 'em. Try to tame 'em. But they always run true to nature."

I study the pale bark peeling off the old eucalyptus tree leaning over the lion cage, smell the stifling exhaust from the ambulance mixed with the cough-drop odor of crushed eucalyptus berries.

"Emilio was Pancho's God," I want to scream.

219

"Park's closed, son—" Mr. Winter says to me. "Time to get along now—"

"No—" I say.

Mr. Winter stares at me. His face softens.

"You were Emilio's friend, weren't you?" Mr. Winter says.

"Yes," I say.

"Well, he didn't have long for this world, did you know that?"

"What do you mean?" I say.

"Emilio was in terrible pain. A very sick man."

I sit at the wet picnic table, glance down at the pink and black scabs on my hands. Slowly, I begin to understand. Dimly. Is this what Emilio was talking about? The dark one— Is this the dark one behind every door? I stare at the flashing red lights as the ambulance pulls away, then down at the dusky heap in the spreading blood, catch a strong whiff of cat urine. Freedom, I think. For what? For whatever we make of it. I had a choice— ride back to the house and fix the halter or make do. I chose the easy way. And for that— I stare at the gray sky through a break in the eucalyptus trees. Stuie had choices. I'll never know why he chose the way he did, but maybe if we'd chosen to treat him for who he was rather than what he pretended to be— Emilio chose between the lion and pain. For Emilio the lion was the way of honor—the bearer of the final mercy. The mouse plays with the cat. The mouse finds honor. And Pancho— Pancho had no choice at all but to follow his nature.

I think of life, death, and choice. Maybe choice is all that stands between us and the animals in their cages. Maybe the power to choose is all it comes down to.

So much has changed. We move down the road even when we think we're standing still. And that in itself is a choice.

Mr. Winter is still staring at me, then he looks off toward the ambulance disappearing between the palms. I see something in his eyes, grief, loss, that I hadn't noticed before.

"We must light candles," I say. "Emilio was very poor."

## QUESTIONS FOR DISCUSSION

1. In *Freein' Pancho* Calvin is confronted with many choices.

- Which choices were the most consequential?

- In each case, what were Calvin's options and what path did he take?

- Why did he choose as he did?

- In each case, did he make the best choice given the circumstances?

- How might his life be different had he'd chosen differently?

2. It seems that Calvin's family is on a downward spiral.

- Why?

- What does each family member contribute to the negative atmosphere?

- What, specifically, is Calvin's role?

- What would it take to heal this family?

3. Stuie Kramer comes across as a bigot and a bully. Yet Calvin wonders if the way the community treated Stuie might have contributed to his behavior and suicide.

- What do you think?

- What is the best way to deal with bigots and bullys?

- Should there be laws against bullying?

4. Both Stuie Kramer and Emilio choose suicide—Stuie, it seems, out of guilt and rage; Emilio out of pain and a personal code of dignity.

- Is one more justified than the other?

- Is suicide ever justified?

5. China sees her riding stable as a place of refuge for troubled youth.

- Does she really make a difference in their lives?

- Are there such places in your community?

6. Calvin's neighborhood is changing from one of horse barns and fenced corrals to one of two-car garages and suburban lawns.

- Are the new homeowners right in trying to ban horses?

- Can you imagine a way in which the two cultures could live together?

- What does the change mean for Calvin?

7. Characters in this novel use terms for different ethnic groups and make comments about women that would be inappropriate today.

- Are they racist? Sexist?

- How would teens today talk about other ethnic groups and women?

- Do you think society is more tolerant today than it was in the '50s? Why?

8. What will happen to Calvin?

www.ingramcontent.com/pod-product-compliance
Lightning Source LLC
Chambersburg PA
CBHW070105260626
47160CB00004B/1330